Generations
and
Other True Stories

BOOKS BY BRYAN WOOLLEY

Nonfiction

Generations
The Bride Wore Crimson
The Edge of the West
Where Texas Meets the Sea
The Time of My Life
We Be Here When the Morning Comes

Fiction

Sam Bass
November 22
Time and Place
Some Sweet Day

Generations
and
Other True Stories

by Bryan Woolley

Introduction by John Nichols

Texas Western Press
The University of Texas at El Paso
1995

First Edition
Library of Congress Catalog Card No. 95-061097
ISBN 0-87404-235-6

∞ All Texas Western Press books are printed on acid-free
paper, meeting the guidelines for permanence and durability
of the Committee on Production Guidelines for Book
Longevity of the Council on Library Resources.

"Generations" originally appeared in *Redbook*; "Herbert
Kokernot, Satchel Paige, and Me" and "How He Played the
Game" in *Tuff Stuff*, under different titles; "A Memoir of
Hamilton and Comanche Counties," also under a different
title, as the introductory essay to *The Way Home: Photographs
from the Heart of Texas*, by June Van Cleef, copyright 1992,
Texas A&M University Press. The other pieces appeared in
The Dallas Morning News and its magazine, *Dallas Life*. I
thank the publishers for permission to reprint my work here.

Contents

FOR TED, PAT, AND CHRIS

the next generation

and in memory of JERRY

who was murdered

Introduction

by John Nichols

Yes, I've known Bryan Woolley for a right long spell, but I think I've only met him twice. His book, *Time and Place*, started the relationship—I really loved that tale of small town west Texas in the Fifties. And then one day we sat down to some serious bourbon in an upscale air-conditioned Dallas fleabag and discovered we had some kindred blood. I liked the dude right off the bat: he knew how to drink and he knew how to tell stories, and he seemed like a real nice guy into the bargain. Later, he suckered me into writing a few book reviews for the old *Dallas Times-Herald*, but I don't hold that against him. And it wasn't long afterwards that I read his small novel, *Some Sweet Day*, and it knocked my socks off. I thought: This man is one of those rough tough gentle souls who deep down isn't much afraid of anything, and he really knows how to see clearly with the heart.

No, I wouldn't call him sentimental, though he is not afraid of nostalgia, either. Bryan's memories of his own childhood are as vivid and moving as the classic sepia prints in an old family album. Seems like he always has an insight into something of value, plus a gift of being able to care about most anything that crossed his path forty years ago...or only yesterday. Respectful compassion lights up the past, the present, and his observations concerning the future. Too, the man goes about his business with a seemingly effortless *savoir faire*, a bullseye instinct for the truth, a rapacious curiosity, and a gratifying tendency to do his homework: the consummate pro.

Bryan doesn't manipulate or stack the odds; he lets you decide. He isn't really a neutral observer, however: the impact almost always evolves out of a quiet place, then hits hard. And, no matter how harsh a story might be, there's always a thread of hope running through it. Even when the outrage is evident the decency of vision keeps a balance. For some reason, that makes me think Bryan would be a handy person to have around in an emergency; he'd keep his head, figure all the angles pretty quick, make sense out of the confusion, decide what to do, and probably save my life.

And even if he blundered and *didn't* save my life, he would probably feel obligated, out of guilt (deriving from the code that requires honor among thieves), to immortalize me in his sweet prose!

So here it is, no literary gee-gaws, do-dads, gimcracks or gimmicks, and no wiseguy fancy stuff, either...though I must admit Bryan is often funny as hell. But he gets you to laugh *with* people, as opposed to *at* the foibles of others. Put another way, Bryan can dissect like a skilled surgeon, but he ain't much for overtly twisting the knife. I don't believe the man has a malicious bone in his body.

Born and raised in the Lone Star state, Bryan naturally considers his roots a most merciful benediction. Yet he never struts them with any of that big bold brassy tacky braggadocio so often associated in our national mythology with the inhabitants of Texas. Hence, anybody who reads this book, even a xenophobic highlander (like me) from the sierras of New Mexico, is bound to enjoy being Texasified, Woolley style—

I guarantee.

Bryan knows his home territory in spades. And you will too, after this intriguing journey. These tales are all over the map and you don't need to read them in order. They've got quirky facts galore, fascinating lingo, and a slew of eccentric, noble, bawdy, reserved, heroic, humble, crazy, intelligent, small town, big city characters. There's even a cowboy poet who grooves on Gabriel García Márquez and T.S. Eliot; there are urban Indians who keep the faith; there's an old time gospel horseback rider who's "very thoughtful of other peoples' beliefs." And just when you think it might be safe to go back into the desert, there's a flying saucer somewhere across the border in New Mexico.

One minute we have a young kid, Bryan himself, watching—in person!—as the immortal Satchel Paige strikes out six major league batters in a row. In St. Louis?...nope, that happened in Alpine, Texas, in 1951. Where is Alpine, Texas? Beats me, but in Bryan's memory, and in his imagination, it's a fabulous place to visit.

Next minute, we jump from Satchel to whooping cranes down in the Aransas National Wildlife Refuge on San Antonio Bay; and from those whoopers Bryan diddy-bops through a riotous elegy (or do I mean eulogy?) for the cartoonist, Gary Larson. (Is Gary from Texas?—I don't know. But so what? There's another nonsequiter riff in here about Dashiell Hammett's Maltese Falcon'd San Francisco.) Then, before you can say *To Hell and Back*," Bryan is over at Audie Murphy's hometown of Celeste learning about that war hero/movie star's hardscrabble childhood, a time when the Murphy family was "as broke as the Ten Commandments." A few pages later, Bryan gives us a jive riff on Kinky Friedman and the Texas Jewboys, after which we gallop right up to a cowboy poet hootnanny...then *zip!*—out west we go to meet a strange guy (in a piece of wild country called the Trans-Pecos) who's marveling at the blossoming *Leucophyllum candidum*...a flower which probably wouldn't mean horsesquat to the maniac Dallas Harlequin rugby players (that Bryan eventually follows all the way to a tournament in Las Vegas, Nevada) for whom mud, blood, and Bud is the name of the glorious game.

By the way, you know what Kinky Friedman thinks of Garth Brooks? He thinks Garth is "a cultural mayonnaise" and "the anti-Hank." I think Garth is...rich.

But these stories are richer, by far. Some are funny, all are interesting, a few will break your heart. The title piece, "Generations," is as lean and poignant as anything I have ever read. A hundred and eighty degrees in the other direction, Bryan's spritz on the arcane double-dealing scuttle-butting backbiting Public Art Follies in Dallas is hilarious. (Show me another town in America that could put seventy bronze longhorn steers on a grassy knoll in front of its Convention Center a couple of blocks from Nieman Marcus and get away with it!)

But it's not funny at all when Bryan tells us about an internationally famous Dallas balloonist who is badly burned in a flying accident: the man's courage sure will make you sit up and take proper notice. And there is no glamour, either, in a short piece on an ex-Pentecostal preacher, abandoned by his church because he's gay, who dies of AIDS. The preacher has the kind of decency that resonates throughout this book.

Bryan moves around easily from a lovely hosannah for Nolan Ryan (the great baseball pitcher) to a history of that zany crazy healthfood water burg, Mineral Wells. And though his take on a steer wrestling school in Madisonville doesn't resort to much hyperbole in the telling, it is graphic enough to leave me feeling black and blue!

One of my favorite moments involves an elderly teacher who remembers a night from her young womanhood when she camped outside in her backyard because of the heat...but still couldn't sleep, the moon was so darn bright. How do you solve a problem like that in small town Texas? She opened an umbrella to shade herself from the moon's brilliant rays.

Do you know who the "Last Cowboy of Brewster County" is? I do now, but I don't want to spoil it, so I'll let Bryan take you there to meet the guy, who right now might be the most famous writer in America. The question is, will Bryan himself be able to track down that elusive celebrity? And, if so, what then—?

Much of this writing is about change. The old days; the new days. Sacred traditions die out; land gets developed; native people decide to assert their rights. After nearly fifty years of Woolley occupation, Bryan's mom sells the family home, and that is a melancholy process.

There's difficult history here—racism, prejudice, reaction, fear of development. But you won't find an ounce of sarcasm, cynicism, or petulant whining from the author. Maybe these days it is old-fashioned (or even the kiss of death) to be honorable, but to my way of seeing, that's what we've got here: this volume is purely intentioned, it is considerate, and that sort of quality is hard to come by anymore. Bryan mocks nobody; he himself is "very thoughtful of other peoples' beliefs."

Still, before you enter these pages, there is one important question I feel compelled to ask: Have you got that "Baptist booster spizerinctum?" I hope so. But if you don't have it yet, do not despair. Because no matter who you are or where you hail from, by the end of this collection of fine stories, you'll have spizerinctum up the kazoo—in your head, in your heart, in your belly, and pulsating neon-bright smack dab in the exact center of your soul—

Guaranteed.

—Taos, New Mexico
April 1995

When Redbook *magazine published this piece in 1981, I called it fiction, but it wasn't. Everything in it happened as I wrote it. I just changed the names.*

Since then, the father of the story and his wife have died. So I've changed the fictitious names back to the real ones, and I'm publishing the story here as the truth, which it is.

Generations

The last place I had seen my father was on the left front fender of the 1939 Chevrolet in front of a tourist court hundreds of miles from the farm where I had lived all my life. It was 1945, not long after V-J Day, and we had moved only a few weeks before — my mother, my grandmother, my younger brothers and sisters, and me. I was eight years old, barely. School had just opened, and my grandmother was my teacher in the town's third grade — one of the third grades; the Mexicans went to another school. My mother took in sewing. We lived in two cabins of the tourist court, so we had two kitchens and two bathrooms. One of the kitchens was my bedroom. Being the eldest, I got to sleep on a cot there. I was the only member of the family who slept alone. Sherry, the baby, slept with my mother, and Linda with my grandmother. My brothers, Dick and Mike, slept together. We were crowded but I didn't know it, for we had been crowded at Carlton, too, in the house on the farm, when my father was living with us.

I didn't know why we had come to Fort Davis, or why he hadn't come with us. If I asked, they didn't tell me. And I didn't know why my father had come now or why he was going away again. I didn't know why we were sitting on the Chevrolet in the dark, he on the left fender, I on the right, or why the other kids didn't come out of the cabins and climb on the car with us. I didn't know someone was making sure we were alone.

Nights were cool in those mountains, even in August. A breeze drifted through the apple orchard that separated the tourist court from the road, and through the huge cottonwood in front of the cabins. It was nothing like the sultry summer nights on the farm, with not a breath of wind stirring in the live oaks. It was a strange place to me, high in those rugged mountains — the first mountains I had ever seen — in that strange town with so many strange brown people speaking a language I didn't understand, where the white boys wore jeans and cowboy boots and hats to school and stared at my farmer's overalls and bare feet. It would have been worse if my grandmother hadn't been my teacher, I guess, and if Clay, the son of a rancher whose big stone house was just over the orchard fence from the tourist court, hadn't been my friend.

If there was a moon, it was hidden by the trees, and I couldn't see my father's face. I asked him, "Are you going to move here too?"

He was a long time answering. "Yes. Maybe."

"When?"

"I don't know. Someday."

"Will you live with us then?"

"I think so."

"When?"

"I don't know. Don't worry."

I don't think that's what he was supposed to say. They wouldn't have kept us alone if he was meant to tell me that. I think he was supposed to tell me I would never see him again.

It was at school, months — maybe a year — later, that I first heard the word "divorce." I was lying belly down on the merry-go-round, dragging my hands in the dirt, when some kid mentioned to another kid that my mother and father had got one. The other kid asked me if that was true and I said yes, although I didn't know what the word meant. And they seemed impressed, as we had been in Carlton when the father of a schoolmate of mine was killed in the war. Well, I guess I did know what it meant, for I never asked. It meant that my father wasn't coming to live with us, which I had begun to suspect anyway, since so long a time had passed and he hadn't come. I had stopped expecting him.

Maybe that was how kids learned about divorce in those days. It was something that didn't happen often. I knew no other kids in Carlton or Fort Davis whose parents had got one. So far as I knew, mine were the first and, until I was much older, the last. And in that time and place it was a dark thing that nobody talked about. Whenever I was reminded by the earth or the weather of my father and asked my mother or grandmother where he was or the reasons for the divorce, their replies were soft and evasive, designed to tell me not to ask. Only once do I remember my mother's mentioning him, and that was two years later, when she discovered I had stolen a pocketknife from a store. She whipped me with my belt, and while I lay on my bed crying, she cried too. Her thin face,

3

tight with fatigue and worry, was wet with her tears, and her teeth, clenched to hold back her anger and grief, ground against each other. She said, "Do such a thing again and I'll send you to your father!"

I can't describe the terror those words inspired in me. The thought of living away from my mother and grandmother and brothers and sisters, having them disappear from my life as my father had, was frightening in itself. But now the man about whom I had ceased to ask, whose features had dimmed in my mind, whom I recalled only as a tall, dark figure trudging across furrowed fields and as a shadow on the fender of the Chevrolet, entered my dreams.

"Will you live with us?" I dreamed myself saying.

"Yes," the shadow replied.

"When?"

"Don't worry."

What had once been a wish was a nightmare, powerful enough to end my experiments in crime. And when months of being good finally cleansed my soul, I no longer had the dream.

My brothers and sisters and I grew up without seeing him again, and I remember only one other mention of him during all that time. I was fourteen or fifteen, and Dick and I had climbed Sleeping Lion Mountain and were resting in the shade of an oak at the top, looking down at the town. Out of the blue, Dick said, "I wonder if any of us look like our daddy."

His words startled me. "I don't know," I said.

When I told Isabel all this, I was almost a year past my own divorce but still deep in its pain, still appalled that I had walked in my father's footsteps. My older boy, Ted, was eight when it happened, the age I had been in 1945.

Patrick was five, as Dick had been then. But the world was used to divorce now. It had happened to friends of my children's; I didn't have to explain what it was. I had to explain why it was happening to them, though, and I tried to be honest. No, I wouldn't be moving to St. Louis with them. I probably would never live with them again, and they shouldn't hope that I would someday. But I would see them at Christmas and in the summers and would always love them. No matter what happened, I would always be their dad.

"I want to go there," Isabel said.

"Where?"

"To Carlton, where it happened. Where you knew your father."

Someday Isabel and I would marry, we had decided. She wanted to know things. "Who do you look like?" she asked.

"My mother," I said.

It was a Sunday, and the day before my fortieth birthday. The late-morning sun glinted off the glass towers of Dallas as we hunted two-lane U.S. 67 in the maze of interstates and freeways. It was the church hour and the highway was almost empty. So was the countryside. The Volkswagen churned past white frame farmhouses surrounded by pickups and station wagons, signs that children and grandchildren had gathered at old family homesteads for Sunday dinner. But they were eating or already watching TV, and no children were out. Not even dogs. The gently rolling fields were pale August green, steaming under the huge, empty, brilliant sky.

"Is this prairie?" Isabel asked. Her Manhattan eyes, not used to horizons, were full of awe.

"Yes."

"It looks like Russia. Something out of Chekhov."

Two hours into the countryside, I expected the scenery to become familiar. I hadn't seen it in more than thirty years, but remembered unpainted houses, ancient cars and farm machinery sitting under trees, hounds lying under porches, cotton fields as brilliant as snow, awaiting pickers trailing long canvas sacks behind them as they moved along the rows on their knees. None of it was there. Where the cotton had been, exotic European cattle grazed on Bermuda grass. The fences that had separated the fields, even those that had divided the farms, were gone. The houses were gone, the sites of some of them still marked by a stand of trees in what had been the front yard or a stone chimney or a cluster of rusting metal. The dogs and people were gone. Everything was gone except the cattle, which hadn't been there before.

"It's all changed," I said.

"Are you sure we're on the right road?"

"I think so."

I found Hico and, farther on, the store at the Olin crossroads. The white frame store that my parents had kept for a short time when I was a baby had been replaced by a squat cinder-block building painted white. It was still a store, but the four or five houses that had stood around it and had been Olin were gone. There was a sign pointing toward Carlton at the crossroads, and the road had been paved. The farms between Olin and Carlton were gone, and much of Carlton was, too. At least it was smaller than I remembered it. But its landmark, the stone bank that had closed during the Depression and later burned, remained, its vault door still hanging rustily, Johnson grass still growing in the cracks of its concrete floor. I remembered some of the houses and even the names of some of the people who had lived in them. One of the grocery stores remained, and the other, across the street, had been converted to hardware. The blacksmith's shop was gone. The variety store was in ruins, like the bank. The Texaco station was still there. Everything still there was closed. No life was in sight. I stopped the car in front of a red-brick building with the word "Cafe" painted crudely on its window.

"This used to be the drugstore," I said. "I got a nickel every Saturday when we came in from the farm, and I would buy an ice-cream cone here. My grandfather died here. He was the deputy sheriff, and he interrupted three burglars here in 1932, just before Christmas. They shot him with his own gun and dumped his body into a ditch. It was snowing. The posse didn't find him for two days. They kept driving past him but saw only his coat, and they thought he was an old car fender. They caught the burglars, though, two Indians and a white man from Oklahoma, looking for drugs. None of them would say who pulled the trigger, so they all got life. That was five years before I was born, when my mother was sixteen. My grandmother gave me my grandfather's pocketknife when I was a kid. I still have it."

Isabel gazed at the building for some time. "Imagine," she said.

"The Depression was rough around here. There were a lot of outlaws. He had no business being a deputy. He was only a farmer, and he took the job as a favor to the sheriff in Hamilton, who was his friend."

"Why don't we get out of the car?" she asked.

"No. That's all there is to it, and it's all different now anyway."

We drove past the Baptist and Methodist churches and the Church of Christ, out the road that memory told me led to the farm. As we were about to pass the old cemetery I pulled over and stopped. "Let's see if we can find his grave," I said.

His family plot was near the road. His stone, standing among those of grandparents and parents and brothers and sisters, was larger than the others, etched only with his name and his birth and death dates.

We found the other too, my father's father, who had owned the farm. "He was a horseman and a hunter," I said, "but he had diabetes and the doctors took one of his legs. When they wanted to take the other one too, he couldn't stand the thought. He put a shotgun in his mouth and pulled the trigger. Before I was born."

The Johnson grass stood as high as the posts along the fences that lined the road, and the great yellow sunflowers stood even taller, drooping from their stalks, nodding. I had forgotten that so many lanes intersected the road, that so many houses stood at the ends of the lanes. Probably fewer than then, but still too many for my memory to cope with. Most of the houses were too new; and others had been abandoned years ago and were rotten beyond recognition. I studied the natural landmarks, the low bluffs, creeks, stands of trees. They all seemed familiar, like photographs of old relatives whose names have been forgotten.

Isabel sensed my uncertainty. "Do you know where you're going?" she asked.

"It feels right," I said, "but I can't be sure. It could be any of these."

I turned into a lane that led to a house old enough to contain someone who might remember. When I stopped outside the fence, two black-and-tan hounds crawled from under the porch and stretched in the sun, just as they used to. A woman's voice spoke cautiously in the dark interior behind the screen door. A man opened the door and stepped onto the porch. He wore a billed farmer's cap and a stubble of black beard. His dark eyes studied my own beard, my long hair, my red VW.

"Sorry to bother you," I said, "but I need directions. I'm looking for a place where I used to live when I was a kid." I told him my name and my father's name and tried to describe the farm to him.

The farm, he said, was still called by my grandfather's name, the Gate Woolley farm. It was sold right after the war, he said, to a fellow named Henson. "I knowed your father once," he said. "Lived over at Stephenville then. Had two sons, I remember. I guess one of them was you."

"No, they would have been by a later marriage."

"Oh. Well, your dad lives over at Meridian now, don't he?" The hounds stood by his legs, wagging their tails.

"I don't know," I said. "I haven't seen him in a long time."

He gestured, directing me past the farms of people I didn't know, telling me to turn left here, left again there, and to go south about a mile. "Turn right," he said, "and in another mile or two you'll see the water tank standing back from the road. You can't miss it."

I thanked him and returned to the car. The man went into the house and the dogs crawled under the porch again.

"They'll talk about us the rest of the day," I said.

"Does he know where it is?" Isabel asked.

"Yeah, *he* does, but I still don't."

We wandered, trying to guess which farm was which, which water tank was the one we couldn't miss. "It's hopeless," I said. "Let's go back. You have an idea what it was like, anyway."

"Ask him," she said, pointing at a pickup coming down the road toward us. "If he doesn't know, we'll go back."

I stuck my arm out the window and waved. The pickup pulled alongside and stopped. The man was big and old, smiling. I asked him if he knew where the Gate Woolley farm was.

His smile widened. "I ought to," he said. "I've lived on it since '45."

"Mind if we go look at it?" I asked. "I lived there when I was a child."

"Sure don't," he said. "Just follow me." He backed the pickup, turned it around in the road and headed in the direction from which he had come.

I would never have found the place. The old house was gone, replaced by a larger, more solid one. The big frame barn was gone, blown down, Mr. Henson said, and replaced by a smaller sheet-metal one. The windmill and tank tower were gone, replaced by an electric pump. Was its small tank the one I was supposed to see from the road? But the fig tree that had grown beside the windmill was there, and the pomegranate bush by the fence, both still yielding, Mrs. Henson said as she poured us ice water in the kitchen.

The Hensons knew our history and the histories of all who had lived around us. Some remained but most had moved away. She mentioned a boy I had started to first grade with. "He's had three wives," she said. "The first one was rotten. She run around on him. The second one died. He's married to a nurse now. Widow with four kids, and three kids of his own. Getting along well, I hear. He sells Fords over at Stephenville. How long have you two been married?"

"We aren't married," Isabel said. "I live in New York. I'm just in Texas for a visit."

"New York! My! You're a long way from home, just to visit!" Mrs. Henson was storing up mental notes. "How often do you see your daddy?" she asked me.

"Not since we left here," I said.

"Really? He lives at Meridian now," she said. "He has heart trouble, they say."

"Mind if I look around outside?"

"Help yourself," Mr. Henson said. "Better stay out of the fields, though. The snakes are bad this year."

Less had changed than I thought. The old corncrib, where my father used to kill rats and copperheads, was still there. So was the stone watering trough, down by the barn, and the weathered old smokehouse, which had served as a storeroom in our day. I had found my grandfather's trunk in there, and opened it and discovered his pipe and reading glasses and straight razor and hypodermic syringes. I took them to my mother and asked if I could have them. She put them back and told me never to open the trunk again. My mother's garden was still behind the smokehouse, still yielding, I guessed from the withered bean vines and cornstalks. Gazing at the far field, down by the creek, I imagined I saw my father on his tractor, and myself carrying him a jug of water.

"We just passed the road to Meridian," Isabel said. "Let's go by."

"Why?"

"To see where he lives. Aren't you curious? We've got time."

I took the road. We stopped in the town square, and Isabel got out and asked an old man where my father lived. "He must be important," she said, getting back into the car. "He asked, 'The business or the residence?' "

The residence was a mile or two outside the town, easily recognized by the neat white wooden fence that the old man had described and the neat white barns and brick house that sat about fifty yards back from the road. Even in the dusk it was obvious that he had prospered. I drove slowly, trying to take it all in and keep my eyes on the road at the same time. As we passed the gate I happened to glance up the driveway.

He was sitting in a chair in his backyard, silhouetted against the buttermilk sunset. From the way he was sitting, the slope of his bones, I recognized him. "That's him!" I said. "I'm going to say something to him!" I turned the car and headed into the driveway.

"What are you going to say?" Isabel asked.

"I don't know." My heart was beating fast. I was almost giddy. I drove up the driveway, into the backyard, and stopped a few feet from his chair. A gray-haired woman was sitting facing him, hidden from the road by a shrub. She looked up, alarmed. I knew then that I couldn't identify myself. She might not know I existed. I got out of the car and walked to my father and stood facing him, my back to her.

He was heavier, a little gray at the temples, but he hadn't really changed. He sat in khakis and white undershirt, barefoot, as he always did. His cheekbones were as high, Indianlike, his eyes as dark and steady through his glasses. He held a chew of tobacco in his cheek and didn't move, only stared into my eyes, never looking away, saying nothing.

"I seem to be lost," I said. "Can you tell me how to get to the Dallas highway?"

"Which way you coming from?" he asked. His voice was as steady and dark as his eyes. It hadn't changed.

"From Meridian."

12

"Well, you missed it. Go back to town. A sign in the square tells you which way. Highway Sixty-seven."

I made no move to go. We kept staring into each other's eyes. He frowned slightly, as if trying to recall something. The woman behind me coughed and shifted in her chair.

"How's that again?" I asked.

"Highway Sixty-seven's the one you want. Go back to Meridian. There's a sign in the square with an arrow pointing to Sixty-seven. Turn that way. When you get to the highway, turn right. It'll take you right to Dallas." He didn't move, didn't gesture.

I waited for him to say more. He didn't. "Much obliged," I said. I felt strangely light, as if relieved of some dark, indefinite duty. I turned toward the car.

Isabel was staring through the windshield, wide-eyed. When we were past the gate she asked, "What did you say to him?"

"I asked directions to Dallas."

"That's all?"

"I asked him to repeat it."

"He knew you. His eyes never left you. It took my breath away."

"Maybe he thought he ought to know me."

Isabel touched my arm. "Don't just leave it at that," she said.

The next morning I wrote to Ted and Pat. "I'm having a special birthday," I said. And I wrote to him and said, "I'm the man in the red car, and I'm your eldest son."

Only Ted and Pat replied.

"Maybe he never got the letter," Isabel said.

"I don't know," I said. "Don't worry."

July 1981

I remember seeing Audie Murphy on the cover of Life *with his Medal of Honor hanging around his neck. The most decorated American soldier of World War II. He looked about twelve years old. As I was growing up, I saw all his movies, I think. Or nearly all. He never seemed to grow older, maybe because he already was old.*

The Hero's Hometown

The young woman at the cash register in Woody's store regards the visitor with blank wonderment. "I never heard of him," she says.

"Audie Murphy. The most decorated soldier of World War II. He was from here."

"Oh. Well, I wasn't born then."

She hasn't read the historical marker that stands forlornly beside U.S. 69 on the southern edge of town: "Most decorated soldier in World War II. Born 4.5 miles south, June 20, 1924, sixth of nine children of tenant farmers Emmett and Josie Killian Murphy. Living on various farms, Audie Murphy went to school through the eighth grade in Celeste — considered the family's hometown."

The marker's flat prose goes on to sketch Audie's childhood of bleak poverty, his war record of extraordinary courage and bravery, his career as a movie actor. He was one of the most popular Western stars of the 1950s, but his most famous role was as himself in *To Hell and Back*, his memoir of his war experiences.

The marker's last lines tell of his death in the crash of a private plane in 1971. He was forty-six years old, survived by a widow and two sons.

To those born after V-E Day, it's just history, as remote from their own lives as the War of the Roses. But a few in the town and the surrounding countryside still remember the baby-faced buck private who marched away to fight the Nazis and the somehow different first lieutenant who returned three years later as the most honored soldier in American history.

Audie was credited with killing or capturing more than 240 German soldiers. He had received a battlefield commission and thirty-three military citations and awards, including the Medal of Honor and every other medal for valor that the United States can bestow, plus three awarded by France and one by Belgium. He was wounded three times. When he was discharged, his face was on the cover of *Life*. And when he came home, he wasn't yet twenty-one years old.

Audie's life was never easy, his old friends say. Even after the war, even while basking in the nation's adoration and winning wealth and fame in Hollywood, he always seemed under an invisible burden that he couldn't lay down.

"He come back here after the war in a brand new Buick convertible and decided we needed to go rabbit hunting in that car that very night," says Monroe Hackney, Audie's closest boyhood buddy. "We went flying over them back roads. We had a ball. But Audie never was really happy

16

after the war. He never could get settled down. The war had a whole lot of effect on him."

"He was a very private person," says Mr. Hackney's wife, Martha. "He was shy. He didn't like the praise he got when he come home. He said the real heroes of the war was those that was killed. He sat down and visited with me for two hours one morning after Monroe had gone to work. He told me things. He wasn't happy with Hollywood. He said, `Martha, I think I should buy a section of land in West Texas, and you and Monroe can live on it. It would be a place for me to hide out. I am so tired of crowds.' "

He never bought the land in West Texas. He never lived again in Celeste after the war, nor in the community of Kingston, where another historical marker stands near the site of his birth, nor in Farmersville, which erected a stone monument to him in its square, nor in Greenville, whose public library has an Audie Murphy Room full of photographs and paintings of him, nor in Addison, where he owned a ranch for six months, then sold it. (His house is now Dovie's restaurant.)

"Every town in this area from Bonham to Greenville claims to be where Audie Murphy lived," says Danny Lipsey, proprietor of Lipsey's Grocery in Kingston.

But Audie remained in Hollywood, a place whose culture he hated, according to his biographers. There he married a starlet and divorced her and married again. He gambled heavily and suffered recurring nightmares about the war, and would wake up screaming, gun in hand, and shoot at mirrors, lamps, and light switches.

But he returned often to visit with those who had befriended him in the days when he and his mother and his eight brothers and sisters were living on the brink of starvation in a country town where nobody else had much, either.

17

Neil Williams, who still lives in a white frame house about a mile from where Audie was born, worked beside him in the cotton fields when they were fifteen or sixteen years old. "Those rows were only thirty-six inches apart," he says. "When you're hoeing cotton up and down them all day, you get to know each other pretty well. Audie and I even had to share the same bed in the upper story of that old farmer's house."

The historical marker is incorrect, Mr. Williams says. "Audie never got to the eighth grade. He had four years of schooling at Celeste and one over there at Floyd. Then his daddy run off, and Audie had to quit school to take care of his family."

Emmett Murphy — a "drinking man," they say in Celeste — simply went away one day and left his wife and children to fend for themselves. Audie, who was about eleven at the time, became the family's chief breadwinner.

"He really come up the hard way," Mr. Williams says. "I mean, just really *hard*. The Depression was on during the time we was growing up, and not anybody had any money hardly. But the Murphys was as broke as the Ten Commandments. They actually didn't have enough to eat sometimes. A fellow I knew had a turnip patch. One winter, when the ground was froze, he looked out the window and saw Audie out there with a short-handled grubbing hoe, trying to dig some of them turnips out. His family was living in a boxcar at the time."

The blackland prairie of Hunt County was cotton country in those days. Little one hundred-acre family farms surrounded Celeste, and the farmers raised enough cotton to keep four gins busy. U.S. 69, the town's main street, was lined with grocery and drugstores, cafes, gas stations, a couple of honky-tonks, and four doctors' offices. When the 1940 census was taken, 730 people lived there.

"It was a good little town," says Bill Caldwell, who grew up in Celeste but lives twelve miles down the road in Greenville now. "We had a hardware store, a washateria, a cafe. There was a place that sold coal and grain. There was a couple of hotels." They all huddled at the foot of a tall water tower in the town's center. "Celeste was poor, but everybody seemed happy," Mr. Caldwell says.

Neighbors gave milk, eggs, butter, and chickens to the Murphys sometimes, and Audie worked for whoever would hire him to do whatever needed to be done. In his spare time, he wandered the prairie with his single-shot .22 rifle, hunting squirrels and rabbits for the family table.

"Audie could hear a squirrel walking two miles away," says Mr. Hackney, who often accompanied him. "He was an excellent shot. You know them Big Little Books kids used to have? Me and him would hold them up and shoot them out of each other's hands with our rifles. That was real stupid, but neither one of us ever got shot."

Audie loved guns, his friends say, and would play dangerous pranks with them, firing over people's heads or near their feet to frighten them. "He always had some kind of firearm close by," Mr. Williams says, "and he didn't seem to fear them much. My daddy taught me when I was a small boy to respect those firearms as dangerous. Audie didn't seem to think they were. He was a good shot, though. He never hurt nobody."

Mr. Caldwell remembers buying a revolver from Audie when he was only twelve years old. "My grandmother had died, and they split up the inheritance," he recalls. "I got ten dollars as my part. Audie had this old pistol that he had gotten somewhere, and I paid him my inheritance for it. Then I got afraid my dad was going to find out about it. I tried to find somebody to buy it off of me, and finally a guy said he wanted it. I sold it to him on credit and never got my money for it."

Although small of stature — 5-foot-7 and 130 pounds when he entered the Army — Audie is remembered in Celeste as a hot-tempered scrapper and a daredevil.

"He had more nerve than anybody I ever knew," Mr. Williams says. "One time him and Monroe, his best friend, and Robert Cawthon climbed the water tower, to that platform that goes around the bottom of the tank, and Robert and Monroe was sitting there with their legs dangling over the side, and they noticed Audie wasn't with them. They went all around that tank looking for him, but he wasn't there. Then they saw this little bitty ladder that led to a big ball on top of the tank. And Audie had climbed that little bitty ladder and was sitting on that ball, right on the tip top of the tower."

When the weather was good, trips up the water tower were almost nightly occurrences, Mr. Hackney says. "Sometimes we would just sit up there and look around," he says. "Sometimes we would throw rocks at the honky-tonk that was down below." The rocks made an awful racket on the sheet-metal roof, and the honky-tonk's patrons would flee into the night. "It was just something to do," Mr. Hackney says.

But there was a bitter underside to this Huckleberry Finn childhood in this poor-but-happy town. Because of Emmett Murphy's bad repute, many parents in Celeste forbade their sons and daughters to associate with Audie and his brothers and sisters.

"When we was starting to school, some of the kids wanted to pull him down because of his dad," Mr. Hackney says. "But they wasn't pulling Audie Murphy down. He had more pride than anybody I ever met. He kept his head up regardless. He was a real nice guy. He had no bad habits or nothing. He didn't use tobacco. He kept himself neat and clean. He was as honest as the day is long. And he wasn't afraid of nothing. He was a little fighting Irishman, a real boogeroo. And you was either his friend or you wasn't. And if you wasn't, look out."

When Audie was sixteen, his mother, whom he adored, died, and the burden on his narrow shoulders grew even heavier. Had it not been for the kindness of his neighbors, he and his brothers and sisters might not have survived.

"Audie Murphy never did forget people that was nice to him," says Mr. Williams, "and he never did forget the ones that *wasn't* nice to him. He would give you a fight, in the church house or anywheres, if you wanted one."

The one hundred-acre cotton farms where Audie worked to feed his family are gone now, swallowed up by much larger operations that grow milo, wheat, and corn, and where cattle graze. Most of the people who lived on the land moved away long ago in search of jobs. "We've got only one cotton gin now, and it's barely getting by," says Mr. Hackney. Most of the old business buildings are empty, and pansies are growing out of the cracks in the sidewalks.

But, oddly, the population of Celeste is 733, according to the sign beside the highway, almost the same as when Audie put his younger brothers and sisters in an orphanage and marched off to war. "A lot of people come back here to retire," Mr. Hackney says.

And as long as there are old folks in Celeste, he says, Audie Murphy won't be forgotten.

"Me and my cousin George was talking about him just the other day," Mr. Hackney says. "His name comes up in a lot of conversations around here. We want to keep it coming up. A country without heroes is hurting. We need to keep him alive."

August 1994

When I was a teenager, my friends Albert Fryar, Horace Crawford, Bill Young, and I used to camp in a tent in Skillman Grove during Bloys Camp Meeting. There we would play penny ante poker, whittle, moon over girls we were too shy to approach, and, like everybody else, go to church. We earned our keep by working in the serving line at the Jones-Espy-Finley Camp at mealtime.

Albert is dead now. The rest of us are grizzled. The girls we mooned over are grandmothers. But Bloys Camp Meeting is vigorous and thriving, now attended by the fourth and fifth generations of the families who founded it.

The Meeting at Skillman Grove

While the wood-smoke aroma of the supper fires still lingers over Skillman Grove, a clanging bell calls worshipers to the tabernacle. "Lift up your hearts," the Reverend Dale Powell tells them, "lift up your minds, lift up your arms, for God is reaching down."

These words begin the 105th session of the Bloys Camp Meeting. Then the people sing *How Firm a Foundation*, the same hymn their ancestors sang when they first gathered under a huge oak in this grove in 1890, the same hymn that has begun all the gatherings in the grove every year since.

Mr. Powell, Presbyterian pastor for Fort Davis and Marfa and superintendent of the camp, which is held the first part of every August, reminds the people of the few simple rules that will govern their six-day stay:

No applauding in church, no alcoholic beverages, no firearms, no boulder-rolling on the mountain behind the camp, no loud noises after 11:00 p.m., no "kodaking" on Sunday, no short shorts on the women, no buying or selling on the campground.

He introduces the four preachers who will take turns in the pulpit during each day's three preaching services. As always, they represent the Presbyterians, the Christian Church (Disciples of Christ), the Baptists, and the Methodists. Bible study will be at 9:00 a.m. each day, as always, and prayer meetings for men and women at 5:00 p.m.

But there's bad news, Mr. Powell says: Estelle Bloys Fawcett is very ill, and unable to attend.

No one remembers when, if ever, Mrs. Fawcett has missed camp meeting before, for she has been accustomed to celebrating her birthday here. "I was told," says Mr. Powell, "that she is very mad about this."

Of the seven children of the Reverend William Benjamin Bloys, the Presbyterian missionary who founded the meeting, and Isabelle, his wife, only Mrs. Fawcett is still living. The birthday she won't celebrate at Skillman Grove this year will be her 102d.

For her and many others whose roots are deep in the rocky soil of Far West Texas and Southern New Mexico, the Bloys Camp Meeting is the hub about which the rest of the year turns, because the meeting — though established, according to its charter, for "the worship of almighty God" — also is a reunion of the now-scattered clans that settled the surrounding mountains and plateaus more than a century ago. And it's a celebration of the order and civilization that a humble missionary helped bring to a wild and violent land, and the tolerance and generosity that he tried to plant in the hearts of his flock.

"From the very beginning, Brother Bloys insisted that members of every denomination would be welcome to worship here," says Fritz Kahl, a recent president of the Bloys Camp Meeting Association. "He believed that the things people have in common are more important than the things they disagree about. I think it's because of this that a feeling of good will, of religion, has been evident in Marfa, in Alpine, in Fort Davis, for over one hundred years. Brother Bloys brought that feeling here. It has affected the way people live to this day.

"If Brother Bloys heard that some boys were mavericking, he would tell them they had to quit. If they didn't quit, he made them leave the country. And to this day, we have few cattle-stealings and few house break-ins. How has this worked over all these generations? I don't know. But I make no bones about it. This meeting is one of the greatest evidences of Christianity at work that I have ever seen."

The grove was named for Henry Skillman, who carried the mail between San Antonio and El Paso before there were any towns in the Trans-Pecos, even before the army established Fort Davis seventeen miles east of the grove in 1854. The spot provided wood, water, grass, and shelter under the oaks, and Mr. Skillman liked to camp there.

By the time Brother Bloys, a native Tennessean, and his family arrived in 1888, the Indians had been driven out of the mountains, replaced by ranchers who had moved their

herds westward during the decades following the Civil
War. But the ranches were scattered and isolated, and the
few settlements that had sprung up were scarcely centers
of civilization.

The adobe village that had grown beside the army post
at Fort Davis had an especially notorious reputation. A
haven for border riffraff, it was infested with gamblers,
prostitutes, bandits, gunmen on the lam, and cattle
rustlers.

"Perhaps no minister since the beginning of time ever
has been set down in the midst of as ruthless, as wild and
disorderly element as was this little pastor, one of the
most orderly and peaceful of men," wrote Will Evans, who
knew him. "Then, it would seem as if the entire region
was overrun by sin. Eleven saloons in the little town of
Fort Davis alone were running full blast to the accompani-
ment of attendant evils. It was a time when the [Texas]
Rangers had to take charge before court could be held."

Brother Bloys seemed an unlikely match for such an
environment. "He was a very small, frail man," says
Vivian Bloys Grubb, his granddaughter, who still lives in
the house the minister built in Fort Davis. Brother Bloys
had wanted to be a missionary to India, but two bouts
with pneumonia while he was in seminary left him too
weakened. He was sent to Texas instead. He got pneumonia again and almost died while living at Coleman,
then moved to higher, drier Fort Davis on the advice of
his doctor.

His small stature and fragile health notwithstanding,
the preacher apparently was fearless, and made a strong
impression on the toughs he encountered. "I have seen
him walk into a saloon full of drunken men, who were
yelling and cursing," wrote C.E. Wray, the first clerk of
neighboring Brewster County. "When he appeared in the
doorway, every curse was hushed; glasses half-raised to

cursing lips were lowered; profanity died half-spoken, and gambling games suspended operations. After speaking with whom he had business, with a friendly nod he went his way."

Besides ministering to his tiny flock in Fort Davis, Brother Bloys carried the gospel by horseback and buggy to the far-flung ranches of the Davis Mountains and the Big Bend, preaching sermons, performing marriages, offering communion, and baptizing children into whatever Protestant faith their parents favored.

"He was very thoughtful of other people's beliefs," Mrs. Grubb says. "I've heard that Granddad and a friend of his, Mr. S.A. Thompson, sat up all one night, studying books, trying to figure out how to do a Jewish funeral for a Jewish fellow who had died."

Brother Bloys nearly always traveled alone, and the ranches were days apart. "He spent many a night just out on the road," Mrs. Grubb says, "but I've never heard of anybody trying to rob him or harm him, like so many bandits would do when they saw somebody camping."

During one of Brother Bloys' ranch visits, his hosts, John Z. and Exa Means, suggested that the preacher hold an outdoor meeting and invite all the region's families to attend. He could give them a large dose of the gospel, and the ranch folk could enjoy a social time as well. Brother Bloys liked the idea and spread the word on his rounds. On October 10, 1890, forty-seven people gathered in Skillman Grove. There the missionary preached three sermons a day, with the shade of an oak as his sanctuary and an Arbuckles Coffee box as his pulpit. The families cooked in Dutch ovens and slept on the ground. Between services, the women — many of whom hadn't seen another woman for six months or more — visited under the trees.

When the meeting ended, the families decided to convene again the next year. Later, they raised $1,250 to buy the section of land on which Skillman Grove stands as a permanent campground, and agreed to come together for a week each year during the idle time between the spring branding roundup and the fall shipping roundup.

As the crowds grew, the oak gave way to a brush arbor, then to a large tent, and finally to a permanent tabernacle, enlarged several times over the years. As other preachers of various denominations moved into the Trans-Pecos to establish churches, they were invited to share the pulpit with Brother Bloys.

The family cook fires grew into huge cooking sheds, where the food still is supplied by the ranchers and pre-pared by their range cooks. It's still typical ranch grub — meat, potatoes, frijoles, chiles, biscuits, and coffee — and still is offered freely to all who wish to partake. Donations are welcome, but not solicited. The bedrolls under the wagons gave way to cots under tents, then to permanent cabins arranged in family groups around the cook sheds.

Today's campground includes more than four hundred such cabins, six large cook camps, an RV park across the road, the main tabernacle and several smaller ones used for services for children and teen-agers, a prayer chapel, a small museum, and a new reading room. It has become a rustic city, inhabited only one week a year by the more than three thousand people who attend the meeting.

In the early times, many families were on the road for several days in wagons and on horseback to reach the grove, spending nights with other families along the way, and joining with them for the rest of the journey. Even the automobile didn't much ease the rigors of the trip, for the narrow mountain roads were still unpaved and the creeks unbridged. People who lived in the Pecos country north of Fort Davis, for instance, had to cross Limpia Creek, which runs through the Davis Mountains, thirty-one times. "Our dread was that Limpia would be on a rampage to delay our trip," wrote Mrs. R.T. Lewis, a pioneer wife. "At times we were held on its banks overnight waiting for the waters to subside after a heavy rain."

Now the interstates come within a hoot and a holler of the grove, and a commuter airline flight is available as close as Alpine, about forty miles away.

Even the preaching has changed. In earlier days, the preachers labored mightily to steer their listeners away from the primitive evils of the frontier into the arms of the Lord and onto the path of honesty, sobriety, nonviolence, and civic order. "In those times, a lot of the people were unchurched," says Dr. Bryan Feille, a professor at Texas Christian University's Brite Divinity School and the Disciples preacher at this year's meeting. "The land was pretty raw. There were a lot of conversions and a lot of baptisms. But now most people have an affiliation with a church, so the preaching is more for enlightenment and nurturing, rather than for conversion."

But even today lives are changed at Bloys, says Dr. Feille, who began attending the meeting with his uncle and aunt when he was seven years old. "It was here that I decided to be a minister. It was here that I first learned to read the Bible. It was here that I learned to really listen to sermons. And it was here that I first experienced the ecumenical spirit. My response to the preachers and the people here wasn't on a basis of denomination at all. In fact, I decided I wanted to be a minister while I was here, but I didn't know what denomination yet. That didn't matter to me."

Brother Bloys died at age seventy in 1917 and was buried in Fort Davis. Two years later, a tall granite monument to his memory was erected in Skillman Grove. It stands beside the tabernacle.

Andrew Prude led the singing at the first meeting in 1890. This year, his grandson, John Robert Prude, donated the new reading room where campers go to read the Bible and the newspapers or to use the telephone.

"I did this to honor Grandmother and Grandfather and Daddy," Mr. Prude says. "With all the generations together, our family has accumulated three hundred years of perfect attendance at Bloys Camp Meeting. The place has been such a blessing to our family that I had to do something for those who made this heritage possible for me."

"Heritage" and "tradition" come up often in camp-meeting conversations, for the meeting is woven so tightly into the fabric of many families' lives that to be absent is as unthinkable for them as it is for Estelle Bloys Fawcett.

"I love a story that my mother tells about my grand-mother," says Ann Espy Duncan, "that they were living in New Mexico, and my grandmother had to miss camp meeting. Mother says my grandmother would go down in the cellar at nine o'clock, at eleven o'clock, at three o'clock, and at eight o'clock and cry, because that's when the services were. I think that's the only camp meeting my mother has ever missed. My dad has *never* missed, and he's eighty-four."

Despite her living for the past twenty-four years in Richardson, Texas, almost five hundred miles from Skillman Grove, Mrs. Duncan has never missed a meeting, either. Her husband, Jim, who like his wife grew up in a Davis Mountains ranching family, has missed only twice, while he was in the army. "He said Christmas and camp meeting time were the hardest times," Mrs. Duncan says. "He knew exactly what was going on, but he couldn't be part of it." Their daughters represent the fifth generation of Mrs. Duncan's family to make the pilgrimage. "I feel like everybody is family out here," she says.

In Mrs. Duncan's case — and many others — almost everyone *is* family, for a lot of courting has been done at Bloys over the past century. "Besides the Espys and the Duncans, I'm kin to all the Evanses and all the Prudes," Mrs. Duncan says. "My gosh. It's mind-boggling."

Fritz Kahl's wife, Georgie Lee, whose grandparents, Mr. and Mrs. W.T. Jones, were among the original forty-seven worshipers in 1890, tries to count her relatives at this year's session:

"Let's see, there's about twenty over there," she says, pointing to a neighboring cabin. "And then Jan and her boys are coming. That would be . . . There's twelve in our family here. Then Alice's family. There's Alice and Bryant and Michelle and Bud, and they have six kids, so that's thirty-two. Then there's Holly and Rick and their five. And there's Amy and Stormy. That's forty-one. Then there's Ruthie and Bryant and their two. That's forty-five. And there's Sargie Ruth and Rue, that's forty-seven . . . . Mamaw Jones was a Jones before she married a Jones. She had a brother, Ed Jones, that married a Means, and they have a daughter, Mary. And she usually brings a grandchild or two. That's all on the Jones side. Then on the Espy side . . . Oh, there are at least one hundred of my relatives here. We count the Pages as kinfolks, too. They're from Eldorado. Papaw Espy and Mrs. Page were cousins . . . . "

Keeping in touch with kin is a big reason Gail Cinelli, one of Mr. and Mrs. Kahl's daughters, journeys from Yarmouth, Maine, for the meeting each year. "It's a good chance to see a lot of family and to stay connected with my roots," she says, "and for my husband — who grew up in Detroit — and my children to get a sense of our heritage and our traditions and what life is like in West Texas."

Children roam the campground in packs, roping each other, pitching washers, whittling, climbing trees and the mountain behind the camp. At night, their flashlights flicker among the oaks like lightning bugs. Their cries pierce the night until the 11:00 p.m. hush hour. "It's wonderful to be a kid out here," Mrs. Cinelli says. "There's a special connection with cousins that happens at camp meeting that they'll have all their lives. That's why the kids want to come — to see their cousins and climb the mountain and go through the bat cave. I like to sit on the porch and talk, and watch the kids climb this tree that's been here forever and that I climbed when I was a kid."

There are few long pauses in the between-services porch visiting at Bloys, few long gazes into distance. Just talk, talk, talk of families, of the events of the past year, and — as always in the ranch country — the weather, which is so dry this year that Limpia Creek has ceased to flow and lightning is setting fires in the mountains.

"Lord," prays a rancher saying noontime grace at one of the cook camps, "we thank you for the rain you're going to give us."

It's a faith to which Brother Bloys might have said, "Amen."

August 1994

Herbert L. Kokernot, Jr., succeeded his father as the owner of the 06, one of the largest ranches in Jeff Davis and Brewster counties, and his family had — and still has — a number of financial interests elsewhere. Naturally, people trying to raise money for good causes often put the touch on him, and — if the cause was really a good one — he never turned them down. He was one of the most generous and most modest philanthropists in all of West Texas. It would be hard to overestimate the good that he did during his long life.

But to the kids growing up in the Davis Mountains and the Big Bend during the 1940s and '50s, Mr. Kokernot's most important contribution was Kokernot Field and the baseball games that were played there.

Herbert Kokernot, Satchel Paige, and Me

The first major league baseball games I saw were in, of all places, Alpine, a small, beautiful cowboy town tucked into the mountains of Far West Texas. Look at a map of Texas, over on the left-hand side, in that broad arm of the state that juts between Mexico and New Mexico. Now look at the part of that arm that seems to sag into Mexico.

That's the Big Bend of the Rio Grande, and that's where you'll find Alpine. And you'll notice that there isn't much around Alpine for miles — a few tiny towns, a few roads connecting them. Nothing else but mountains and desert.

In the early 1950s, the region was much more isolated than it is now. The interstate highway system hadn't been built. There was no television because the video waves couldn't get over the mountains. KVLF, "The Voice of the Last Frontier," was the only radio station. Alpine and the other little towns — Fort Davis, Marfa, Marathon, Presidio, Sanderson — resembled the towns in the Gene Autry and Roy Rogers movies of the time. The people who lived in the towns dressed much like the people in those movies, but not as fancy.

In those days, the major leagues stopped just west of the Mississippi River. The Cardinals and the Browns of St. Louis were the westernmost big league teams. But we kids in the Big Bend, closer to the Mexican frontier than to any American city, considered them our "home boys." Somewhere in the dim North, we knew, dwelt the White Sox and the Cubs, and eastward were the Reds. The other teams inhabited darkest Yankeeland, a country we could hardly imagine.

Still, we didn't feel as isolated as we were, for a big league game came to us every day via KVLF on the Liberty Baseball Network. Announcer Gordon McLendon, unbeknownst to us, wasn't even at the ballpark. He was in the basement of a hotel in Dallas, reading play-by-play accounts of the games off of a ticker tape and re-creating them. But his studio sound effects were so vivid and his voice was so filled with drama that his broadcasts were at least as exciting as those by Red Barber and Harry Carey and the other announcers who were really watching the games.

On the Liberty Baseball Network, the crack of the bat
was as crisp as a rifle shot, the roar of the crowd was as
overwhelming as a tidal wave, and Musial, Robinson,
DiMaggio, and Feller stood as tall as McLendon's voice
and our imaginations could make them — taller than any
mortal stands now or ever will again.

Gordon McLendon made baseball fans out of us, way
out there in the wilderness, and prepared us for Herbert
Kokernot, who was more important to the kids of Far West
Texas in the early '50s than Santa Claus could ever hope
to be.

Mr. Kokernot was a rich rancher who loved baseball. But
baseball teams were as scarce in our country as opera companies. So Mr. Kokernot assembled a bunch of high school
coaches, college kids, gas pump jockeys, and ranch hands
and organized a semiprofessional team. He named them
the Alpine Cowboys and pitted them against any foe he
could find — Air Force teams from Texas bases, the House
of David (a touring team from an odd religious institu-
tion), and other community semipros such as the Big Lake
Oilers. Anybody who had a bus and could find Alpine was
on the schedule.

He built a baseball stadium in Alpine and named it
Kokernot Field. It was modeled after Chicago's Wrigley
Field, which was then the classiest park in the major
leagues. Some of the major leaguers who later came there
said Mr. Kokernot's field, with its high stone walls decorated with iron baseballs and his "o6" cattle brand, was
superior to any of the big-time arenas.

In those days, a lot of the major league teams held their
spring training camps in California and Arizona. When
their camps ended, they traveled back to the East by train.
And every year, Mr. Kokernot somehow — perhaps by
standing on the tracks and waving — would persuade a

couple of the teams to stop in Alpine and play a game on his field.

Christmas was nothing compared to this. Schools from Odessa to near El Paso — two hundred miles from Alpine — would declare a holiday and fill their buses with boys and a few girls, each happily toting a dollar bill for pop and peanuts, and a fielder's glove to capture the official major league foul ball that was bound to fall into it. Our buses moved along the narrow highways like yellow insects following some inexplicable migratory urge, headed toward the biggest day of the year, always sunny, always noisy, always perfect.

Mr. Kokernot also made sure that the Cubs, the White Sox, the Browns, and the Pirates didn't dismiss our day as just another exhibition game in another tank town. He offered incentives — a hundred dollars to the pitchers for each man they struck out, fifty dollars to the fielders for each put-out, a thousand dollars for every home run. This was in the days before major leaguers became millionaires, and Mr. Kokernot's incentives were big money even to them. So they always played their best.

I witnessed three of those games. I have memories of them all. Nellie Fox of the Cubs, I remember, carried the biggest chaw of tobacco in his jaw that I had ever seen. I remember Ralph Kiner, the great home run hitter of the Pirates, muffing an easy fly in the outfield. It just bounced out of his glove and some of the people in the crowd booed. I thought they were edging close to blasphemy, booing a major leaguer.

The images of those games blend and change in my mind like the glass chips in a kaleidoscope. I don't recall the scores of any of them or who won, but it doesn't matter. What mattered then — and still matters to me now — is that a kid from one of the most isolated spots in North

America saw some of his heroes up close, face to face, and they were real. Men who had been demigods, known to me only in the dramatic recitals of Gordon McLendon and as pictures in sports magazines, their glorious deeds performed far, far away in a land I had never seen, had come to Alpine and shown me that they were flesh and blood.

The greatest player of them all was Satchel Paige.

In 1951, the year I saw him, Paige was pitching for the St. Louis Browns, the worst team in the majors. They were pitiful, the perennial doormat of the American League. Since the Browns were so bad, their owner, Bill Veeck, who's generally considered the greatest showman in the history of baseball, was resorting to outlandish measures to attract fans to their games. They were written up in *The Sporting News* and the sports magazines, and we read about them even out where we were.

But I recall only two: Eddie Gaedel, the midget whom Veeck hired to lead off his batting order (he walked in his only plate appearance and was replaced by a pinch runner), and Satchel Paige.

Paige in 1951 was either forty-five or fifty-one years old, depending on which of two disputed birth dates is correct. But we didn't know that. We just knew he was old, very old, because Bill Veeck kept telling everybody that he was ancient, a Methuselah in a baseball uniform. And he was colorful.

For instance, Paige had given all his pitches nicknames. He threw a changeup that he called a "two-hump blooper," and a medium fast ball named "Little Tom," and a hard fast ball called "Long Tom," and a pitch called the "hesitation pitch" that nobody else threw. And he always was saying wise, funny things relating to his age, such as his classic: "Don't look back. Something might be gaining on you."

The sportswriters loved him. Whenever Paige took the mound, Gordon McLendon always had a funny Satchel story or two to pass on to us, gathered around our radios. We kids came to regard him as a sort of wise, funny Uncle Remus of baseball, a clown that Bill Veeck had invented to put a few bodies into his empty ballpark.

We didn't know Paige was one of the greatest pitchers in the history of the game. We had never heard of the Negro Leagues. We didn't know about the decades that Paige had spent pitching for the Birmingham Black Barons, the Nashville Elite Giants, the Pittsburgh Crawfords, the Kansas City Monarchs, and a half-dozen other teams whose games were never re-created on the Liberty Baseball Network. We didn't know that he had toured with the great Dizzy Dean after the 1934 season and won four of the six games they pitched against each other. We didn't know that after Joe DiMaggio faced him in an exhibition game in 1935, Joltin' Joe had called him "the best I've ever faced, and the fastest." We didn't know that after Jackie Robinson cracked the color line in 1945 and later became the first black man to play in the majors, Paige already had been a hidden star for almost twenty years.

But while our bus moved slowly through the mountains toward Alpine, where the Browns were going to play the Pirates, it was Satchel Paige we talked of, Satchel Paige we wanted to see. His was the only familiar name on the pitiful Browns' roster. And the Pirates, except for Kiner, were almost as bad.

Because our high school coach played for the Alpine Cowboys, our seats were on the first base line, not far from the Browns' dugout, and before the game we crowded there, getting autographs from anyone who would sign our programs. "Is Satchel here?" we asked. "Did he come?"

And the white guys would grin and reply, "Oh, he'll be along. Old Satch, he's so old it takes him a long time to get dressed."

Then he appeared: A very tall, very dark man who seemed to be all arms and legs, greeting us with the kindest, gentlest smile I had ever seen on a man. He didn't look old. He looked . . . wonderful. He stood by the fence, signing our programs, talking softly, patiently, making sure he didn't miss anybody. Then, while the National Anthem was playing, he disappeared into the dugout.

I don't remember much about the game except Kiner dropping that fly and us hollering, "We want Satchel! Let Satchel pitch!" Then, late in the game, the announcer told us: Satchel Paige was coming in for St. Louis.

He was driven from the dugout to the mound on a golf cart — Bill Veeck's way of showing us how old Paige was. Everybody laughed. He threw a few warmup pitches, using an awkward, old-fashioned windmill windup that exaggerated his lankiness and made us laugh more.

Then he faced his first batter, and struck him out. Suddenly, I realized that when Paige finished that crazy windmill motion and let the ball go, I didn't see it again until it hit the catcher's mitt. He quickly struck out the side.

The golf cart moved to the mound and carried him back to the dugout. And, because we yelled for more, it took him back to the mound for another inning, and he struck out the side again.

This time, as the cart was bringing him from the mound, several of the Browns lifted a huge, upholstered chaise longue out of the dugout and set it on the grass near the fence, then lifted Paige from the cart and laid him on the chair, as if he were too old and tired to move.

Paige was smiling, going along with the gag. But I was close enough to see that he hadn't broken a sweat. He could have pitched all afternoon and not one of those Pirates, except maybe Kiner, could have touched the ball.

I knew then that I was looking at a great man. And it was a great day for me when, in 1971, the first real hero I had ever seen was named to the Hall of Fame.

December 1992

*For many years, Dallas pretended it was part of the sophisti-
cated East, not rough-around-the-edges Texas. Then, in the
1970s, cowboy boots and big hats became a fad in the East,
and being Texan was perceived as a good thing. So always-
fashionable Dallas started wearing boots and big hats, too. It
even imported a small herd of longhorns to stroll along the
Trinity riverbank during the Republican National Convention
in 1984.*

*Then the fad passed, and Dallas was left confused. Some of
its citizens wanted to remain part of Texas, some wanted to be
sophisticated easterners again, and some started talking about
Big D becoming an "international city," whatever that is.*

The following piece reflects that confusion.

*Incidentally, the lawsuit filed against the city went nowhere,
and the bronze steers are very popular with the tourists.*

The Art Snobs Meet Frankensteer

A few years ago, Tex Schramm was reminiscing about
the coming of professional football to Dallas. One of his
duties as general manager of the team was to give it a
name: "So I said, 'Damn it, what's the first thing people

think of when they think of Texas? Cowboys!' So I called them the Cowboys."

But the team hadn't come to Texas. It had come to Dallas. To Mr. Schramm's surprise, dozens of Dallasites took pen or phone in hand to express dismay. "Dallas was where the East ended!" he remembered them telling him. "It was cosmopolitan, for God's sake! Fort Worth was the West! And they were saying, 'Cowboys? Jesus! That's not Neiman Marcus!'"

That was thirty-three years ago. A few months ago, bulldozers began tearing up a parking lot in front of the Dallas Convention Center and building a hill of dirt. The lot is about to be transformed into a four-acre park called Pioneer Plaza, in honor of the early settlers of Dallas, some of whom are buried in the adjacent cemetery.

The finished park will feature a twelve-foot waterfall over a limestone cliff, a rushing stream, a reflecting pool at the corner of Young and Griffin streets, trees, seats for tired tourists, a plaque about the history of Dallas, and a miniature prairie planted in buffalo grass.

But the centerpiece of Pioneer Plaza, its *raison d'etre*, if you will, is to be . . . cowboys. Three of them. One white, one black, one Hispanic. In bronze. Ten and a half feet tall in the saddle. And . . . cows. Well, steers. In bronze. Seventy of them. About six feet tall at the shoulder. Driven by the three cowboys, the steers will appear to be meandering down the new hill, through Pioneer Plaza on their way to market. Just a few blocks from Neiman Marcus.

The whole project is supposed to cost about nine million dollars — about five million dollars for the land, provided by the city, and about four million dollars for the landscaping and the sculpture, to be provided by the Dallas Parks Foundation.

The sculpture, the first pieces of which are now being cast at the Eagle Bronze foundry in Lander, Wyoming, is the brainchild of the foundation, a private, nonprofit organization that raises money from private sources to help out the city of Dallas in such projects as developing parks and planting trees on public lands.

Or, more precisely, it's the brainchild of real estate developer Trammell Crow, chairman of the foundation's board of directors, who with a single application of political clout may be turning eastward-looking, sophisticated, cosmopolitan Dallas into Cowtown East.

At least that's the view of the Public Art Committee, an adjunct of the city Cultural Affairs Commission, whose job it is to look artistic gift horses in the mouth and advise the City Council whether to accept them. In this case, the committee's recommendation was a resounding no, on grounds that the sculpture is bad art, bad history, and a possible hazard to the public safety. But the Cultural Affairs Commission overruled the committee and recommended that the City Council approve the project, which it did.

Agreeing with the Public Art Committee is a group of Dallas artists who believe the shortcut path that the Dallas Parks Foundation took through the City Hall bureaucracy was an illegal one. They've filed a lawsuit against the city to halt the project.

They also condemn the Parks Foundation's image of Dallas and its past as historically incorrect. And, because of the way the sculptor is planning to create the animals — by making an assortment of steer horns, tails, and hooves and attaching them in various combinations to ten basic steer bodies, instead of sculpting each beast individually — they refer to the project as "Frankensteer."

On the other hand, the member organizations of the city's tourist business establishment — the Central Dallas Association, the Dallas Convention and Visitors Bureau, the Greater Dallas Chamber of Commerce, and the

Hotel/Motel Association of Greater Dallas — all have issued statements in praise of the project. Les Tanaka, executive vice president of the Hotel/Motel Association, went so far as to declare that because of Pioneer Plaza, we Dallasites already "have become the envy of everyone in the tourism industry, throughout the country."

And those most intimately involved in the project — Jack Beckman, president of the Mesquite Arena, home of the Mesquite Championship Rodeo, who is co-chairing the project for the Dallas Parks Foundation, and Robert Summers, the Glen Rose artist who is creating the steers and their herders — say it's time for Dallas to dismount its cultural high horse and admit at last that, yes, it's part of Texas.

"Dallas has always tried to be the New York City of the West, the most sophisticated city in the West, and there's nothing wrong with that," Mr. Summers says. "But it's a mind set. It's a facade. When we were kids we called it 'play like.' The fact remains that Texas was started on cattle. And Dallas is part of Texas. What hurts me more than anything people are saying about the art is that people don't want to admit their heritage. And this *is* the heritage of Dallas, whether they like it or not."

Besides, adds Mr. Beckman, Pioneer Plaza isn't really about art anyway. "This isn't just a piece of art, sitting out there for people to see its artistic value," he says. "This is supposed to look like a real cattle drive, not something somebody made up. Those cows are supposed to look like damned old longhorn cows or steers or whatever. You can call it art or you can call it crap. Either way, that's just your opinion. To me, it's sort of a ghost of our past, telling where we came from. And it'll be at the front door of the Convention Center, where many, many people from all over the world are coming to visit."

According to the Parks Foundation, that's why Dallas —
the part of it in front of the Convention Center, anyway
— is suddenly shucking its snooty cosmopolitan pose and
becoming part of cowboy Texas: because Texas is what the
tourists who come to Dallas want to see.

In 1990, says Paula Peters, executive director of the
Parks Foundation, the Convention Center and the
Convention and Visitors Bureau conducted a survey of just
about everybody who attended a convention in Dallas. "It
was something like two million people," she says, "and
they asked them some questions about Dallas: What did
you come here to see? What did you expect to see? What
didn't you like? What did you expect to see that you did-
n't see? What would you like to see more of?

"The overwhelming response they got was: Where is the
West? Not only Where is the West? but Where is Dallas
history? Did the city spring fullblown as a twentieth-cen-
tury city? Was it constructed in 1960? Where are the historic sites? Where's the story of how Dallas came into
being? And that was the seed of Pioneer Plaza."

A few years earlier, the City Council had hoped to lease
the parking lot as the site for a new convention hotel. But
when the oil bust came and the Dallas economy took a
dive, the city's negotiations with developer Vance Miller
and the Marriott Corp. fell apart. So when the master plan
for expansion of the Convention Center was completed in
1989, the four-acre plot was designated a green space.

Some critics of Pioneer Plaza have claimed that Mr.
Crow and the Dallas Parks Foundation offered to develop
the site as a means of preventing a hotel being built there
in the future — a hotel that would compete with the
Loews Anatole, partly owned by Mr. Crow's family, and
with the Hyatt Regency, which is owned by the Woodbine
Development Corp., whose president is John Scovell,

whose wife, Diane Scovell, is co-chair, with Jack Beckman, of the Pioneer Plaza project.

Mr. Crow (who was in Russia and unavailable for comment) has denied this. "There should be a beautiful entry to the Convention Center," he told reporters last May, after a briefing at which the City Council thanked him officially for developing Pioneer Plaza. "That's what started us putting a sculpture out there."

Ms. Peters denies it, too. "The city turned to the Parks Foundation and asked if we would help them develop that green space," she says. "The hotel-motel tax is being used to retire the indebtedness of the Convention Center expansion, but there was no money available for any improvements to that site. They needed us to come up with some private funding."

In 1991, during the early discussion with city bureaucrats and politicians about just how the plaza was going to be developed, apparently little was said about sculpture, and nothing about cowboys or steers. "The original proposal did not include an art project associated with it," says A.C. Gonzalez, the assistant city manager in charge of the Convention Center. "The first concept drawings had to do with landscaping work, a water project, and at the time of the actual presentation before the council for the contract, there was some thought about it being an art project, a sculpture or what-not, but nothing had really been decided."

However, Carl Lewis, a member of the Public Art Committee, says Ms. Peters broached the idea of a cattle drive sculpture to the group around January 1992, before the contract was signed. "We all chimed in," he says, "and our response was that there are already a number of projects that have to do with cattle in other cities. Besides, the history of Dallas is not one of cattle.

"It came past us again later in the form of a proposal," he says. "We asked to see a maquette (a small model), and we asked to see a resume of the artist and other things. There was a certain amount of information that we needed in order to make an appropriate assessment as to whether this was a viable project. The Parks Foundation kept promising they would have a maquette soon, but they kept putting us off. Then we read in the newspaper and in the Parks Foundation newsletter that the contract with the city had been signed (by the city manager's office) and the landscaping was under way. I said, 'Wait a minute. How can you have a contract if the project hasn't gone through the appropriate review process?'"

The contract that the city signed with the Dallas Parks Foundation on March 26, 1992, says Mr. Gonzalez, "was simply to develop that site. There were no details in it about what kind of development Pioneer Plaza was going to be, and no specific mention of any artwork.

"For that reason, there really wasn't anything to take before the Public Art Committee or the Cultural Affairs Commission," he says. "The contract anticipated, however, that if there was going to be some art feature, that feature would be coordinated with the Public Art Committee and the Cultural Affairs Commission."

The Parks Foundation already had begun its search for an artist. After conferring with galleries and collectors of western art, it had put together a list of some twenty sculptors who had done monumental bronze pieces. "We were committed to hiring an area artist," Ms. Peters says. "We went in person to look at the works of eight artists, and finally narrowed it down to two." Robert Summers, whose monumental works include a statue of Byron Nelson at Las Colinas and one of John Wayne at the

Orange County Airport in California, kept coming up on everybody's list, she says.

The foundation also hired historian A.C. Greene to write a report on the early history of Dallas, with emphasis on the trails that ran through the town in its early days. The gist of Mr. Greene's report was that Dallas became an important town because it stood at the junction of several trails that carried settlers, freight, and cattle to and fro in all directions across the Texas frontier.

John Neely Bryan, Dallas' first settler, had reached his new home on the east bank of the Trinity via an old north-south Indian trail called Coffee's Bend Road. An east-west trail called the Kickapoo Trace ran along what is now Commerce Street. Another north-south route called the Preston Trail ran along what is now Preston Road and brought thousands of settlers across the Red River into North Texas.

But the foundation was less interested in the trails that brought settlers into Dallas than in the Shawnee Trail, a trace that South Texas drovers used to herd cattle to markets in Missouri before the Civil War. The Shawnee originated in Brownsville, came north through Austin and Waco, crossed the Trinity near the present Hyatt Regency, went through downtown Dallas, and continued northward along Preston Road to the Red. The first herds moved along the trail in the 1850s, and until the opening of the war, it was the only route to the northern cattle markets.

But its fame was brief, and its role in the history of the West — and the history of Dallas — was minor. Cattle raisers in Missouri, whose more expensive livestock had to compete with the cheap Texas cattle on the market, claimed that the longhorns were infecting their cattle with Texas fever, a disease carried by ticks, which apparently didn't affect the wild longhorns but was fatal to more domestic stock. After a number of armed confrontations between Texas drovers and Missouri farmers, the Missouri markets were all but closed to Texas cattle.

Furthermore, the Texas cowboy hadn't yet become a folk hero. It wasn't until after the Confederate surrender, when war-impoverished Texans began moving cattle up the Chisholm Trail to Abilene, Dodge City, and the other Kansas railheads, that the cowboy grew in the American imagination into a romantic knight of the prairie.

"Dallas had a cattle trail before Fort Worth did," Mr. Greene says, "but by the time the Chisholm Trail opened in 1867, all the cattle and everything else had moved west. That's why Fort Worth, and not Dallas, became Cowtown."

Instead, Dallas became the mercantile and financial center for cotton-farming East Texas and, later, the burgeoning Texas oil business.

So when a cousin called Robert Summers in Glen Rose and told him that Dallas was about to commission a trail drive sculpture for downtown, his reaction was: "Are you sure it's *Dallas*?" And when his cousin sent him an August 1992 newspaper article describing the project, he said: "This must be a misprint. Three horses and riders and *seventy* longhorns?"

Not long after the article appeared, Jack Morris of the Altermann & Morris Art Gallery in Dallas, which represents Mr. Summers, called and asked him if he would be interested in the job. He said, "Sure." And last fall, Mr. Morris and his partner, Tony Altermann, landed the commission for their client.

"When I went to Trammell Crow's office, an architect had designed a scale model of the plot," Mr. Summers remembers. "They already had a bunch of little half-inch steers arranged on it like an army marching across a flat field. They asked me, 'What do you think of this?'

"And I said, 'That's probably the most uninteresting thing I've ever seen.'

"And they said, 'Well, what would *you* do?'

"They had some buckets of sand there, so I dumped one of them on the desk and started making a hill out of it. We spent two hours playing with the sand and the steers, and they took pictures of it, and that was it."

Mr. Summers went home to Glen Rose to start work on his maquettes. He says he would prefer not to have to assemble the steers from interchangeable parts, but the cost of seventy individually sculpted steers would be prohibitive.

When Mr. Beckman presented the maquettes to the Public Art Committee, the steerhockey hit the fan.

"The first reason was safety," says Sharon Leeber, a Dallas art consultant and a member of the Public Art Committee. "They said they would blunt the horns of the steers so people won't be impaled on them, but the sculpture is certainly going to cause a safety problem. You can have massive internal injuries from falling on anything blunt. The other thing is people falling off of them. What are they going to fall onto? Prairie grass? Mud? First, they said the steers were going to be a storybook thing, with kids climbing all over them and getting their pictures taken. Then they said, 'No, nobody is going to be allowed to climb on them.' Well, who's going to enforce that? And if, during some Texas-OU weekend, a drunk falls off of one of those steers and breaks his neck, who's going to be liable?

"The second reason was the maintenance cost," she says. "The Dallas Parks Foundation was predicting between five thousand dollars and ten thousand dollars, basically for washing and waxing the steers twice a year. That didn't include any repair or any other maintenance that might have to be done. So nobody knows what the maintenance really will be. And the money has to come out of the Convention Center budget."

She's talking about why the Public Art Committee voted not to recommend the project to the Cultural Affairs Commission. "We also had some questions about the manner in which they chose the artist and the landscape architect, Slaney Santana. We found difficulty with quite a bit of what they were proposing. Prairie grass and some of the other things they were proposing were not in keeping with the overall view of the space. We felt they didn't fit an urban space.

"And fourth," she says, "the project didn't meet the aesthetic standards that had been set for Dallas. We saw a maquette. I can't remember which one it was. It was not a good maquette. I think it was a steer we saw. I've blocked it out of my mind very successfully. The man basically is not a good sculptor. I've seen his John Wayne piece in Orange County, and half the town considers it a laughing-stock. Why do we need seventy steers? If it's really good art, we don't need seventy of anything. A good artist would be capable of making a statement with seventeen or twenty or whatever."

Finally, she says, "This is not Dallas' history. Steers have nothing to do with Dallas. If Mr. Crow wants something like this to happen in Dallas, none of us is opposed to him buying a space downtown and putting that project on it. But from my standpoint as a citizen of Dallas, it's not a good thing to put in front of the Convention Center. I don't think this is what Dallas really *wants* as its image. Years ago, Dallas *fought* this image. Immense energy was dedicated to keeping Fort Worth Fort Worth and Dallas Dallas. There was a huge effort to make sure you knew where you were."

So the Public Art Committee was surprised and dismayed when its parent body, the Cultural Affairs Commission, voted on March 18 to recommend that the City Council approve the Pioneer Plaza project, cowboys, steers, and all. "If my memory is correct, that's the first time we've been overturned during my five years on the committee," says Carl Lewis.

The Public Art Committee is a subcommittee of the Cultural Affairs Commission. Both are advisory. The City Council isn't required to follow their recommendations. Says Phil Jones, director of the Office of Cultural Affairs, "A city ordinance provides that the two bodies will review and make recommendations regarding any proposed donations of artwork to the city. In essence, that's what happened. The project was reviewed. The Public Art Committee had concerns about it. The Cultural Affairs Commission reviewed the recommendations of the committee, looked at a couple of maquettes, heard city staff address other concerns that had been raised, and then voted to recommend approval. This process fulfilled the foundation's responsibility to confer with the two bodies. Pioneer Plaza is the responsibility of the Parks Foundation now."

In any case, Mr. Jones says, Pioneer Plaza already was a "done deal." The contract had been signed before either advisory body could vote on the art proposal. A negative vote by the Cultural Affairs Commission wouldn't have affected its validity.

Dallas sculptor Greg Metz doesn't buy that argument. He and two other artists, Rowena Elkin and Harrison Evans, filed a lawsuit in Denton County in June, claiming that the city "illegally implemented the Pioneer Plaza Public Art Donation Project . . . by failing to initiate the project through the Public Art Committee and to secure its approval for location, design, and commission of the artist."

The three are asking a Denton County judge to declare the Pioneer Plaza contract null and void. They filed the suit in Denton, Mr. Metz says, hoping it might be concluded there more quickly than in a Dallas County court. Since a tiny portion of the city is in Denton County, a court there may have jurisdiction in the case.

Mr. Metz also is collecting signatures on a petition demanding that the City Council terminate the Pioneer Plaza project.

Although Mr. Metz is the one who dubbed the project "Frankensteer," he says his objections have nothing to do with Mr. Summers. "Artists believe that every artist should get his due," he says. "We believe that every artist is entitled to create what he wants to create. But I and anyone else who wants to give artworks to the city have to go through the process. When you go before the Public Art Committee, you have to have a model, you have to have specifics, you have to have letters of recommendation for the artist, you have to have the funding, you have to have all kinds of stuff. But Trammell Crow didn't. The process was abused. And when you abuse what little advocacy the visual arts have with this city, you abuse every artist in town, because you disempower them. It sends a message that if you have enough money and you want to do something that might not get past the Public Art Committee, you can do it another way."

Jack Beckman acknowledges that the path his steers took through City Hall may have been a bit off the beaten trail, but he makes no apologies.

"There are people appointed who appoint other people who sort of sit around and listen to other arts groups," he says. "I call them artsy-fartsies. And we sort of bypassed the artsy-fartsies. Probably at first we didn't do it deliberately. But this thing went on for a year before anybody from the arts groups said anything. Then I went and visited with the Public Art Committee and they were ticked off because we didn't consult with them. But the City Council approved it. We've got an absolutely ironclad contract. We did it in open meeting. I don't know what the artsy-fartsies are squawking about."

Then he adds: "The longhorn cattle drive was a fact of our past. I don't know why anybody would be ashamed of it. I don't think most of the people of Dallas are. I'll bet you that when the thing is installed, all those people who are against it now will run and hide. Or they'll jump on the bandwagon and say, 'Oh, yeah, I was for this all along.' "

Well, it worked for Tex Schramm.

August 1993

I was pretty familiar with the musical career of Kinky Friedman and the Texas Jewboys back when they were playing at the Lone Star Cafe in New York and recording their songs. Many of the songs were funny, but they were never merely funny. They always had a satirical bite to them.

The same is true of Kinky's mystery novels. I've read them all because they're fun to read. They're perfect airplane books — books that are entertaining and make time pass quickly and don't tax the brain much. But Kinky's books have an edge to them, too, which puts them above most airplane books.

I had wanted to meet the Kinkster for a long time. Finally I did.

Kinky in Character

The Kinkster deplanes at D/FW holding the remains of a used Honduran cigar that he has been holding since Chicago. He greets me with a handshake that might be the secret sign of recognition of the Odd Fellows or the Knights of Pythias. It requires the clasping of hands as in the classic soul handshake, but with Kinky somehow snapping thumb and middle finger together at the same time, an impressive feat of digital dexterity that duplicates the sound of knuckles cracking.

"That's the Kinkster's good-luck handshake," he says.

Then he gives me a guitar pick with his name on it. "It's a Kinkster good-luck plectrum," he says. "That particular one was used by Roger Miller when he was writing *England Swings*. You may expect your good luck to begin within forty-eight hours."

So this is Kinky Friedman, legendary band leader, singer, composer, author, amateur sleuth of uncanny skills, appreciator of cats . . . .

The Kinkster's dressed in black jeans, black boots, a black belt heavy with silver conchos, a black tuxedo jacket, a purple shirt, and a black cowboy hat adorned with a silver band and several feathers. One of the feathers, he points out, looks like two feathers that have sprouted from the same quill. "The feather of the emu," he says, "the only bird that can do that."

We saunter to the baggage carousel in company with Lenore Markowitz, who calls herself an "author escort." She has been hired to ferry Kinky about the Dallas area in her Suburban during his tornado-like tour of local media and bookstores, flogging his new mystery novel, *Armadillos and Old Lace*.

The book's something of a Lone Star literary event for Kinkster fans, for it's the first of his seven whodunits to be set in his native state instead of New York City's Greenwich Village and environs. A serial killer is murdering little old ladies in the Hill Country, and it's up to the Kinkster and several real-life "Kerrverts," as the author calls residents of Kerr County, to stop him.

In all the Kinky mysteries, most of the characters are based on the author's friends, neighbors, and relatives, and they're called by their real names. Kinky feels free to do this, he says, "because there is very little innocence to protect."

The cast of characters in *Armadillos and Old Lace* includes Pat Knox, who defeated Kinky in his effort a few years ago to become a Kerr County justice of the peace; Frances Kaiser, the county's female sheriff; and the author's own father and sister. He even drags two dogs, a cat, several children, and an innocent armadillo into his plot.

"I've been a fan of yours for a long time . . ." I say, intending to elaborate. My fandom, I'm about to tell him, dates back nearly twenty years, to the days when Kinky and his band, the Texas Jewboys, were riding the crest of the urban cowboy bizarreness, singing *Get Your Biscuits in the Oven and Your Buns in the Bed* at the Lone Star Cafe in New York. The song had the same effect on the feminists of the day as a sharp stick poked into their nest has on wasps.

"A man of impeccable taste," Kinky interrupts. He has spotted an emergency exit and darts through it to the sidewalk outside and relights the Honduran butt, leaving Lenore and me to watch the carousel for his bags and guitar.

It's about noon when we arrive at his hotel, and his room isn't ready yet. "This is a horrible inconvenience for the Kinkster," he mutters. He checks his bags with the bellman and changes out of the tuxedo jacket into an iridescent little number that might have come from a garage sale at Hunter Thompson's place. It shimmers soft-neon reds and greens on a field of black.

While a dose of enchiladas and tacos at El Fenix is restoring the Kinkster's good spirits, I ask him: "Did you get another cat?"

As Kinky readers know, his cat is an important character in all his novels. But his sixth book, *Elvis, Jesus and Coca-Cola*, contains a moving epilogue in tribute to Cuddles, who died in January 1993 at age fourteen.

It's immediately evident that Kinky doesn't want to talk about Cuddles. He says he had three cats and still has two of them, plus two dogs, at Echo Hill, the family ranch and children's camp near Medina, Texas, where he grew up and where he lives now.

"The cats are wonderful cats," Kinky says. "The dogs are wonderful dogs. But Cuddles . . . Cuddles was the first cat I ever had. She's the one who lived with me in New York. She was my best friend. She fought the drug wars with me. She put up with me during the period that I was flying on all kinds of herbs and spices. I was halfway through *Armadillos and Old Lace* when Cuddles went to Jesus. I kept her in the book. She's in the next one, too, which will be called *God Bless John Wayne*."

Unintentionally, my question seems to have kicked us into a mood of general mourning. "I mourn the passing of the undecaffeinated era of country music," the Kinkster says. "The cleverness has gone out of it. These young people in the business now, the thing they have in common is that they grew up on Dan Fogelberg. They hate Lefty Frizzell. They hate Hank Williams. They hate Ernest Tubb. They hate twang-twang. They're kind of savvy enough to know the good stuff by Patsy Cline and George Jones and a few others, and that's about it. That's the extent of their emotional history. Garth Brooks is a cultural mayonnaise. His fans would just as soon be wearing mouse ears at Disneyland."

He pauses, grinning. "I'm trying to keep this light, or anything you say or I say will make us look like old geezers who are sucking sour grapes."

Kinky will turn fifty on November 1, "just a step away from the Shalom Rest Home," he says. He's puffing so fast and furiously on a fresh Honduran cigar that even the other folks in the smoking section are giving us the eye.

"Garth Brooks is the Anti-Hank," he announces. "I'm sure there are millions of lost country music fans out there, waiting for me to lead them into battle against the Anti-Hank. But I'm not going to. I thank the Lord that the Texas Jewboys were not a big financial success. Otherwise, I'd be playing Disneyland with the Pips."

I try to imagine a crowd of Disneyites in mouse hats gathered in front of the Magic Kingdom, swinging and swaying to Kinky's rendition of *They Ain't Makin' Jews Like Jesus Anymore.*

"Being able to write these novels twenty-four years later and have some success at it," the Kinkster continues, "is my attempt to prove that there can be a second act in America, to prove F. Scott Fitzgerald wrong about that. There *can* be a second act, and I'm living proof of it. My books are selling so well these days that I'm in danger of losing my coveted cult status."

While Lenore is driving hell-for-breakfast toward KRLD, I ask Kinky how he decided to write mysteries. He shoots me a dark, mysterious look. "I saw a rodeo in Bandera when I was a kid. It was a very seminal experience for the Kinkster. They had an act called 'Shoshone the Magic Pony.' It was this real old man with this horse that looked like two men dressed up in a horse suit. The horse did tricks, crossed its legs and stuff like that. At the end of the act, the old man took his outfit off, and he was a young girl. And she took the saddle and blanket off of Shoshone, and he was a real horse. That really stayed with me.

"Later I refined what it meant to me — that nothing is what it appears to be. Now, if you get a story where nothing is what it appears to be, you've got yourself a great mystery, regardless of plot. Plots are for cemeteries, as George Bernard Shaw said."

At KRLD, he gets permission to ignore the This-Is-A-Smoke-Free-Building sign, shakes hands with talk-radio host Jody Dean, goes on the air and shouts in a falsetto squeak: "I like it here. Be kind to me, Jody."

He sings *The Ballad of Ira Hayes*, throws out one-liners like Mardi Gras beads, tells a story about eating monkey brains in Borneo when he was in the Peace Corps — "They taste a lot like chicken-fried steak," he says — plugs his book, and suddenly we're on our way to the Irving Public Library to tape a cable show called *Conversations with Pam Lange*.

"Is there somebody who can give me a papal dispensation to smoke in here?" the Kinkster asks.

"No way. No way," Pam says. "Just chew. Don't inhale."

Several children peek at the Kinkster from behind the stacks. He waves at them. "Would you like me to sing *Ol' Ben Lucas Had a Lot of Mucus*?" he asks. "Do you know that song, boys and girls?"

"No," says a shy young girl.

"Well, it's one of Kinky's songs for children. I wrote it when I was eleven."

He removes his hat and shows the TV camera his long, kinky hair, which he calls his "Lyle Lovett starter kit," points out the Star of David and the star of Texas on his belt buckle, tells Pam that his new book is about "old ladies being dispatched to Jesus on their seventy-sixth birthday," then it's back to the hotel.

The Kinkster's room is ready. He and Lenore go over his schedule for the next two days, which includes such nightmares as a 5:30 a.m. TV show in Fort Worth followed by a 7:00 a.m. flight to Austin. We make arrangements to meet again for his evening gigs at Borders Books & Music and another show at KRLD, and we leave the Kinkster to get some rest.

But when we see him again, he seems wearier than when we left him. His face is clouded in a grief newer than those that we've spent the day discussing. He has had a phone conversation of the unhappy kind, he says. A romance has soured. A sweetheart has told him goodbye. "I am semi-brokenhearted," he says.

But the shows go on. All of them. And the Kinkster leaves everybody laughing, as usual.

Nearing midnight, we say goodbye and do the Kinkster's good-luck handshake.

He smiles wanly. "I really learned it from Mexican parking lot attendants in L.A.," he says.

October 1994

If you're ever fortunate enough to see a whooping crane, you'll never forget it. The magnificent white birds, some of them five feet tall, seem like creatures from another world. Despite their size, they seem delicate — fragile, even — and somehow sad, as if they know how precarious their existence is in this world.

Working on this piece gave me a new and deeper understanding of the crisis around us, and the incalculable value of the treasures we're losing to our stupidity, ignorance, and greed.

The Long Journey

Through the telescope, sunlight turns the ripples of the stream to mirror shards almost too bright for the eye to endure. Heat rises from the water, making the air ripple, too, like a gauzy curtain in a breeze. On a sand bar in the middle of the South Saskatchewan River, nine huge white birds pace with slow deliberation. Isolated in the wavy round image of the telescope, on their sliver of sand in the middle of the broad river, they resemble priests of some lost religion, performing a ritual long forgotten by all but themselves.

"They're early this year," Brian Johns says. "I don't know what that means. An early winter or something?"

It's late September. The wheat harvest is under way in Saskatchewan, and so is autumn. While the daily highs still range into the nineties in Texas, the leaves of the mottes of trees that dot the prairie here are already a blaze of red and gold.

And the whooping cranes have begun their annual journey from their summer home, only four hundred miles south of the Arctic Circle, toward their winter quarters in the warm bay waters of the Texas Gulf Coast.

The first whoopers usually don't arrive in Saskatchewan until the first of October, but this year Mr. Johns, a Canadian Wildlife Service biologist, already has spotted eighteen, these hanging out on the river, others in a few small lakes around Saskatoon.

They travel in pairs, or in family groups of three, or in bunches of five or six, like human families taking their vacations together. The largest single group ever spotted near Saskatoon was thirteen, Mr. Johns says, and the largest he has seen was eleven. So the tall white birds preening and pacing along the sand bar in the river are, as whooping cranes go, a sizable conclave.

"They leave their nesting grounds, arrive here three or four days later, spend anywhere from a few days to a few weeks fattening themselves on the barley and wheat in the fields, then take off for Texas," Mr. Johns says.

The nests they've left behind are in a huge wetland in Wood Buffalo National Park, on the border between Alberta and Canada's thinly settled Northwest Territories. The nests are widely scattered, and because of the vastness of the marshes in which they lie, the soft ground and fallen timber, the nesting ground is inaccessible to humans except by air, and so remote that no one knew where it was until a pilot discovered it by chance in 1954.

The end of their journey will be quite a different kind of place. On the Aransas National Wildlife Refuge, twenty-six hundred miles south on San Antonio Bay, northeast of Corpus Christi, and the offshore islands of Matagorda and San Jose, the cranes will live much closer to each other and will be surrounded by the commotion of human activity. There, those who survive the long flight will spend the winter fishing for clams and blue crabs, watching towboats shove oil barges along the Intracoastal Waterway, and posing for birders who come by the boatload every winter, like the whoopers themselves.

Come spring, Nature always tells the cranes to return to Canada. Last year, 136 whoopers departed Aransas for their northern breeding ground. In June, Canadian Wildlife Service biologists counted thirty-five new chicks following their parents about the marshes. But by the middle of August, only thirteen were still alive.

"There's no way to know what got the rest of them," Mr. Johns says. "The only place we can get an accurate count of the whoopers is at Aransas, where they aren't so widely scattered. Their survival is measured by the number of chicks that make it to Texas."

If all 136 cranes who left Aransas in the spring are still alive, and if all the thirteen remaining chicks survived until migration time, 149 whooping cranes have left Canada for their long journey to Texas. How many live to arrive won't be known until mid-December, when U.S. Fish and Wildlife biologist Tom Stehn will take his annual census.

Except for a few in zoos and in experimental captive breeding programs, these are the only whooping cranes left in the world. They're the only ones still attempting the arduous and dangerous trek across Saskatchewan, the Dakotas, Nebraska, Kansas, Oklahoma, Wichita Falls, Dallas-Fort Worth, Waco, and Austin, as their ancestors did thousands of years before such names had been given.

The books say there probably never were a lot of whooping cranes. Some authors guess that maybe two thousand were scattered in small flocks across the continent when the first Europeans reached North America. They probably ranged from the Great Salt lake in Utah to New England in those days, and down the Atlantic seaboard, and over huge swathes of Canada and Mexico.

Wildlife biologists estimate that by the 1850s and '60s their number had been reduced to fourteen hundred or thirteen hundred, but their breeding grounds still stretched from Alberta and Saskatchewan eastward as far as Michigan and Illinois, and many flocks still wintered along the coast of South Carolina and Georgia and all along the Gulf from Florida into Mexico.

But as settlers spread across the midwestern United States and the Canadian prairies, the cranes began declining. Farmers hunted them, and drained the marshes where they bred. Museums had them killed and stuffed and placed in glass cases. Egg collectors robbed their nests. Milliners used their long white plumes to decorate ladies' hats.

Although whoopers are wary birds and not easily hunted, by 1900 they were in danger of disappearing from the earth. By 1941 only twenty-two were left. Six were in a Louisiana flock that would be extinct by 1949. The other sixteen were wintering on the Blackjack Peninsula, a maze of marshes and bays in Aransas, Calhoun, and Refugio counties on the Texas coast.

On the last day of 1937, while eighteen whoopers were wintering there, Pres. Franklin D. Roosevelt had signed Executive Order No. 77841 declaring 47,215 acres of the peninsula a wildlife preserve. His decree gave the whoopers a chance to struggle back from the edge of extinction.

But man's efforts to aid the recovery of the species was hindered by the fact that the location of the whoopers' breeding ground was their secret. When the few remaining cranes lifted off from Aransas each spring and headed north, no one knew where they went.

In 1945, Canadian pilots and biologists began crisscrossing the prairie provinces where cranes had been sighted, scanning the wilderness for signs of the mysterious last remaining nesting ground of the species. In 1952, biologist Robert Smith spotted two whoopers on the ground, thirty miles apart, near the Great Slave Lake in the Northwest Territories, but subsequent flights to confirm his sighting failed.

Then, on June 30, 1954, pilot Don Landells and forester G.M. Wilson were flying over the same area in a helicopter, checking on a wild fire that was burning in the wilderness below. Along the Sass River, in the wildest, most remote region of the Wood Buffalo National Park, they spotted adult whooping cranes and their new chicks, browsing in the marshes. The secret breeding ground had been discovered.

"Wood Buffalo had been a national park since 1922," Brian Johns says. "That part of it also turned out to be the whooping cranes' nesting ground was pure coincidence."

Since the discovery, biologists have been able to study the breeding and feeding habits of the birds in their secret hideaway, searching for ways that science may help the whoopers to multiply themselves off the Endangered Species List someday.

Mr. Johns, who now heads the whooping crane program for the Canadian Wildlife Service, has been a member of the crews that helicopter into the nesting ground each summer to catch the fledgling chicks and place identification bands on their legs, so their lives can be chronicled by the biologists.

"The young birds can't fly yet, and we chase them around the marshes on foot," he says, "slogging through mud up to the knees, getting tangled in the growth, falling down. When we capture one, we weigh it and put the bands on its legs. Thereafter, when we spot them from a distance, we can tell who they are, where they were banded and the nest sites they came from."

Whooping cranes mate for life. Each couple stakes out its own territory, to which it returns each spring to build a new nest of bullrushes, sedges, and cattails. The breeding pairs migrate from Texas first, in late April and early May. By the middle of May, all the nests that are going to be built have been, and each hen has laid her usual two eggs. Only then do the younger, nonbreeding birds — those under four years old — begin arriving at the grounds.

Except in May, when biologists fly into the marshes to test the hatchibility of the eggs that have been laid, the birds spend the summer in peace. "Very few people who have come to the park have ever seen the cranes," says Dave Milne, a Wood Buffalo park warden. "In fact, a lot of people who work for the park have never seen the cranes." Except for the small craft used by the biologists in their work, airplanes must be at least two thousand feet up when they fly over the nesting ground.

"Nearly all the eggs hatch," Mr. Johns says. "But the survivability of the chicks is what will determine whether we're going to have twenty young or five young from one year to the next. More survive in years when water in the wetlands is high. It's harder for wolves and bears to reach them then."

The biologists have learned that although both eggs in a nest usually hatch, most crane parents don't want to rear twins. The second hatchling rarely survives. So in recent years biologists have taken one egg from each of the nests and tried to hatch them in captivity, to ensure the survival of the species if catastrophe should happen to the Aransas flock.

68

A flock of eight whooping cranes now spends its summers in Idaho and its winters in New Mexico. It was created by placing whooping crane eggs in the nests of sandhill cranes. The sandhill cranes hatched them and took care of the chicks, but the whoopers have never paired off and bred. They even have a different call than the Aransas cranes. "Maybe because they were raised by sandhill cranes," says Mr. Johns. "There's some behavioral problem there."

Also, last winter thirteen young birds were released in Florida in an effort to restore a nonmigratory whooping crane flock that once lived there. So far, bobcats have eaten eight of them. If the remaining six survive, they won't reach breeding age for three more years.

For the whooping crane to be upgraded from "endangered" to "threatened" status would require that at least forty breeding pairs show up at Wood Buffalo for ten consecutive years, and that there be two other breeding flocks of twenty-five pairs or more.

So far, all efforts to create those new breeding flocks have failed. "All our experiments are fraught with difficulty," says Mr. Johns.

But the wild flock is doing well. More than forty breeding pairs have shown up at Wood Buffalo two years in a row now, and in recent years the whoopers have experienced a population explosion. Twenty years ago, there were only forty-nine cranes in the Wood Buffalo flock. Throughout the 1960s and '70s their numbers hovered in the forty-to-sixty range, seemingly unable to grow further.

"It hung there for a long time, and then they got over that hump," says Tom Stehn, the refuge biologist at Aransas. "For years, it was cause for celebration if the flock increased two or three birds. Now they're in kind of a geometric progression." Between 1981 and 1990, the size of the flock doubled, from 71 to 146. With good luck in

Canada, Mr. Stehn believes the wild flock soon could produce as many as twenty-five chicks in a single year.

"The problem now is we've been getting pretty high mortality," he says. "Over the last three or four years we've been losing like ten birds a year that leave here in the spring and then don't show up again in the fall."

What happens to them? A network of observers has been set up throughout the entire migration corridor. Biologists check every report of a whooping crane sighting to ascertain whether the birds are really cranes and whether anything in the area might harm them. They notify hunters in the area to take extra care not to shoot them. Yet the birds disappear, and nobody knows why.

But, Mr. Stehn says, there are clues.

In 1982, when there were only seventy-three whoopers in the world, Mr. Stehn was part of a team tracking a family of three cranes from Wood Buffalo to Aransas. During the summer, Canadian biologists had captured chicks and attached lightweight solar-powered radio transmitters to their legs. The trackers chose one crane family to be followed in the air by a pilot and an observer in a small plane with antennae mounted on the wings. They could pick up the chick's signals at a distance of fifty miles. When the birds would land for the night, the air crew would radio their location to biologists on the ground, who would find the group and observe them until they took off again the next day.

"We knew where their general flight path was, but we didn't know much about their behavior during migration," Mr. Stehn says. "What did they eat? Did they have traditional stopping places that we might need to protect, or did they stop at random? What kind of dangers did they encounter on the trip?"

The birds lifted off from Wood Buffalo, flew 175 miles the first day, landed and rested for five days, then took off again. That evening, they landed in Saskatchewan, where they hung out in Midnight Lake for eighteen days, making short flights each day to feed in the farm fields.

Then, on a routine feeding flight, the chick they were following crashed into a power line. The tracking crew took the injured bird to a veterinarian, but it died six days later.

So the crew switched its attention to the radio signal of another chick that was feeding in the area. This chick and her parents made it safely to Aransas.

The following year, the trackers decided to follow the same bird, now seventeen months old, on her first solo flight from Canada to Texas. Somewhere along the way, the crew lost her signal. Days later, they found her dead under a power line near Waco.

"We think the No. 1 cause of loss of whooping cranes is collisions with power lines," Mr. Stehn says. "They just plumb don't see the lines, either toward dusk or in a snow storm or fog. It happens when they're stopping for the night during their migration, and when they're flying to and from the fields where they feed."

The cranes' other great danger is still people with guns.

In 1918, a farmer named Alcie Daigle helped the Louisiana flock — one of only two flocks left at the time — along the road to extinction by shooting twelve whoopers he found feeding on rice that had fallen from his threshing machine. So far as the biologists know, such mass avicides don't occur anymore, but whooping cranes are still being shot, and no one knows how many.

"I used to think that shooting was a rare exception," Mr. Stehn says, "but now I don't know. We have fewer and fewer wetlands, and as the hunting pressure concentrates, whooping cranes are bound to be shot by mistake. A lot of those guys aren't real hunters. They're just shooting at whatever flies over. And when they discover they've killed a whooper, they hide the evidence."

Most of the whooping cranes that have been shot — at least of those reported to authorities — were killed in Texas, including the two most recent.

In January 1989, Mario Max Yzaguirre, a Houston lawyer hunting on San Jose Island, just outside the Aransas refuge, shot a four-year-old whooping crane hen. He said he thought she was a snow goose, a bird less than a third the size of a whooper.

The crane had just arrived from Canada with her first chick. Had she lived, she might have produced ten to fifteen more chicks during her breeding years.

A federal judge fined Mr. Yzaguirre $15,000 and ordered him to pay the state $6,480 restitution for the dead crane.

And in 1991, Billy Dale Inman of Marble Falls, Texas, was sentenced to sixty days in federal prison and two hundred hours of community service, fined $15,000 and ordered to pay $8,100 in restitution for killing a whooping crane on a dare.

Curtis Collier Sayers, who was fishing on the Colorado River with Mr. Inman and dared his companion to shoot the bird, was sentenced to twenty days in jail, three years probation, a two thousand dollar fine and two hundred hours of community service for his part in the crime.

They had buried the dead whooping crane, but Raena Wharton, an English teacher at San Saba High School, had witnessed their deed. Ms. Wharton said she was standing outside her home admiring the cranes flying over when she heard the shot and watched the bird fall. She went inside and called a game warden, then saddled her horse and rode down to the river to keep an eye on the men. She saw them bury the bird.

"I couldn't believe someone could shoot anything so beautiful," she told the court.

Whoopers and their relatives always have fascinated people. A thousand years before Christ, Homer wrote of cranes in the *Iliad*, and Jeremiah spoke of them in his prophecy. Theophrastus says sailors used them to predict the weather. When cranes headed out to sea, then turned back, it was unsafe to leave port, but when they departed and didn't return, it was a sign of fair weather.

The Greeks and Romans thought cranes to be wise, intelligent, sociable beings, capable of helping tired or wounded companions, and willing to let smaller birds ride on their backs when they became weary.

The call of the whooping crane, which gives it its name, is made by a large, long windpipe that curls like a French horn in the whooper's chest. It can be heard for two miles. About one hundred years ago, a sportsman named Theodore S. Van Dyke described it as "the blast of a silver horn."

He was writing of his observations of a flock of whooping cranes that were strutting about, calling to each other. Then they took to the air. "It seemed wicked," he wrote, "to spoil anything so rare and so beautiful as that sight." But he shot two of them anyway, causing them to "relax hold on the warm sunlight."

Though smaller in number now, the whoopers continue to fascinate all who see them, and on the Texas coast their arrival is awaited with high anticipation. "Once you spot a whooping crane, you know it couldn't be anything else," says Ted Appell, captain of the *Skimmer*, one of four boats that run whooping crane tours out of Fulton and Rockport, just down the coast from the refuge. "There's no other bird like them."

Captain Appell had the *Skimmer* built "especially for the birdies," he says, with a shallow draft so he can work it into the waters of the back bays. It carries eight thousand birders a year from all over the world to see the magnificent white birds, North America's largest, four and a half feet tall, wading in the shallow water, warning interlopers away, teaching their young all the ancient crane ways.

"I've been looking at them for twenty-something years," Captain Appell says, "and when a whooping crane flies across the bow of my boat, I still get cold chills right up my back, just like I did the first day I saw that beautiful bird."

In 1972, when he started working on a birding tour boat, the whooping cranes numbered in the twenties. Over the years, he has watched the flock grow. An avid birder himself, he has formed attachments to certain birds he has watched from year to year.

One of his favorites was the young hen killed by Mr. Yzaguirre on San Jose Island.

"That family of birds was a young male and female that I had watched as young chicks growing up," he says. "They paired off, and they came down. She was an extremely young crane, only four years old. And she had successfully bred and brought her chick all the way down here. People called them 'Ted's family.' They were *my* birds. So my friends and I had a memorial service for her. It went nationwide on the television news. It brought a very large awareness to the public and to hunters that it is time to pay attention to what they are shooting. It's gotten to the point where if we don't do something strong . . . . "

Captain Appell and his family — his daughter Deanna also holds a captain's license and sometimes commands the boat — are cleaning up the *Skimmer*, preparing for the beginning of their new season. "I have a contract with the cranes," he says. "And they'll be here soon."

Few of his passengers, he says, will be casual tourists, just looking for entertainment. "They'll be serious people, involved in conservation and wildlife matters. In the last ten or fifteen years, I've seen an enormous change in people's attitudes toward these things. A lot more people are getting involved in their environment and are more aware of what they've got around them."

And just up the coast on the refuge, Captain Appell's friend Tom Stehn and his crew are mowing around the water holes the cranes will use, so bobcats can't hide near them, and burning the tall grass in the oak brush and upland areas of the reserve, so the cranes can more easily find the acorns on the ground.

It's early yet, but they're on their way, and Mr. Stehn says he already has "whooper fever." His eyes keep drifting upward in search of the first flash of long white wings.

"About twenty minutes before they start their migration," he says, "they suddenly become very alert. They start milling around. They preen. They straighten all their feathers. There's an energy in the air. The male tips his head and looks up into the sky. Then they line up, and the male will take those running steps and lift off into the wind. And the others will follow."

November 1993

One day Mary Lynn Sharp, the daughter of my first grade teacher, phoned me. She told me that my teacher, Mrs. Miller — or "Miss Gertrude," as we called her — was living in Dallas, not far from my neighborhood. I had seen neither Mrs. Miller nor Mary Lynn since 1945.

I went to Mrs. Miller's house one afternoon, and the three of us talked about the long-ago lives we spent together in a place that has almost disappeared.

A few months later, Mrs. Miller died.

Mrs. Miller

Mrs. Gertrude Miller gives me a big hug. She says she wouldn't have recognized me if she hadn't known I was coming. I'm not surprised. We last saw each other in 1945. I was seven years old then.

I would recognize her anywhere, I tell her. I think I would. She has aged, too, from forty-three to ninety-one, but she still smiles the same smile, still laughs the same laugh. And her voice . . . "I've forgotten so many of the children," she says, "but I sure do remember you." Do you forget the voice of your first teacher?

Fifty years ago last fall I enrolled in Mrs. Miller's first grade class. I rode to school that day with my grandmother, who was a teacher, too, and a friend of Mrs. Miller's. In my lap lay a wooden box that contained my school supplies: scissors, two yellow pencils, a jar of white paste, a box of Crayolas. All new. Pristine. I also had a new Big Chief writing tablet with a picture of an Indian on its cover, and a green lunch box containing a thermos of milk, two sandwiches wrapped in waxed paper, a red apple, and a Hershey bar.

My grandmother was telling me what to expect when we reached the school — a gloomy two-story stone building on a hill at the edge of Carlton, about eighty miles southwest of Fort Worth — and how I was to behave when I got there.

Mrs. Miller greeted me at her classroom door. She smiled and bent to my level to talk to me. I knew her already. Her husband, Steve, was pastor of the Baptist church, which my grandmother and I attended. The younger of her two stepdaughters, Mary Lynn, was starting the first grade with me that day. She also was in my Sunday School class. I was jealous of her because she could color within the lines and I couldn't.

It was Mary Lynn who called me, all these years later. Mrs. Miller was living in Dallas, not far from me, and would love to see me, she said.

So here we are, the three of us, in Mrs. Miller's living room, looking through a stack of first-grade school pictures, trying to remember names for the young faces in them.

Mrs. Miller talks of her friend, my grandmother. She remembers rooming with her one summer in Denton, where they were taking some college courses, trying to accumulate semester hours toward their degrees, as so many teachers did back then. My grandmother had been teaching since she was seventeen. Maybe Mrs. Miller had,

too. "The place where we stayed was so hot," she says.
"One night we took our mattresses out and put them
under some trees in the backyard so we could sleep. But
the moon was shining so brightly that I couldn't sleep. I
opened my umbrella to shade me."

She says she and my grandmother chaperoned a bus-
load of kids who came up to Dallas for the great Texas
Centennial celebration in 1936. "The school children
massed on the football field at the Cotton Bowl to sing
Texas, Our Texas," she says. "It was so hot. Kids were faint-
ing all around. None of our kids fainted, though."

She speaks of my grandfather, the deputy sheriff who
was shot to death by robbers in a Carlton street one snowy
night just before Christmas in 1932, and Jim Pierce, the
posse member who made the robbers think his flashlight
was a gun and arrested them with it. "I remember that just
like it was yesterday," she says. "Those were hard times, I
tell you. Scary times."

As the afternoon slips away we talk of other times, of
the time we spent together in the stone schoolhouse. Of
cold mornings when the janitors would pour coal into the
huge black stove in our room until it glowed red. Of the
wooden privies — one for the girls, one for the boys —
that stood at opposite corners of the school ground. Of
the piano that Mrs. Miller played, and our "rhythm band"
sessions when we banged on wooden blocks, sticks, and
metal triangles. Of the patriotic posters that hung in our
hallways in those World War II days, and the savings
stamps we bought and pasted in little books. When a book
was full, we traded it in for a twenty-five-dollar war bond
to help our boys overseas.

"I have a memory of you standing by a chart at the
front of the room," I say. "It has the letters of the alphabet
on it. You're teaching us the sound of the letter B. 'Bu, bu,

bu,' you say. And then you say, 'Remember seeing your father, when he gets to the end of the row in the field? He picks up the water jug and takes a drink out of it. What sound does the water make as it comes out of the jug? 'Bu, bu, bu.'"

"Phonics," Mrs. Miller says. "It was new then. Uncle Bob McDaniel, he was a carpenter there in town. A fine man. He and his wife had their grandson to raise. They called him Sonny Boy. He was smart as a whip. And Uncle Bob made a complaint to the superintendent, Mr. Huffman, that Sonny Boy didn't have a book to bring home at night. Well, I didn't give my pupils a book until they knew how to read. They learned the alphabet, and how to sound out words on the chart, then I would give them a book. Mr. Huffman told Uncle Bob, 'Well, you just go up there and visit someday.' So Uncle Bob and his wife came and sat in on my class. Little Sonny Boy's hand kept going up. He was smart as could be. They went home just elated. That was a new way of teaching to them. Phonics was the new way of doing in those days."

Mary Lynn and I remember the first book she gave us. *We Look and See.* About Dick, Jane, Baby Sally, Mother, Father, Spot the dog, Puff the cat, and Tim the teddy bear. I read the whole thing aloud to my grandmother that night.

We laugh, the three of us, remembering the school that closed so many years ago, in the little farm town that has almost disappeared. "We had so many kids in those days," Mrs. Miller says. "We were just swamped."

Two years after I enrolled in Mrs. Miller's first grade, my family moved away from Carlton. So did the Millers. But on this afternoon, the place and all its people are alive again.

"The Lord has been so good to me, to let me live this long and have the friends I've had," Mrs. Miller says. "I go to bed some nights, Bryan, and I can't shut my mind off. Things will come up that I remember . . . a family will come to mind, and I'll think, 'How many were in that family? What were their names?' And I'll start naming them off. And there'll be one whose name I can't remember, and I'll think about it and think about it. And after a while the name will come into my mind, and I can go to sleep."

January 1994

In a time when more and more people are spending their lives flipping burgers and staring into computer video monitors for a wage, it warms the soul to know a man who has a great job, knows it and loves it. To wander the mountains and deserts of the Trans-Pecos with Benny Simpson is like accompanying a child into a huge toy store. The joy generated is the next best thing to being young again.

The Plant Hunter

Benny Simpson is driving a rented van along one of the emptier roads in Texas, somewhere between Hallie Stillwell's ranch and the Mexican village of La Linda, in the magnificent desolation of the Big Bend. Suddenly he stomps the brakes, slams the van into reverse, and speeds backward up the hill he has just passed. He swerves onto the shoulder, cuts the engine, jumps from the van, and scrambles up the steep, rocky slope.

A tourist, if one should pass, might think him a rancher, searching for a sick calf, perhaps. Ruddy face. Faded jeans tucked into the tops of scuffed brown boots. White hair held down by a sweat-stained straw hat that looks as if it were trampled by a herd of wild burros.

But Benny stands reverently before a bush with grayish leaves. It's a cenizo called violet silverleaf, about as high as his knees and not much wider than his hat. Tiny flowers the hue of Elizabeth Taylor's eyes adorn the bush and lay a sweet, wild aroma into the still desert air.

"Isn't that a beauty?" Benny exclaims, unlimbering his camera. "Boy! Isn't it a knockout?"

He turns to his companions, who have struggled up the slope behind him. "*Leucophyllum candidum*! I tell you, I am admiring this! This is *nice*!"

Cenizo is a common shrub in the Big Bend and some other areas of West Texas. Its vivid blooms are one of the blessings that rain brings to these arid parts. Whenever a good rain falls, the cenizo will follow a few days later with its splendid little flowers, no matter the time of year.

The hillside where Benny and his friends are standing is almost covered with the gray bushes, their dominance broken only here and there by stands of cactus and sotol and greasewood. Normally after a rain, the slope would be robed in the violet blossoms of *Leucophyllum candidum* and the rosier hues of its close relative, *Leucophyllum frutenscens*. Sometimes their flowers last for a week or ten days before they fall. Other times, a heavy wind will wipe them out in a day. On this day, nearly all the bushes are bare of blossoms. Only a few others bear any flowers at all, and this one alone is in full flower.

"Odd," Benny says. "Maybe the others already have bloomed and gone. Maybe we just caught the tail end of it."

Or maybe the perfect glory of this one bush is the answer to some prayer that Benny has been muttering under his breath for the past two days while he and his companions trudged up mountainsides, canyons, and dry creek beds in search of desert flora in bloom.

He had heard that Far West Texas had just had a wet season. He has brought his five companions — most of whom have never been in the Big Bend before — from Dallas and College Station, expecting to show them the mountains and the desert in their glory.

But not as many plants are flowering as he hoped to find. The Big Bend is always a gamble, he has told his friends as he maneuvered the van across the barrens. You never know what you're going to find, and you can see only what's there.

Now he's vindicated. He leads his friends back down the slope to the van and climbs in behind the wheel. "Good!" he says. "Now you know I'm not a complete blathering idiot!"

One perfect *Leucophyllum candidum*.

It's enough to make a six hundred-mile journey worthwhile.

Benny has worked at the Texas Agricultural Experiment Station on Coit Road in Dallas since 1954, when he arrived from Texas Tech with a brand new B.S. degree. The station was called the Texas Research Foundation in those days. It was a private research center, located in a tiny farming town called Renner and funded by downtown Dallas businessmen. "Back then, agriculture was important to Dallas," Benny says. "Now it couldn't care less."

In 1972 the Texas Research Foundation donated its land and buildings to Texas A&M University and became a part of the university's vast research and extension system.

Although some scientists there still study such conventional agricultural subjects as cotton and grain, the focus of much of the station's work has evolved along with the countryside around it. While Renner has been swallowed up into Far North Dallas and the ever-advancing bedroom sprawl has surrounded the station's fields and barns, it has become a nationally renowned center for the study of urban agriculture — the plants that live among us in our yards and parks and along our streets.

Benny's official titles there are "research scientist" and "ornamental horticulturist." He calls himself "plant hunter," and he could be called "crusader" as well, for he's a man with a cause.

"One thing that Texas doesn't have and never has had and never will have is enough water," he says. "Someday we're going to be in the same fix as California and Arizona. People don't want to face up to that, but it's a fact. It's going to happen. So it's getting to be important that we save as much water as we can, and grow the kind of plants that can survive on very little when they have to."

Unfortunately, whatever knowledge Californians and Arizonans have accumulated about plants that will thrive in their arid climates is of no use to North Central Texas. California's is a Mediterranean climate in which rain falls in the wintertime and not in the summer. Arizona is warmer than North Texas. Anything brought from there is likely to freeze in the winter.

Most plants from the northern and eastern parts of the United States don't do well in Dallas, either, because they come from acid soils. Many of them also can't take the hot summers.

"Where we need to look for plants for Dallas is in Iraq and Turkey and that Russian country next to Turkey and the pampas of Argentina and Paraguay, but we don't get along with any of those people," Benny says. "Everybody wants to go to Mexico and look for plants, and that's all right for Houston and Brownsville, but not many of them are going to work here in Dallas."

So for twenty years Benny has roamed his native Texas, searching out wild trees and shrubs that not only are beautiful but also might be able to grow in the waxy black soil of North Central Texas and survive the extremes of heat and cold that torture so many plants here.

Even that hunt hasn't been easy.

"I spend a little time in South Texas, just to keep from being ignorant of what's there," Benny says. "But by the time I get to San Antone, I'm just kind of kidding myself about anything I bring back to Dallas, because winter's going to get it. I spend a little time in East Texas, but within thirty miles of Dallas I start hitting acid soil, and our soil here is highly calcareous. It has a high limestone content. Although I think the wax myrtles I brought back from East Texas are going to grow in this old black soil, most of the things that grow there just will not make it here."

Of the five thousand plants that are native to Texas, he says, maybe twenty-five hundred are worth looking at as possible domestic landscape ornamentals.

"But the really good ones, I doubt if you're talking more than 250 to 300 species."

And most of those will come from regions of the state where most residents of the Dallas area have never gone and have thought of as barren — the far reaches of the Panhandle plains and the deserts and mountains of the Trans-Pecos.

"Most of the stuff I bring back is from the Rolling Plains, the Caprock Escarpment, the Glass Mountains, the Apaches, the Del Nortes, and the Guadalupes," he says, "because they grow in limestone."

Benny finds the best specimens he can — often at the end of a lonely ten- or twelve-mile hike up some remote canyon — and brings cuttings or seeds from them back to Dallas. He plants them at the experiment station to see if they can take the Dallas weather and soils and water. If one flourishes and shows promise of looking pretty in somebody's yard, he'll try to propagate it. And if it propagates easily, he'll release it to the nursery trade and try to persuade nursery owners to propagate it themselves and offer it for sale to the public and to professional landscapers.

The grounds of the A&M Research and Extension Center are landscaped with his experiments, and a tour of them on his golf cart offers a botanical atlas of Central and West Texas:

"That dalea there is a ground cover from the Alpine area. This true sage — *Salvia gregii* — is in the trade now. Those madrone trees were grown from seed from the Hill Country near Medina. That Apache plume is from the Guadalupes. That lantana is from Langtry. Here are several species of the forty-seven oaks that are native to Texas. This big-toothed maple is from the Guadalupes. Have you ever been in McKittrick Canyon when the maples are in color? Awww, man, isn't that something? American smoke trees from Boerne. The pink, white, and purple cenizos. Shedscale. None of this stuff takes any water. Bitterweed from West Texas. Mexican hat. Black persimmon trees from the Hill Country. Animals just love them. Sabal — this is the closest thing we have to a native palm tree in Texas. Dogweed. Wax myrtles. Spice bush. Walnut. Indian cherry. The seven roses that are native to Texas. Doveweed from the Hill Country. Whitethorn. Four-nerve daisies. Arizona cockroach plant. Hawthorn . . . . "

Benny estimates that he has collected and experimented with more than five hundred species of plants during the two decades he has been roaming Texas.

"I used to have a little old white Chevrolet pickup," he says. "I put 347,000 miles on it, most of it going out to the Big Bend, the Davis Mountains, the Guadalupes. I'm the only one in the state doing this, growing this many plants, going this far to find them. This work isn't for people who want fast results. Garden clubs come out to the experiment station, and they want to see the greenhouse because they just know they're going to see pansies blooming and roses blooming. But all I've got is a bunch of little old seedlings that don't show anything yet. No flowers, no nothing. Some of them might not show anything for twenty years. Not many people want to wait."

So far, Benny has released nine formerly wild species to the nursery trade of Texas and the Southwest as suitable for city landscaping. Five of them are cenizos, relatives of the beautiful gray-leafed shrub he has found on the La Linda road. The others are a mountain sage, a false indigo, and two desert willows.

Texas A&M has trademarked the cenizos as Green Cloud, White Cloud, Silver Cloud, Rain Cloud, and Thunder Cloud; the sage as Mount Emory; the willows as Dark Storm and White Storm; and the false indigo as Dark Lance. Framed pictures of them hang on Benny's office wall.

"I grew up out on the Rolling Plains right at the foot of the Caprock in Motley County," he says. "A little place called Northfield. Our place was so small we didn't call it a ranch. Out there, anybody who didn't have a very big piece of ground, you didn't dare say you were a rancher. They'd laugh you out of the country. The old Matador sat on one side of us — 800,000 acres — and on the other side of us was the Mill Iron, which was also several hundred thousand acres. So we just told everybody we were farmers."

He was born sixty-four years ago. Not such a long lifetime ago, but long enough to have been a different world to grow up in.

"Some things stick in your mind," he says. "I can remember when I was a little boy, one night a big wad of cowboys slept out on our front lawn, and the next morning before daylight they got up and ate breakfast. That was one of the last cattle drives to Estelline."

Northfield, which never was much, almost has disappeared. He says, "We lost our school, and then my mother lost her church. She's Baptist, and they even came out and moved the church house away. My daddy was Campbellite — Church of Christ — and my granddad built the Campbellite church, and they held on a few years longer, and the building is still there, but nobody goes to it because there's no one there."

He's leaning back in his office chair, drinking coffee, just talking. "And then we lost our post office. Our mail's put in a box on the road, you know. Boy, that hurts. It really does. My mother's eighty-five. She lives out there all by herself. She says she's happier there than she would be in town. Man, it's lonesome country. We're a long way from anybody. You can look off in the distance and see the Caprock Escarpment and the Quitaque Peaks. When you drive up to them, the Quitaques are just kind of pimples, is all they are. But from one hundred miles off they look like mountains. They're famous in that country. The only place we had a tree — unless you want to call a little old runty mesquite a tree — was down on the river. Our place is on the North Pease River. In the canyons we had a few little hackberry. But on the river, boy, you'd run into cottonwoods and maybe a maple and some shinnery oaks that would get pretty big. It was like going to another world when we would go down to the river."

Many years later, in 1988, Benny published a book called *A Field Guide to Texas Trees*. It's a thick volume devoting a page to each of the trees native to Texas, with color photographs and maps of their habitats. It seems a strange work to have been written by one who spent so many years in a treeless country, but Benny says that may be the very reason he did it.

"I was so enthralled when we would go down to the river. Even though it was on our own ranch, we didn't see it often. It was sandy country, and we didn't know about Jeeps or four-wheel drive, so we couldn't get down to it in a vehicle. And in a wagon it took all day to go down there and back, so we didn't go often. What we went there for was the wild flowers, which always bloomed about the Fourth of July. And I'd get to see the trees and sit under the trees, and I never forgot that."

After high school, he enrolled in Texas Tech, expecting to become a journalist. But World War II was still on, and he dropped out to join the Marines.

"I got in in time to get the Victory Medal, but not soon enough to be involved in the war," he says. "I spent most of my hitch out in Los Angeles. When I saw how people lived in town, I decided not to become a journalist after all. I said, 'Man, I don't want any of this damn stuff!'"

After two years, he was discharged and went back to Texas Tech. He hadn't been there long before he discovered he had made a mistake. "When I was getting my discharge from the Marines and was about to go out the door," he says, "there was a guy signing men up for the Reserves. And I was fool enough to do it."

When the Korean War broke out, he was recalled into the service and assigned to the first Marine helicopter transport squadron ever formed. "But the reservists soon were let go," he says. "A little over a year, and I was out again. I never got a chance to be a hero."

He returned to Tech again, this time majoring in agronomy and farm machinery. His plan was to finish his degree and go back to the family farm in Motley County. "But I graduated right in the middle of the drought of the '50s," he says, "and Daddy didn't even know whether he was going to be able to keep the farm or not. There just wasn't a place for me there. So I went to work for the Texas Research Foundation for $3,200 a year, and I've been here for thirty-eight long years."

In 1973, not long after Texas A&M took over the research foundation, Benny got the idea that has consumed his life ever since.

"It's written down and approved by the hierarchy all the way to the Agriculture Department in Washington, D.C.," he says. "It's called *New Landscape Plants for Texas and the Southwest.* That's my project. It's my job. And I'm the only one doing it."

Like many pioneers, Benny found little understanding among his colleagues when he first began tramping about the wild places of the state in search of plants that might adjust to city life.

"Boy, it was rough the first few years," he says. "I didn't seem to be getting anywhere, and people were shaking their heads at me like they didn't know whether I was wasting the state's money or not. People were saying to me, 'Hell, we're just paying you to camp out.' For the first ten years, I tried to talk everybody in the A&M system into going out to the Trans-Pecos with me, but nobody would go. They didn't think anything was out there. Or maybe they just weren't interested. So I quit asking."

Contrary to popular belief in the Trans-Pecos as a barren place, at least half of all the plants that are native to Texas are found there, and Benny estimates that about 50 percent of his work has been done in that supposedly empty region. "The Trans-Pecos is a meeting ground," he says. "Plants come in from the Rockies, they come across the deserts from the West, they come up the Rio Grande."

Experience has taught him that he's probably better off working alone, for searching for plants out in the vastness can be a lonely, tedious, exhausting business, not suitable for the fainthearted.

"First you have to do your homework," he says. "You read the literature, and you find out where a certain oak tree, let's say, is supposed to be. If you can, you find somebody who has seen it up in that canyon where you think it might be. Sometimes the ranchers have seen the tree, but they don't know what you're talking about because they don't call it the same thing you do. Then the next thing is getting permission to get on the place. Sometimes getting permission is the hardest and longest part. When you get permission, then you've got to crawl up that ten-mile canyon to see if that oak's really there. Sometimes it's not. You can't find it. Then you go back a year later and you find it. You don't know why you missed it the first time. If it's not in fruit, you have to go back another time to get the acorns. You get somebody up a trail about fifteen miles in one hundred degrees, and you find out real quick how strongly he wants to do this."

In his younger days it wasn't uncommon for Benny to get out of bed at four o'clock in the morning, make his trek up a canyon, and return at midnight with one plant, maybe, or a handful of acorns.

"On most of my trips I'm looking for a particular plant," he says, "but then I'll take anything that occurs when I get out there. I always try to come back with something."

He wraps his cuttings in plastic bags and puts them in an ice chest for the trip home, in hope that in twenty or twenty-five years their progeny may be growing in the back yards and office parks of North Dallas.

"A lot of the work is done on my own time," he says, "and a lot of it is done on very short notice. If somebody calls and says, 'Hey, the plants are in bloom,' I drop everything and go. I tell you, it sure does help to be a single man. I don't know that a married man, if he wants to *stay* married, could do this kind of work. You have to put first things first. I had a girlfriend once. I was getting pretty serious. And then she says, 'You spend too much time out there in your damn flowerbeds.' I thought about that a *looooong* time, and then decided: 'Well, if she's going to be that way, we may just as well put an end to it.' I was married once, years ago. Eight years. Too long. I figured: 'If I do *that* again, it's my fault for sure.'"

If, after a quarter-century or so, a tree or shrub has proved it can survive in North Texas, A&M will put a trademark on it and Benny will release it to the public. But that doesn't guarantee a happy ending to his years of labor and care.

"Releasing a plant involves a whole lot of paperwork and a whole lot of cussing and crying and getting chewed out," Benny says, "because every nurseryman will tell you he wants them, because he's afraid his buddy will get them and he won't have them. But you give them to them, and nine times out of ten, the nurserymen won't do anything with them. They won't propagate them. They'll sell the first ones and forget it. I swear, I don't know what to do about it. I've tried for twenty years, and I can't get people to grow them."

At least his A&M colleagues no longer are skeptical. As the trees, shrubs, and wildflowers that Benny has planted on the grounds of the Research and Extension Station have matured, they've provided glorious proof that his work hasn't been in vain. "Now," he says, "this is becoming the 'in' thing to be doing, with all the interest in the environment."

But he's sixty-four. Thoughts of retirement cross his mind from time to time. And he has no idea who — if anybody — will take the long hikes up those canyons to continue the work he has begun. That, he says, is for someone else to decide. "I plan to go back to the family place in Motley County. I can get down to that river easier now than I could in the old days."

He's in the Davis Mountains, on top of a mountain where he has never been before. The ridge hasn't been grazed, and the grasses stand long and lush. "Bluestem grama. Sideoats grama. Delea, highly beloved of livestock. Sprucetop grama. Boy, you have to be up pretty high to find sprucetop."

Benny moves among the flowers, shrubs, and trees like a child in a wonderland.

"Golden ball lead tree. Scarlet bouvardia. Look at that vivid red flower! It's know locally as 'firecracker bush.' Three-leaf sumac. Emory oak. The Apaches lived off of them. Wherever Apaches lived, there you find the Emory oak. Oh, man! This is some place! See how blue the agrita is? And this little plant they call 'high mass.' Catclaw mimosa. Gray's oak. Buckwheat. It has nothing to do with the buckwheat up in New York that the bees make honey out of. They're not the same species. Besides, the one in New York is an interloper from Europe. We have several species of this little fellow in Texas. Wolftail. Acacia, closely related to the mesquite . . . . "

He mutters their Latin names under his breath like an incantation. As if in reply, thunder rolls through the deep canyons below.

"Just knowing what's growing out here is valuable," he says. "*Somebody* ought to know."

So, for a while longer at least, the hunt goes on.

January 1993

Some people are heroes because of what they do. Others are heroes because of what they endure. Dr. Coy Foster is both. He's recognized worldwide as one of history's great balloonists. But I admire him even more for his courage in the face of utter disaster. In all my years as a journalist, I've never known anyone who endured so much physical pain and ruin with as much grace as he.

I'm happy to report that in June 1994 Coy began piloting balloons again, and in early 1995 returned to medicine as a family practitioner. He still hopes that someday he'll recover some of his surgical skills.

An Ordeal By Fire

AUGUST 15, 1992

It seems a good day for a balloon race. The skies over Tyler, Texas, are clear. The early morning is comfortably cool for August. The crowd of spectators is large and happy. And one by one, the gaily colored balloons rise from the park, their propane burners roaring, shooting long tongues of flame upward, warming the air that keeps the huge craft aloft.

One of the most famous balloon pilots in the world, Dr. Coy Foster, is piloting the *Patty*, owned by the Owens Sausage people. It's the most easily identified of the fifty or so balloons drifting over the city. Instead of the bulbous shape of most hot-air balloons, the *Patty* is a long cylinder, a gigantic replica of the packages of Owens Sausage that you see at the supermarket.

Months later, Gordon Trosper, Dr. Foster's crew chief, will say that its peculiar shape makes the *Patty* more difficult to handle than most balloons. "It's very small and doesn't have a tremendous amount of lift," he says. "It goes up and down very fast, and it takes a lot of skill to fly it. But Coy had flown it many times. He was very good at it."

On the day of the race, Mr. Trosper and the other members of the crew, including Dr. Foster's fiancee, Caroline Street, are tracking the *Patty* in a truck. As with all of Dr. Foster's flights, their job is to maintain radio contact with him, follow his balloon to wherever it might land, take it apart, and load it onto the truck for the return home to Dallas.

"We stopped so we could watch the balloon," Ms. Street will remember later. "The members of the crew were standing outside the truck, talking. I heard Coy on the radio say, 'Do you have a visual on me?' And I heard Gordon say, 'Yes, I do.' And then he said, 'No, I don't.' Then we heard a popping sound. Gordon yelled, 'Get in the truck! Get in the truck!' Then we saw the smoke."

The huge sausage tube rises again above the trees and drifts on, but the wicker basket in which Dr. Foster was riding no longer is hanging under it. The crew finds it lying against the curb in a small residential street, under electrical power lines, engulfed in flames.

"Coy was thirty or forty feet away from it, lying on the ground," Mr. Trosper will say later. "I ran up to him. He had been rolling in the grass. The fire was out, but the back of his shirt was still smoldering. He was conscious. I asked him what he wanted us to do for him, and he said, 'Put cold water on my hands.' One of the other guys there had a cooler, so we started dousing cold water on his hands and tried to make him as comfortable as possible. We could hear the paramedics' sirens coming."

OCTOBER 17, 1991

Pictures of balloons are hanging all about Dr. Foster's waiting room. Some are antique prints of early French balloons in the eighteenth century. Even his calendar has pictures of balloons on it. On the walls of his office, which isn't far from Presbyterian Hospital in Dallas, rows of certificates attest to his medical training and to the records in altitude, distance, and duration that he holds in ballooning.

Dr. Foster, a plastic surgeon who also specializes in the treatment of burns, is sitting at his desk, talking about balloons for a magazine story — especially about a very small one-man balloon with a three-foot-in-diameter basket in which he's planning to attempt a new altitude record. He's aiming for thirty-nine thousand feet, he says. He has been test-flying the balloon since early in the year, but there are still several bits of equipment — an oxygen regulator, a transponder — that he needs before he can make a serious attempt. And he's looking for the right kind of weather. "Very nice, gentle winds," he says. "Cool temperatures."

"The view, when you're five, six, seven miles up, is spectacular," he says. "You're in the stratosphere. You can almost see the curvature of the earth. The winds that high can be 100 to 150 miles an hour. So although I'm trying to go straight up and come straight down, I can cover a great distance. Trying to go straight up and straight down,

I've sometimes traveled seventy-five or eighty miles across the country."

He already has broken forty-nine world records in hot-air balloons, helium balloons, and blimps, and even more national records. How many does he still hold in 1991?

"I really don't know off the top of my head," he says. "Possibly about twenty world records. Some of the records that I have are records that I have broken of my own. I've set more world records than anybody in the two hundred-plus-year history of ballooning."

All the balloons in which Dr. Foster has set his records were custom built for him by Per Lindstrand of Oswestry, Wales, who himself holds many ballooning records. In 1987 Mr. Lindstrand was the first to cross the Atlantic in a hot-air balloon. In 1991 he became the first to cross the Pacific in such a craft. Dr. Foster, Mr. Lindstrand says, is "not only a great balloonist, but one of the last true amateurs of the sport."

"Most people do ballooning to make money out of it now," he says. "Ballooning is almost like motorcar racing today. You can't sustain it without having sponsorship. But Coy does it purely as a hobby, purely because he loves it. He has had no financial gain out of it. In fact, he has paid for it out of his own pocket. He just has enjoyed the challenge."

Dr. Foster's fascination with flying goes back to childhood, he says, when he was growing up in Houston after World War II. He read everything he could find about airplanes, built balsa wood models, would go to the airport to watch planes take off. He thought of becoming a jet pilot when he grew up, but decided on medicine instead.

After medical school in Galveston and an internship in San Francisco, he went to work for NASA in flight medicine, taking care of the Gemini and Apollo astronauts, then decided to specialize in plastic surgery. He went to

Phoenix and to the University of Texas Southwestern
Medical Center in Dallas for more training, practiced for a
short time in Southern California, where he also finally
got his airplane pilot's license, then moved back to Dallas.

"The first time I ever saw hot-air balloons was in
Phoenix, from a great distance," he says. "I thought, 'Hey,
when I get some time, that would be a great thing to try.'
Then sometime in the mid-1970s, not long after I came
back to Dallas, I was driving to my dentist's office and
happened to see a sign that said `Balloon Port of the
Southwest.' I thought, 'Wow!' I had a little extra time, so I
went to check it out. I went to the gentleman there at the
balloon port and said, 'Tell me about this balloon stuff.'
And he said, 'Well, I've got one in the back. Come and
look at it.' I looked at it and asked many, many questions.
And he said, 'You should come out and see how we fly
and help us out.' I did, and six months later I had my balloon pilot's license."

After a few years of piloting the big, colorful pleasure
balloons that carry five or six passengers, Dr. Foster
became fascinated with one-man craft, and in the early
1980s, he began his assault on the world records. In 1982
he set his first one, flying a tiny AX-2 class balloon 22.8
miles through the arctic air over Sweden, establishing a
new distance mark for the class. He went on to capture
nearly every record in the diminutive AX-2 through AX-4
classes, including those for altitude, duration, and distance.

Most of his records have been set in tiny craft. Indeed,
one in which he set an altitude record consists only of a
plastic playground swing seat, a modified parachute har-
ness, and an aluminum backpack that holds the propane
tank. When he was sitting in the swing seat, Dr. Foster's
head was only a few inches under the gas flame that kept

the balloon inflated. That one, he says, probably will be in the Smithsonian someday.

In 1988 the Federation Aeronautique International in France, the organization that certifies world ballooning records, presented Dr. Foster the Montgolfier Diploma, which is recognized around the world as the top award in ballooning. Named after the Montgolfier brothers, who are credited with inventing the hot-air balloon in 1783, the award is presented each year to individuals who have expanded the scope and capabilities of hot-air balloons.

"My motivation is real simple," Dr. Foster says, sitting in his office. "It's to do something nobody has ever done before. It's a dream. Many, many people don't have dreams anymore. It's dangerous, I know. I know very, very definitely that anytime I take off I could not survive the flight. I accept that. I don't consider myself a thrill seeker, but I do know that the reality of the situation is that I can be killed or seriously maimed. At any moment, this thing can fall apart on me. Or it can turn into a ball of flame."

DECEMBER 1, 1992

This is the way physicians like Dr. Foster figure a patient's chances of surviving a bad burn: They take the victim's age and the percentage of his body that has been burned and add them together. If the sum is less than one hundred, the victim may have a chance at survival. The smaller the number, the better the chance.

When his balloon hit the power lines on August 15, 1992, Dr. Foster was fifty-one years old. He suffered third-degree burns over 80 percent of his body.

Score: 131.

"That's way off the scale," he says. "I'm not supposed to be here."

He remembers taking off in the *Patty* and flying along on a straight and level course. "I was doing well that morning," he says. Then he remembers a downdraft grabbing the balloon like a huge hand and pushing it into the power lines.

"He lost altitude real fast and was unable to compensate for it," Gordon Trosper says. "Other pilots in the immediate area said there were some squirrelly winds which were causing the balloons to react strangely."

The impact wasn't strong enough to break the lines, and Mr. Trosper, who arrived within a minute or two, says Dr. Foster apparently wasn't touched by them.

"The power lines carried 69,000 volts," he says. "If Coy had gotten directly across one of them, it would have just blown him apart."

Instead, the highest of the three power lines burned through the flying wires — the stainless steel cables that attached the basket to the balloon — and sent the detached balloon sailing off across the city. At the same time, the lower power lines arced through the wicker basket, burned holes in the *Patty's* fuel tanks, ignited the propane inside and turned the basket into a ball of fire.

"I remember an explosion," Dr. Foster says. "I remember searing heat and pain. I remember falling with the basket, and saying to myself, 'You've got to get this fire out.' I remember rolling in the dirt."

People ran from houses along the street and pulled him farther away from the burning basket. His crew arrived and poured cold water on his hands. An ambulance came and took him to a hospital.

"They took X-rays," he says. "They put a tube down into my lungs to breathe for me. After that, I couldn't talk. I vaguely remember getting lowered onto the helicopter, and they gave me some morphine, and that's the last thing I remember."

The doctors who met him at Parkland Memorial Hospital in Dallas told his family and friends not to expect him to live. "And if he lives," they said, "there's no way to know what he'll turn out to be."

He spent two months in a coma in the Parkland intensive care unit. Per Lindstrand flew to Dallas to sit at his bedside. Caroline Street came to the hospital three and four times a day — as often as Parkland would allow. *Balloons and Airships* magazine in England declared "Coy Foster Day" among balloonists in Europe and America. Letters, cards, faxes, and gifts arrived at Parkland from balloon pilots all over the world.

"And I wasn't aware of any of it until I woke up," Dr. Foster says. "I received letters from other balloonists who had had accidents similar to mine. They wrote straight from the heart. It was very emotional, very personal to have someone share their innermost feelings with me. They were looking back at it. I was still in the middle of it. And it was very helpful to me."

After he awoke from his coma, he says, "I knew I was going to make it." He spent another month and a half in the hospital, regathering his strength, undergoing skin-graft operations. So much of his skin was damaged that his body couldn't provide enough for the grafts. The surgeons had to take only tiny pieces of what remained and send them to a laboratory in Boston, where scientists have learned to grow sheets of new skin from samples of the patient's own cells. The lab-grown skin then was shipped back to Dallas and grafted to Dr. Foster's body.

On the day he's telling about this, he has been out of Parkland only two weeks. He's sitting at a table in the Charles Sprague Physical Medicine Rehabilitation Department at Zale Lipshy University Hospital, where Carol Cook, an occupational therapist, is helping him try to make a fist with his left hand, a feat he won't achieve for another month.

"That's my main hand," he says. "I'm a left-handed surgeon, and my worst burns were on the left side. When I climbed out of the fire, I wouldn't have given you anything for that hand. I thought I was going to lose it."

Kathy Tisko, a physical therapist, is with him, too, massaging him, moving him through exercises to stretch the scarred and grafted skin, guiding his workouts on the bicycle, the treadmill, and other machines to help him build up the strength and mobility of his body.

"That's my job right now, is to get well," Dr. Foster says. "And when you're in the shape I'm in, you've got to start from ground zero. I have to learn to go to the bathroom — which is not easy, by the way. I had to learn how to walk, to balance myself, to climb stairs. It's like being a baby again." He hasn't yet learned to feed himself. He hasn't yet learned how to write, which frustrates him. "I'm going to have to work very, very hard for months and years to see how much I can get back," he says.

Both his elbows have been locked by abnormal bone growth caused by the fire. He won't be able to move them again until surgery frees them. He has bad days, he says, when he's discouraged and depressed. But he's happy to be alive. His therapists and his friends say that most of the time his mood is upbeat and determined.

"He's got tremendous courage and fortitude," Mr. Trosper says. "He's doing everything possible that he can do to make the best out of a bad situation, to regain as much as he can of his former self."

"After I woke up," Dr. Foster remembers, "the very first thing I decided was that I wouldn't worry about anything on the business or professional side of it. It would be foolish of me to start worrying about that now. It's not a priority. I'll practice medicine in some way, I think. But will I be a plastic surgeon again? I don't know. I have to take it day by day."

Ms. Tisko estimates that he will be doing physical therapy all day and into the night, every day and every night, for six to eight months, minimum. "This man works hard," she says. "He already has made impressive gains. He gets ten gold stars."

FEBRUARY 8, 1993

Caroline Street rises at 5:15 a.m. and gets herself ready for the day and makes breakfast. At 7:00 a.m. she gets Dr. Foster up and helps him dress. He eats, then she drives him to Zale Lipshy and leaves him there. At 8:00 a.m. his therapy begins. At noon Ms. Street returns to the hospital and has lunch with him. At 1:00 p.m. Dr. Foster returns to the Physical Medicine Rehabilitation Department and continues his therapy until 3:30 or 4:00 p.m. Ms. Street drives him to the home they share in Highland Park, helps him with his bath and changes all his dressings. Then Dr. Foster starts all over again, stretching, bending, keeping his parts moving so that he doesn't become stiff.

"Coy is dependent on me now," Ms. Street says. "He needs me. It makes me very careful, because I don't want him to feel that I begrudge doing things for him, or that I'm doing it because I have to. I'm not. I do it because I want to do it, because I care."

They have dinner together, watch a little TV, then Ms. Street helps Dr. Foster prepare for bed.

"We don't go out a great deal now," Dr. Foster says. "We spend a lot of time with friends — about twice a week. And Caroline and I spend a lot more quality time together than we used to. Our relationship is much, much closer now, and the love is much, much more. It's more defined for me now than it was before the accident."

106

On January 18, he underwent surgery on his left elbow, to free it from its locked position. Temporarily, the operation has made his home routine even more complicated than before. As soon as he returns from the hospital in the evening, he must strap on his CPM, a battery-operated continuous passive motion machine which extends and flexes his left arm every ninety seconds, to keep the freed elbow from freezing up again.

He must wear the machine every night from 5:00 p.m. to 7:00 a.m. Sleeping while strapped to several pounds of moving metal isn't easy, he says. "When you turn out the lights and everything is quiet, it sounds like somebody's driving a tractor around the room." And he worries that if something goes wrong with the CPM, it could injure him without his knowing it. "I have no feeling in my fingers. If they somehow got caught in the machine, it could chew them up without even waking me."

But his years as a young intern and resident physician prepared him somewhat for the ordeal. "In my surgical training, we slept on little single beds in call rooms when we were on emergency call," he says. "So I can sleep on a rock and lie still. I rarely move at night. I may sleep eight or ten hours without moving."

In several weeks he will undergo surgery on his other elbow, and there will be more surgeries over the next two or three years, but most of them will be minor compared to those he already has undergone. He's proud of his progress. But the better he does, the more he must preach to himself to be patient.

"I'm anxious to get back to work," he says. "At times I'm very frustrated, very irritated that I can't do what I did before. But my slate was wiped clean by the accident. I couldn't do anything except breathe. And I had to learn how to do that again after being on the machine all those weeks. It's way too early to decide what occupation I'll follow for the rest of my life. Whether I'll ever be able to do plastic surgery again, I don't know. But I don't think there's any question that it will be in medicine."

Despite his losses and his uncertain future, his love for the sport that nearly killed him is still strong. Nor is he yet through with it.

"Many people think the feats I did during the '80s were risky," he says. "And I've proven by my own experience that the worst can happen on a nice day on a fun flight just as easily as if you're flying for a world record. I can say right now, officially, that I'm retired from world records. I've done enough. I don't need to do any more. But I have every intention to go up in a balloon again. It's much more likely that you'll be injured seriously or killed if you get in your car than in a balloon. I'll take the odds on a balloon anytime."

Per Lindstrand is so sure that Dr. Foster someday will take to the skies again that he has reserved for his friend "Serial No. 1" of a new series of balloons.

"The type of balloon that I build will be up to Coy," he says. "I'll hold that serial number for him until he's fit enough to see and tell me what he wants to do. But there's no doubt at all that he will go up again. None at all. He's got that old Texas spirit, you see."

April 1993

There are better detective stories than The Maltese Falcon, *I suppose, but I don't know what they are. Dashiell Hammett's tale has everything a reader could desire: sex, greed, betrayal, murder, a great cast of characters, and — the icing on the cake — a jewel-encrusted bird intended as tribute to a medieval king.*

It also has San Francisco, the perfect setting for such a story.

Where The Falcon Dwells

It's still the perfect spot for a murder. The lights from Bush Street barely penetrate the gloom, barely illuminate the graffiti near the alley's mouth and the fire escape that zigzags up the wall at its dead end. Anything could happen here in the black, smelly emptiness, and no one would know for hours.

The wooden railing that Miles Archer broke when he fell and the steep hill down which he rolled are gone. The spot where he died is covered by an ugly building as dark and forbidding as the alley. Its sign, around front on Stockton Street, advertises the Green Door, a massage parlor that promises "A Touch of Ecstasy."

But the small bronze plaque, high on the alley wall, reminds of the death: "On Approximately This Spot Miles Archer, Partner of Sam Spade, Was Done In By Brigid O'Shaughnessy."

Mr. Archer lived and died only in the imagination of Pinkerton-detective-turned-writer Dashiell Hammett. But in the centennial year of Mr. Hammett's birth, pilgrims from all over the world have journeyed to this spot to imagine that foggy night in 1928 when Mr. Archer caught a bullet.

"Hammett fans aren't like Elvis fans. They don't swarm," says Don Herron, who leads grueling three-hour walking tours up and down San Francisco's steep hills to places where Mr. Hammett lived and worked before his death in 1961, and where the characters in much of his fiction hatch their intrigues and bump each other off.

"Hammett fans appear alone or in pairs," Mr. Herron says. "They're quiet. They're devout. Last May, I had a guy from Glasgow, Scotland, who had saved up for twenty years to come and visit the Hammett sites. You should have seen him. He had an epiphany. He was in heaven."

In *The Maltese Falcon*, in which Mr. Archer meets his doom, and four other novels and dozens of short stories, Mr. Hammett invented an enduring hero — the hard-boiled private eye — who, along with the cowboy, has become a symbol of America around the world.

Many detective-story devotees consider *The Maltese Falcon* one of the greatest crime thrillers ever written. It's also one of the most popular. Originally published as a serial in *Black Mask* magazine, the novel appeared in hardcover in 1930 and has sold well in several languages since.

In it, Mr. Hammett created the cynical Sam Spade, destined to become grandfather to hundreds of wisecracking, tough-guy sleuths who have spellbound readers, radio listeners and movie and TV viewers for more than sixty years.

Millions who have never read the novel have seen the 1941 movie, starring Humphrey Bogart as Sam Spade, Mary Astor as the murderous Brigid O'Shaughnessy, and Sydney Greenstreet and Peter Lorre as villains in pursuit of a mysterious black bird. The ancient jewel-encrusted statuette is worth a limitless amount of money and blood.

Even the foot-high falcon made for the movie is worth a small fortune. Christie's, the New York auction house, has announced that it will sell the prop on December 6. Once the property of the late William Conrad, who himself played a hard-boiled detective on TV, the bird is expected to fetch between thirty thousand dollars and fifty thousand dollars.

In the late 1940s and early 1950s, families gathered around the radio to hear actor Howard Duff play Sam Spade on a weekly radio mystery sponsored by Wildroot Cream Oil hair tonic.

But it's the book that draws true Hammett fans to San Francisco, the scene of its crimes, a city drawn so vividly it becomes one of *The Maltese Falcon*'s strongest characters. Sam Spade's "burg," as he calls it, is full of fog and darkness. Its alleys, streets, and back rooms simmer with intrigue.

And the city that still draws Hammett fans has changed amazingly little from the clammy night when Mr. Archer was murdered.

"Nearly all of San Francisco was built after the 1906 earthquake and fire, and not much has been torn down since," says Joe Gores, who, like Mr. Hammett, is a private-eye-turned-mystery-writer. "The faded signs of long-gone businesses are still visible on a lot of the buildings. Hell, a lot of the businesses from Hammett's era are still where they were then."

Mr. Gores is sipping a Bloody Mary at the bar in John's Grill, a dark-paneled restaurant where Sam Spade dines on chops, a baked potato, and tomatoes in *The Maltese Falcon*. The meal is still on the menu, where it's called "Sam Spade's Chops." The bartender also will mix a "Bloody Brigid," which comes in a souvenir glass with a black falcon on it.

Outside on Ellis Street, John's sign advertises the restaurant as "The Home of the Maltese Falcon." An upstairs dining room is decorated with poster-size stills and pages of dialogue from the Bogart movie. A glass-fronted bookcase holds copies of Mr. Hammett's novels and a copy of *Hammett*, a novel written by Mr. Gores in which the tough-guy detective is Dashiell Hammett himself.

So far as Mr. Gores knows, John's Grill is the only Dashiell Hammett museum. The restaurant, which is called by its true name in *The Maltese Falcon*, is next door to the Flood Building, where the Pinkerton detective agency had its office when Mr. Hammett was on the payroll. But the names of most of the buildings in which Sam Spade fends off unfriendly cops and too-friendly women and plays cat-and-mouse with the villains of *The Maltese Falcon* are disguised.

Mr. Gores, working from internal evidence in the novel, has identified nearly all the hotels, office buildings, restaurants, theaters, and apartment buildings involved in the chase after the black bird.

Most are still serving the same purposes. The St. Francis and the Sir Francis Drake, which are fancy hotels (under different names) in the novel, are still fancy hotels. The Geary Theatre is still a theater, though now closed for renovation. The Cathedral Apartments, which in the book is the Corona, Brigid O'Shaughnessy's building, has gone condo and is still a swanky place to live. The Hunter-Dulin

Building, the home of Sam Spade's office, is still an office building.

And 891 Post Street is still a nondescript apartment building with a laundry on its ground floor. "I've spent whole days just walking the 800 block of Post street, feeling the past," Mr. Gores says.

In the novel, Sam Spade lives in a fourth-floor apartment in the yellow brick building. In the late 1920s, Dashiell Hammett lived there. It's where he wrote *The Maltese Falcon*.

The white marble lobby with its white columns — surprisingly elegant, considering the building's dreary exterior — resembles a little Greek temple. It's locked to visitors. A sign visible through its glass door advertises studio apartments for five hundred dollars a month.

"There's a guy who got an apartment there, he has convinced himself that it's the one Spade lived in," Mr. Gores says. "This guy, he shows up at conferences and stuff, all dressed up as Sam Spade. He has cards printed that say he lives at Sam Spade's address. Suddenly his life's work is to live in that apartment and look as much as possible like Sam Spade."

Mr. Gores, a disciple and scholar of Dashiell Hammett, has published eleven hard-boiled detective novels of his own. He takes quiet pleasure in the fact that critics often compare his work to his hero's.

"Hammett is one of the world's great writers," he says. "And Sam Spade is a wonderful character. Hammett always said Spade is the guy that private eyes would like to have been, and thought they were in their gaudier moments."

Yet, judged by the standards of modern, real-life private eyes, Mr. Spade would be a failure, says David Fechheimer, one of the best-known private detectives in San Francisco.

"Detective fiction, film, and television are all about mistakes," he says. "A real detective's work is almost entirely cerebral, not physical. If a detective does his job right, there's nothing to see. There's no action. It's when he makes mistakes that there's lots of action. Would you want to hire some guy who went out and got in fistfights and got thrown through windows and wrecked cars and shot people? It doesn't work that way. A good day for me is a day when nobody knows I was working."

Yet, Mr. Fechheimer says, Sam Spade is the reason he's a private eye.

About thirty years ago, he was a graduate student at San Francisco State University, studying to become an English professor. He read *The Maltese Falcon* and got caught in its thrall.

"I called Pinkerton and asked if they needed someone who had no experience and a beard," he says. "I called them because they were Hammett's company. To my surprise, they said they needed somebody with a beard that day. I thought I would do it a couple of weeks as a goof. It looked like fun, being Sam Spade. Pinkerton put me undercover on the docks, and I was hooked. I never went back to school. I never finished my degree."

Sam Spade may break all the rules of the private-eye business, but Mr. Fechheimer says he has always been sure that the tough guy's creator was a very good detective.

"I never had any doubt about it," he says. "I know Hammett was a good, reliable Pinkerton because the details are always right in his books. And he's one hell of a writer."

To Mr. Gores and other Hammett devotees, *The Maltese Falcon* epitomizes San Francisco.

"Every time it's a foggy night," he says, "I really expect to see Sydney Greenstreet or Peter Lorre come trotting down the street with a bundle under his arm."

October 1994

Not many of us think of American Indians as urban people. Living in the suburbs, commuting to jobs and worrying about bills and taxes don't fit the stereotypes that non-Indian writers and filmmakers have created. When I began interviewing people for this piece, some were nervous and reluctant, and I wondered why. They later told me they had been interviewed before, and that no matter what they said, it was the stereotypes that kept appearing in print.

I was relieved and proud when a number of Indians praised this story and told me they had sent copies to friends and relatives.

It also has been used at the Dallas Police Academy to help train officers to be more sensitive to the ethnic and cultural diversity of the city.

The City Tribe

The singer has sung a gourd dance song, honoring warriors. The elders have told him the song was made by Quanah Parker, the singer says. He doesn't explain who Quanah Parker was. He doesn't have to. The man to whom he's speaking is Dennis Wahkinney, a great-great-grandson of Quanah.

"Years ago, when these songs were made," Mr. Wahkinney says, "nobody knew they would someday be played over the airwaves in a metroplex of four million people."

He sounds a little wistful. He doesn't explain that Quanah was the last war chief of the Comanches, their leader in that terrible time when the U.S. cavalry slaughtered their horses in Palo Duro Canyon, destroying their economy and their way of life forever. Most Texans know that, and most Indians. On this Sunday afternoon, in the studio of radio station KNON-FM, 89.3 on the dial, it's Quanah's song that has survived and is important.

The program is *Beyond Bows and Arrows*. "The only American Indian radio program in the state of Texas," Mr. Wahkinney calls it. It has been on the air every Sunday afternoon for ten years, and its popularity is growing. About eight months ago, KNON increased the show's air time from one hour to two, and on this Sunday Mr. Wahkinney sounds especially happy. The community station's fund drive has just ended, and *Beyond Bows and Arrows* listeners have pledged $3,350, more than triple the program's $1,000 goal.

For what other station may an Indian call and request a song by the Eagle Claw Singers, or Bad Medicine, or the Black Lodge Singers, or Whitefish Bay? Where else may an Indian call and ask, "Would you play some Navajo music?" or "How about a song in Lakota?" Where else may Free Spirit call to ask the DJ to pass on her happy birthday wishes to Spirit Hawk and play a birthday song by Red Bull?

Between songs, Mr. Wahkinney and his wife, Cindy, read the Indian news, about the legal, medical, and social services available to Indians living in the area, about events at the Dallas Inter-Tribal Center and the American Indian Center in Grand Prairie and the doings of the

American Indian Chamber of Commerce and some of the local Indian churches, about upcoming powwows in North Texas, Oklahoma, and more distant parts. And from time to time, visitors drop into the studio to perform live, like the singer of Quanah's song, or just to chat with the Wahkinneys and their radio audience.

From 4:00 to 6:00 p.m. on Sunday, *Beyond Bows and Arrows* is one of the liveliest times on North Texas radio, and many Indians set aside those hours each week to relax and enjoy this small taste of their native culture, this invisible gathering of the tribes.

According to the 1990 census about sixty-five thousand Indians live in Texas. Of them, a few hundred live on the reservations of the Tiguas at El Paso, the Alabamas and the Coushattas at Livingston, and the Kickapoos at Eagle Pass. Others live in Houston and San Antonio or are scattered about the state. But forty thousand make their homes in North Texas, most of them within the reach of Mr. Wahkinney's radio show.

"Rise and be recognized," he urges them as he signs off, "and let us grow stronger and stronger together."

But it isn't easy, staying Indian in the metroplex.

Richard Lester and Pat Peterson, brother and sister, say they were the first Indians in Dallas. They laugh, because it isn't strictly true. Many years ago, Comanches, Kiowas, Caddos, Kickapoos, and Tonkawas were wandering about this neck of the prairie, following the buffalo, harrying the white settlers, doing business with John Neely Bryan, the founder of Dallas, and other traders. Eventually, however, the federal government moved them all beyond the Red River. So when Dick and Rebecca Lester and their two children, a Choctaw family from Oklahoma, stepped off a train at Union Station in 1957, they may indeed have been the only Indians in town.

Pat was nine years old when they arrived, Richard was eleven. "There was a big hoopla," Ms. Peterson recalls. "The newspapers sent photographers to take pictures of us. Then somebody from the Bureau of Indian Affairs took us to the West Dallas housing projects and showed us three or four apartments. They had a lot of furniture we could choose from, and they set up housekeeping for us."

The Lesters' arrival was part of a relocation program run by the federal Bureau of Indian Affairs in those days. Under the program, Indians living in the Oklahoma nations and the reservations in the Dakotas, New Mexico, Arizona, and other states were persuaded to sign contracts to leave their homes and relocate in Dallas and half a dozen other cities around the country. In return, the BIA agreed to find them housing, pay their way through vocational schools, and find them better jobs.

"In short, it was to urbanize the Indians," says Bob Colombe, who was eighteen when he left the Rosebud reservation of the Sioux in South Dakota and came to Dallas to enroll in barber college. "The BIA gave you housing, a clothing allowance, and sent you to school to learn how to be an auto mechanic, a nurse, or whatever. But the plan didn't go far enough. If a guy hadn't been to town before, it was kind of difficult. The people who were running the program were inadequate. It was a typical government deal."

The BIA neglected to tell the Indians that the housing they would be provided was in the projects. "We were just dumped there," Mr. Lester says. "Once the BIA got you into the projects, they just went off and left you alone. The schools were segregated at that time. The Mexicans and whites went to Thomas Edison. We were the first Indians there. The very first day I was in the housing project, I got in a fight. We were always getting into trouble because we were brown, but didn't speak Spanish. But the tribes kept coming in. We had Cheyennes, other Choctaws, Creeks, Seminoles, Sioux, Eskimos. We had everybody. Pretty soon, the whole project was alive with Indians."

Almost immediately, the Lesters and a few others began organizing Indian cultural groups. In 1958 they started the Thunderbird Indian Club at the Elmer Scott Community Center in the project where they lived and planned events to bring the Indian people together and keep their community intact. Dick Lester also organized the first multiracial football and baseball teams in the projects.

"The Elmer Scott project was Mexican, the George Loving project was white, and the Andrew Ward project was black," Richard Lester says. "The teams my father started were the only racially integrated athletic teams in Dallas until the schools desegregated. We had a West Dallas league."

The relocation program somehow worked for the Lesters and Mr. Colombe, but it failed for many others, and the government abandoned it about ten years ago. "The whole idea was for the Indians to assimilate, to get on their feet economically and socially, but they put us in a Catch-22 situation," Ms. Peterson says. "When they placed you in the projects, your rent was based on your income. As your income increased, your rent increased. Many never reached the point where they could remove themselves from that situation and get out. So they gave up and went home."

Even if the Indians completed the training they had come to the city for, the BIA's promise of a good job was seldom fulfilled. "You'd go to the job placement office to try to get a job," Ms. Peterson says, "and the job placement people would be reading the want ads in the newspaper. That's where they found the jobs. You got no help."

Mr. Colombe says half the Indians who went to barber college with him never got jobs in Dallas.

And many who stayed still maintain some ties with the places whence they came, even after so many years. Mr. Colombe used to spend every vacation on the Rosebud reservation, and still takes his son hunting there every year. Many families in Dallas and Fort Worth journey to Oklahoma almost every weekend to participate in pow-wows and visit family.

"A lot of people who live in Dallas, whether they be Navajo, Sioux, or whatever, they go home for sweat lodge ceremonies to revitalize spiritually," says Ms. Peterson. "They call it 'getting smoked.' They go home, go through the ceremonies, and come back totally different people. It's a cleansing. It's a spiritual experience. You don't get that here in Dallas. You have to go home."

"But," Mr. Lester says, "they're faced with the economic necessity of coming back to Dallas, because the jobs are here."

Mr. Lester, Mr. Colombe, and Ms. Peterson are sitting in the North Dallas office of the American Indian Art Council, which they helped establish. Mr. Colombe is its president, Ms. Peterson its vice president, and Mr. Lester its director. For the past three years their organization has run the American Indian Art Festival and Market, which attracts Indian artists, craftspeople, dancers, and musicians from all over the country and Canada. They exhibit and offer their works for sale in Artist Square, next door to the Meyerson Symphony Center.

Part of the reason for the event is to educate the non-Indian public about the beauty of the American Indian culture and destroy stereotypes. During the festival, visiting Indians appear before school classes and other groups to explain their heritage and their ways of life. The art show also gives Indian artists an opportunity to bring their works to the city and perhaps make a little money.

But to the show's organizers, who over the years have become as urban as they are Indian, the festival also carries a personal meaning. "Our parents taught us to be proud of the fact that we're Native Americans," Ms. Peterson says. "We've got to make sure we don't forget who we are. It's important to me that I do whatever I need to do to maintain my Indianness and to feel fulfilled as an Indian and as a person. And I don't want my children ever to forget who they are or what their culture is. But they were raised here in Dallas, and this is what they consider home. It's going to be important for the second and third generations of Native American families that there be something established here that they can identify with. This is something I see the American Indian Art Council accomplishing over the long haul."

Her brother nods agreement. Then he says, "I want to see the Choctaw tribe do well, and if there is anything I can do to assist them, I'll do it. But I have no desire to live in Oklahoma. I'm thoroughly acclimatized to Dallas. You can't help who you are."

Henry Johnson, like Pat Peterson and Richard Lester, is Choctaw. His wife, Bernice, is Seminole and Chickasaw. About a century and a half ago, their people traveled the Trail of Tears to Oklahoma, Mr. Johnson's people from Mississippi, Mrs. Johnson's from Florida. In 1963, Henry and Bernice and their six children traveled another trail from Ada, Oklahoma, to Dallas, looking for work. They were part of the relocation program that already had brought the Lester family and Bob Colombe to the city.

"We came here with a very young family, and we've raised all our children here in Texas," Mrs. Johnson says. Four of the children, now grown, still live in Dallas. The two eldest sons have moved back to Oklahoma. Two foster children, younger than the others, still live with Mr. and Mrs. Johnson in Grand Prairie.

The contract that Mr. Johnson, a truck driver, signed with the Bureau of Indian Affairs promised him a better job in Dallas than he had in Ada. But the job the BIA found for him paid only one-third as much as he had made in Oklahoma. The BIA promised to find him a better one in a few weeks, but failed. So he went out and found one for himself. "I had to find a better job because I wanted to get my family away from that project," he says.

Despite the hardships, the Johnsons never were tempted to give up and go home. "There were a lot of educational opportunities here that my children didn't have in Oklahoma," Mrs. Johnson says. "It seemed that there was a junior college or a vocational school everywhere you turned."

Over the years, the Johnsons have participated in most of the American Indian activities in the Dallas area and have worked to find help for Indian families in need. Mrs. Johnson was one of the founders of the Dallas Inter-Tribal Center, which offers health and educational help to Indians. "So they would stay here, instead of go home to what they left behind," she says.

Although their children grew up in the city, and all of them eventually married non-Indians, they've neither ignored nor forgotten their Indian heritage. "My parents told us about the Seminole whipping tree, and what the green corn dance stands for, and all those things," Mrs. Johnson says. "And we tell them to our children and our non-Indian in-laws, because they need to know, too. And our grandchildren need to know."

Mrs. Johnson makes silver jewelry and beadwork and sells them at powwows and Indian art shows around the country. Her husband makes the elaborate feather bustles and headdresses that powwow dancers wear.

It's a craft he learned out of necessity. The Johnsons' eldest son, now thirty-four years old, became a dancer at age eight. His expensive bustles kept falling apart after only a few dances, so Mr. Johnson made a study of them and found ways to make them stronger. Other dancers admired his work and asked him to make bustles and headdresses for them. So Mr. Johnson took feathers with him on his truck-driving runs and worked on them at night in the motels where he stayed. Since his retirement from truck driving, he gets orders from Indian dancers all over the United States and Canada, and even from Indians serving overseas in the armed forces. He has taught his sons to make their own dance dress.

The Johnsons have been the organizing force behind the Texas Red Nations Powwow, which for the past three years has attracted dancers and musicians to Dallas. Proceeds from the event are used to help Indian students in the Dallas Independent School District. The Johnsons also encourage DISD teachers to come and learn about the Indian culture, take pictures to show to their classes, and arrange for Indian performers to come to their schools.

"I think interest in the Indian culture has increased in recent years," Mrs. Johnson says. "Sometimes I think it's becoming *too* popular. It's kind of a fad. Here in Texas, there are a lot of want-to-bes and fake Indians who are doing a lot of inappropriate things that they think are Indian. And when the fad is over with and gone, the damage is done, and we have to be the bearers of what's left."

She's especially critical of non-Indians who try to imitate Indian art or Indian religious ceremonies and desecrate such sacred objects as the smoking pipe and the eagle feather. "To do these things is just outrageous," she says. "To us, it's like a slap in the face. Only certain people may use the pipe. Only medicine men known to the tribe are allowed to perform certain rituals. And this is the way we teach our children. 'This is not for you to do,' we tell them. 'If ever one day you have the honor of being selected, *then* you can do these things. But if you aren't, then you honor the ones who are.'"

"When you sing an Indian song," Mr. Johnson says, "you better know the language of what you're singing. If you don't know the language, and you don't know what you're singing, you don't amount to nothing. You're just a want-to-be. You've got to know who you are and where you're from."

Because of stereotypes that white people have created of the American Indian, sacred traditions and Indian dignity are violated almost every day without a thought or a care, Dennis Wahkinney says. He tells of a torrid, dry afternoon when he was listening to the radio and the disc jockey suggested that the city find an Indian to make it rain.

"Then some guy called in and told the disc jockey, 'Offer them a fifth of whiskey and they'll do it.' And another guy called and said, 'If you want a downpour, you have to offer more than just a fifth.'"

Then Mr. Wahkinney called in and explained that the rain dance is sacred to those tribes who practice it, that it's a ritual of prayer, and nothing to joke about.

"You know what the disc jockey replied? He said, 'You ought to learn to laugh at yourself.'"

He tells of a company in New York that markets a drink called Crazy Horse Malt Liquor, billing it as "The Drink of the Warrior."

"A court has ruled that it's OK," Mr. Wahkinney says, "that it's freedom of speech. But would they be permitted to produce Martin Luther King Malt Liquor, 'The Drink of Basketball Players'? They couldn't do that to any other

124

race. But people still have it in their minds that it's OK to belittle the Indian people."

Mr. Wahkinney grew up north of Lawton and went to a small country school in Elgin, Oklahoma "The prejudice there was very bad," he says. "There was no getting around it. I grew up with an inferiority complex because of it, and for a while, when I was a young adult, I didn't really identify much with the Indian culture, because to me it was just problems. It lessened my image of myself, my self-esteem. I didn't learn much about the Indian culture until I became a member of the Baha'i faith. Baha'i puts an emphasis on individuality. One of its basic teachings is unity in diversity."

He tells of going to the Choctaw reservation in Mississippi and viewing a video made by a Baha'i friend. "The video showed all the Indian people from different tribes dancing in their native dress. Eskimos dancing in the big fur coats, Navajos with their headbands and silver belts, others dancing in their feathers. But they were all dancing in such incredible unity. This feeling just overwhelmed me that it was OK to be an Indian person. It was OK to be a Comanche. It was then that I began to really want to learn about the Comanche people, to learn about Indian culture."

So when his employer, the Internal Revenue Service, transferred him from Oklahoma City to Dallas in 1984, he volunteered to help with *Beyond Bows and Arrows*, which had been started a couple of years earlier by Frank McLemore, a Cherokee and a prominent leader in the Indian community. When Mr. McLemore left the program, Mr. Wahkinney took it over.

He would go to the Dallas Public Library to research the program, to learn about the different tribes. Then he started going to powwows and manning an information booth about his program. Then he started taping the music at the powwows to broadcast for his audience.

"People think that because I do the radio program, I know a lot," he says, "but I'm just learning a little here and there. It's through getting involved in the community that I'm learning the most. But I don't feel that I need to live with it all the time, the way a lot of people do. It's not that ingrained in me. That bothers me sometimes. I don't feel that I can be as traditional as a lot of people I know, simply because it will never be as much a part of me as some other Indian people. I kind of backed into it. I've had to find ways to get in touch with the Indian culture so I'll know about the people I serve. I find peace in that."

Ken Brown is one of those who goes to Oklahoma to the powwows. He also goes to powwows in Texas and Colorado and many other places. He loads his feathers into his van and goes, often with relatives and friends riding with him.

"The powwow world is a pretty big world," he says. "A lot of people in the non-Indian world don't know about it. They don't know that many Indian people depend on the weekly contest powwows for a living, like rodeo performers make their living on the rodeo circuit."

A recent powwow that Mr. Brown attended in Tulsa attracted more than five hundred dancers from the United States, Canada, and Mexico, and a half-dozen drums. A drum is the Indian equivalent of a band. Six or eight or ten men sit in a circle, beating a single drum and singing. At the larger powwows, there are northern drums, which specialize in the high-pitched, falsetto singing style of the northern tribes, and southern drums, who sing the lower-pitched songs of the southern Indians. Many of the songs are old, many are new, and they're sung in many languages. The drums take turns performing, and the dances alternate between social dances, in which anyone may participate, and the contest dances, in which the professionals compete for prize money.

Many powwows also include sessions of gourd dancing, which honors military veterans. In gourd dancing, the people simply stand in a circle and shake rattles, sometimes for three or four hours. "Non-Indians come in, watch awhile, get bored, and leave," Mr. Brown says. "They want to know, 'Where are all the feathers?' The southern tribes love to gourd dance. And it appeals to a lot of older people."

Around the fringes of the dancing arena, vendors sell food, Indian jewelry, beadwork, leatherwork, clothing, pieces of art, and tape cassettes of the more popular drums and their singers.

Traditionally, powwows were held in open fields, and some still are. But many are in downtown urban areas now, in air-conditioned convention centers. Hundreds, sometimes thousands, pay admission to watch the dancing. Profits usually aid some Indian cause.

Mr. Brown is Sioux and Creek, originally from the Pine Ridge reservation in South Dakota. But his father didn't like life on the reservation, so the family moved to Oklahoma, and eventually to Dallas when Ken was in the third grade.

"My father was fairly independent," Mr. Brown says. "He didn't like the government at all, the BIA programs and stuff. He didn't want us kids to be influenced by them, for fear that we might have the desire to 'go back home,' as they say. He loved Texas. He had this fascination with the state. And he wanted us to be able to handle city life. My dad's whole thrust was: Stay in school, get your education, learn how to handle things. It was a wise plan."

Mr. Brown started dancing when he was five or six years old and his family was living in Anadarko, Oklahoma. But

his father died when Ken was fifteen, and the Indian influence on his life "took a nose dive, because with his death
we lost any connection we had with the reservation. It
was difficult to make the Indian way a lifestyle in Dallas.
But it's real healthy if you can balance those things — city
life and the Indian things."

Mr. Brown works in the display department of the
Dallas Public Library, and spends much of his spare time
trying to educate both non-Indians and Indians — especially children — about Indian culture.

"Dancing gives self-confidence to kids," he says, "and
there's nothing wrong with that, especially for Indian kids,
who tend to be more shy than most because we're such a
small percentage of the population. Sometimes you're
afraid to let anybody know about your Indianness,
because then everybody focuses on it and wants to know
every answer in the whole wide world about every Indian
tribe. And if you're a kid, like I was, you can only speak
for your own tribe. If something else comes up, about
totem poles or canoes, then a kid can be embarrassed
when he shouldn't be. Sometimes it's good to ask a question back. If they ask, 'Were you born in a tepee?' I ask,
'Were you born in a covered wagon on the prairie?'"

He's one of those who drops by KNON to chat with Mr.
and Mrs. Wahkinney. "The program does a lot to make the
Indian culture more recognizable and not so mysterious,"
he says. "That's what I hope I'm contributing to. I can't go
back to the homeland, the Dakotas, and be everything I
want to be there. Since I can't, I try to influence as much
as possible, in a good way, the culture of Dallas."

And he loves the powwows, where, he says, "I can
socialize with other Indian people, dance whenever I feel
like it, and not have to worry about anything. Just for
those few minutes that I'm dancing, I can lose myself in
the music and get away from everything."

128

🐦   🐦   🐦

"The drum is the heartbeat of Mother Earth," Linda Durant is explaining. She's a Delaware-Shawnee-Creek-Chickasaw, sitting in the grandstand at the Tulsa powwow, watching her friends and several hundred others dancing an intertribal dance to the music of Whitefish Bay, a drum from Canada. "Gathering around this drum, we're trying to keep in balance with Mother Earth. We feel that.

"And the medicine wheel you see so many people wearing as an ornament is a circle. It represents the whole universe. It has a point in all the four directions. It represents balance and harmony in the universe. All the four-legged animals, all the two-legged animals are part of it. We're all the same. And the air and the land and everything. We're all part of the universe."

She smiles. "But I'm also a native Dallasite, Texan, American Indian. And a native of Oak Cliff. I have a lot of different worlds. Most people do. And we're shaped by those worlds.

"It's hard to keep the Indian sense of balance in a city like Dallas. It's hard to maintain your connection to Mother Earth. You have to be strong spiritually. The drum, the dance, all this helps us do that."

September 1993

*Some would say that cowboy poetry isn't really poetry.
Others would say that poetry, like beauty, is in the eye of the
beholder, or reader, or in the ear of the listener. I think the real
poetry is in the soul of its creator, and that the best of the cowboy poets are true poets.*

*To a journalist of my type, working on a story such as this is
just about heaven: hanging around people with whom you're
instantly* simpático, *talking about something that means a lot
to all of you — the West, its history, its culture, its peculiar arts
— and laughing a lot.*

*I became a fan of the people I interviewed for this story, and
still read their work.*

Poets Lariat

"This friend of mine, Jack Douglas, he lives up there by
Littlefield," J.B. Allen is saying. "I come to find out that
he's been writin' songs a long while. He's an artist kind of
feller. Plays guitar. Anyway, I was helpin' him brand one
time, and we was settin' around after dinner, and he said,
'I been writin' some poems.' and I looked at him kinda
funny, you know. Cowpunchers ain't supposed to write
poems. But anyhow, he read one or two of 'em off to me,
and they was purty good. At the time, I was nightwatchin'

at a feedlot and had a lot of time on my hands, and I just wrote a li'l old silly poem 'bout somethin' that happened to me down on the river one time. One thing led to another and I got to writin' a lot of 'em. I wrote two or three hundred the first two years. I just couldn't hardly write fast enough to get 'em all out of there."

Mr. Allen's voice is a kind of music not heard often in cities, deep as a cello but full of space and distance and weather. It's a voice born of thirty years or more of hollering at cattle, fighting blizzards and drought, and swapping stories over cups of strong black coffee in ranch-house kitchens and auction-barn cafes.

He's of a family of cowhands "on both sides of the tree," and has spent all his fifty-five years, except for a hitch in the Navy, on the plains of Texas and points west, working and bossing on ranches. Now he and his wife, Margaret, have a place of their own, "a little cow-and-calf operation" he calls it, near Whiteface, between Lubbock and the New Mexico line.

He's as cowboy as they come. But on that fateful night at the feedlot, he became a poet, too. And during the few years since then, he has become one of the more original and authentic practitioners of the peculiar folk art called cowboy poetry that has lived quietly in Texas and the West for over a century, but is just now entering the consciousness of the rest of America.

"How do I go about writin' it? I *don't* go about writin' it," he says. "The way I do it, a line will come to me in my head, and I'll write that down. And then another'n. And another'n. A lot of times the thing'll take off in a different direction than what I thought it was goin' to. Halfway through the poem, I still don't know how it's gonna end. But I git there."

Somehow, the music of his voice gets transcribed to Mr. Allen's pages, where the vowels are just as strong and the g's are just as missing from the ends of words as when he's speaking. For his poems, like all cowboy poems, are meant to be spoken aloud.

"I kind of spell things like we talk," he says. "You can git away with that with this kind of poems. I tell some of them boys from up north there in Montana and Idaho that they talk so good, puttin' the g's on the end and all, that it hardens up the sounds. I'm always hoorawin' 'em about talkin' funny."

Mr. Allen's poems also are written in capital letters, for a purely practical reason. "I type with one finger of one hand," he says. "I don't know how to type no other way. And it's easier to push that little deal down there and then go tap, tap, tap. That way I don't have to mess with nuthin'."

On the day he's telling these things, Mr. Allen is one of the featured poetry reciters at the Red Steagall Cowboy Gathering and Western Swing Festival, billed as "a celebration of cowboys and culture," at the Fort Worth Stockyards. He figures it's about the sixteenth such event he has attended this year. Similar gatherings are springing up all over, even in the Deep South and Deepest Yankeeland. There's even talk of a "cowboy poetry movement," and everybody, it seems, wants to join it.

"This Fort Worth deal is one of the gooduns," Mr. Allen says. "Ol' Red knows who the realuns are. But the 'cowboy poet' label has gotten to where it covers everbody and his frazzlin' dog that ever wrote anything. Some people claim to be cowboys who ain't, and some people runnin' gatherins don't know the difference."

Tradition says it was a newspaperman who attached the label "cow boys" to the horseback laborers who drove the first Texas herds to the Kansas railheads after the Civil War. He probably didn't mean it as a compliment. The austere Midwestern townspeople and farmers considered the "cow boys" to be rowdy and dangerous border riffraff and avoided their company, except while separating them from their hard-earned wages.

True, the "cow boys" weren't the cream of society. They were young, usually uneducated men — many of them orphans, runaways, ex-slaves and peons — who signed on with the trail bosses to do grueling and often deadly work. A few were outlaws who found the herds good cover for getting out of the reach of Texas law.

After months of dust, lightning, swollen rivers, stampedes, hard work, loneliness, and little sleep on the trails, the "cow boys" tended to get a little wild when they arrived in town, where they became the victims of saloon keepers, gamblers, prostitutes, and unscrupulous merchants. Many of the boys got into trouble. Some were killed. As soon as their money was gone, the survivors would ride back to Texas.

Despite what "civilized" people considered to be the wretchedness of such a life, there was something about the young "cow boys" that inspired the imagination. The way they dressed, the swagger with which they carried themselves, the horses they rode, the humor and courage with which they did their work, the troubles and tragedies they suffered, their days and nights spent under wide skies and bright stars, wandering the endless, unfenced plains — all this suggested a kind of adventure and individualism and freedom that tamer town-bound and farm-bound men could only dream of.

And around their chuck wagons and campfires, the "cow boys" were creating a culture of their own that ignored what was happening in the towns.

"It started with the influx of the Celtic peoples into West Texas from the eastern coast of our country and also from the Old World," says Red Steagall. "A lot of West

134

Texas was owned and operated by British concerns, and they would send over people to take care of their interests. They brought with them a love of poetry, of Keats and Burns and all the great masters. And most of what we now think of as the old cowboy songs are derived from old English, Irish, Scottish, and Welsh ballads. The cowhands entertained themselves at night reciting poetry and singing songs. They didn't have guitars. Hollywood invented the cowboy with the guitar. The cook might carry a fiddle or a banjo, or a cowboy might carry a mouth harp in his bedroll. They played the Old World songs and recited the Old World poems. As they became adapted to their new life, they rearranged those poems and songs so that they talked about things important to them now. *The Streets of Laredo*, for instance, started out as a shanty song in Ireland, became a seafaring song, and was changed to a cowboy song when it got to Texas. Later on, they wrote poems and songs strictly about the New World and their life on the range."

When dime novelists and Buffalo Bill's Wild West Show embraced the Texas drover, dressed him in dashing duds and introduced him to the urban East and to Europe, the despised "cow boy" laborer became a romantic cowboy hero and an American myth. Hollywood and its big silver screen enlarged him into a demigod.

By then, the trail herds and the open range were history, and the real cowboys were hunkering down to the unglamorous tasks of building fence, repairing water gaps, oiling windmills, and doctoring sick calves. Around the turn of the century, Texas folklorist John Lomax had begun collecting and preserving the old cowboy songs that had never been written down, and a few cowboy poets such as Bruce Kiskaddon, Curley Fletcher, Henry Herbert Knibbs, and Badger Clark were publishing small volumes of verse about their former lives on the now nonexistent open range.

"Kiskaddon moved to Los Angeles and wound up being an elevator operator at the Ambassador Hotel," Mr. Steagall says. "He would write poems going up and down that elevator, thinking about his old life as a cowboy."

Outside the ranch country, neither he nor any cowboy poet ever was known. So as the real cowboy disappeared from public view into the fenced-in ranches of the sparsely populated West, the six-gun-toting, guitar-strumming Hollywood cowboy captured the movie and TV screens of the world and became the false stereotype of the American Westerner.

"All them silly songs they sang, like *Ridin' Down the Canyon*," says Mr. Allen. "That's the stupidest thing I ever heard. After a feller has put in a ten- or twelve-hour day on a horse, he ain't gonna want to go ridin' off down the canyon to watch the sun go down. The humor has went out of ridin' by then."

Despite the recent miniresurgence of the Western film, traditional cowboy stories and songs are almost absent from mass entertainment these days. Gene, Roy, Hopalong, and the other fancy-dressed stars of the formulaic B movies that established the false cowboy image are gone, too. But the sales of cowboy hats, boots, big belt buckles, and pickup trucks are stronger than ever, and their market has spread far beyond their western homeland.

"Today 'cowboy' is almost a state of mind," says Mr. Steagall. "The *real* cowboy who still works on a ranch sets himself apart from the cowboy who just puts on boots and a hat and goes to dances on Saturday nights. But the cowboy is about independence and individualism. He's seen as the last free American. And everyone, regardless of what walk of life he's in or where he lives, wants to feel like he's an individual and he's independent, even if it's just on weekends."

Like J.B. Allen, Mr. Steagall grew up in the ranch country of Northwest Texas, where his father worked in the oil fields. After he graduated from West Texas State University, he sold agricultural chemicals and rode bulls in rodeos for a while, then, in 1965, he struck out for California to seek his fortune in show business. He later moved on to Nashville.

He recorded a number of country hits, wrote several more that other singers recorded, performed twice at the White House, and discovered Reba McEntire and helped promote her to stardom. But in 1977 he bought a small ranch near Azle and moved back home. "I really love North Texas," he says. "This is where I belong, and this is where I'm going to stay." For several years he raised cutting horses, but now his livestock consists of only four horses, two buffalo, one seventen-year-old longhorn steer, and a dog. He still records his songs and tours about 250 dates a year, but his songs now are in the traditional cowboy vein, not the slick country hits they used to be.

"All those years when I was writing songs, I was very conscious of whether or not they were commercial," he says. "If they weren't commercial, I didn't even bother to finish them. I threw away thousands of ideas that I'll never get back, that are gone forever."

In 1985, Mr. Steagall attended the first Cowboy Poetry Gathering in Elko, Nevada, the event that many cite as the beginning of the cowboy poetry movement. "I got all caught up in the spirit of the poetry," he says, "and I realized that's where my ideas belong. I just absolutely fell in love with it. For five years after that, I didn't write a song. I didn't write anything but poems. It's the greatest creative release I've ever known."

137

Earlier this year, Texas Christian University Press published *Ride for the Brand*, a collection of Mr. Steagall's songs and poems, and for four years he has run his own version of a cowboy gathering in Fort Worth. His features lots of cowboy music — especially western swing, which originated in Fort Worth — a two-night ranch rodeo, a special performance by Baxter Black, the Colorado veterinarian who has become probably the best known of the cowboy poets, and a chuck wagon cook-off in which ranch cooks compete against each other. An addition this year was the Cowboy and Cowgirl Poetry Contest, in which 1,374 children from forty-nine West Texas towns submitted their work.

But the centerpiece is always a day-long string of cowboy poets from Texas and the Southwest, who stand before crowds of hundreds and recite their horseback-rhythmic rhymes about life, work, and death on the range.

"A lot of people refuse to acknowledge that cowboy poetry is a real art form," Mr. Steagall says. "For generations now, some people have refused to accept country music as a musical art form, and western novels as literature, and western art as art. It doesn't bother me. The people who don't like what we're doing, I don't identify with their life, either. But I accept the fact that they have one. Cowboy poetry and music have their own audience, and it's expanding rapidly. Those are the people who want to know something about our heritage, something good, something solid, something real American. Cowboy poetry, you don't have to wonder what it says. You don't have to look for any hidden meaning. It jumps right up and hits you in the face."

Or, as J.B. Allen puts it, "These learned kind of fellers seem to put more value on poetry that don't have no rhyme or meter to it than they do on poetry that has it. I don't see why one has any more value than the other. I like a poem that sounds like a poem, not just a bunch of jumbled-up words throwed out there in the clear blue sky."

The movement began as a small scholarly project. Hal Cannon, a Nevada folklorist, discovered that a lot of cowboy poetry had been published in the past, but nobody had bothered to collect and preserve it. So he got a little grant and began searching for as many cowboy poems as he could find.

"Everything," he says, "from the first stuff that was published in Texas in the 1880s and '90s to modern cowboy poetry that we found in small-town newspapers, livestock magazines, and self-published books. Then we started doing field work all around the ranching country, trying to find ranch people who either wrote poetry or cowboys who recited old poems. We wanted to record and document those memorized poems that sometimes were never written down, that just existed in the memory of the cowboys."

At first, the ranchers and cowboys were skeptical of the scholars. "They didn't trust that anybody was going to interpret them correctly, because everybody came to them with their stereotypes," Mr. Cannon says. "They were surprised when we said, 'Well, we don't even want to tell your story. We want you to tell your story.' It was a stunning thing that happened when that was the request, rather than 'Tell us your story, and then we'll make it into whatever we think will sell.' One of the successes of this whole movement is that it's really born in the culture itself."

In January 1985, Mr. Cannon put together the first Cowboy Poetry Gathering in Elko, a town of about eight thousand in the ranch country of northeastern Nevada.

He invited some of the cowboys who had recited their poems for him to come to Elko and recite them in public.

Just before the gathering, Mr. Cannon was standing with his friend Waddie Mitchell, a cowboy — or "buckaroo," as they're called in the Northwest — in the back of the hall where they had set up two hundred chairs. Mr. Mitchell looked at Mr. Cannon. "We should put some of these chairs away," he said. "This is going to be embarrassing."

"Just then, ranchers and cowboy families started filling the chairs," Mr. Cannon writes in *Buckaroo*, a fancy new anthology of cowboy poetry, stories and art. "We organizers stood back, amazed at the fifteen hundred people who entered the auditorium, having traveled in the middle of winter to the middle of nowhere, for a poetry reading. These people had convened to recite their own poems, to tell their own stories and to sing their own songs."

The crowds have grown each year since, and by early fall every hotel room in Elko already had been booked for the next gathering. "We have people calling every day," Mr. Cannon says. "We're putting them on waiting lists. We're trying to get people in Elko to open up their homes. The event has outgrown the town."

One of those attracted to Elko was a stove-up cowboy from Amarillo named Buck Ramsey. When he was a young man, Buck spent his days punching cattle and snapping out broncos on the big ranches along the Canadian River in the Texas Panhandle. But thirty-one years ago, when he was twenty-four, the rigging broke on the bronc he was riding. The resulting accident left him confined to a wheelchair.

Since then he has made his living as a writer. Today he's also in demand as a performer — as a poet and musician

— at cowboy gatherings, folk festivals, and museums, including the Smithsonian.

Mr. Ramsey is a maverick in cowboy poetry circles. In his saddlebag on the day his bronc's rigging broke, he carried a copy of *The Rebel* by the French existentialist philosopher and novelist Albert Camus. He loves the poems of non-cowboy Wallace Stevens and the fiction of Gabriel García Márquez and Jorge Luis Borges. "If you want to write, you've got to keep your head full of good language," he says. He was a charter subscriber to *The New York Review of Books*, and he "used to get drunk and drive a lot of people out of bars by reciting *The Love Song of J. Alfred Prufrock*," T.S. Eliot's bleak poem. One of Mr. Ramsey's poems includes a line he stole from *The Canterbury Tales*. He found the rhyme scheme of his most ambitious and most popular work in an English translation of Aleksandr Pushkin.

Mr. Ramsey is an intellectual cowboy, an image that doesn't fit the stereotypes, but one that fits more than a few cowboys he has known. "I've heard cowboys discuss the merits of different translations of the *Iliad*," he says. "And there are a lot of Bible scholars among them. Some read the Bible to prove it's all true, and some read it to prove it's all not true. Cowboys read more than any other occupation I've been around, and some of it is pretty heavy stuff."

Mr. Ramsey's poem *Anthem*, which may be the most formal and lyrical of all cowboy poems, has become an anthem of sorts for the cowboy poetry movement, because it captures the feelings of freedom, individuality, integrity, and closeness to the land that are in every good cowboy poem, and in a more musical way than most. It's about a band of cowboys, riding.

"I got to thinking about leather creaking," Mr. Ramsey says, "when you have to get to the back of the pasture before daylight, and you're riding out, and it's dark, and everybody's in a saddle trot, and there's the creaking of the saddles and the jingling of the spurs. It was the creaking that got the poem going."

Written in the fourteen-line rhymed stanza that he found in the Pushkin translation, *Anthem* doesn't sound like a traditional cowboy poem, so when Mr. Ramsey pulled it out and read it for the first time at the 1990 Elko gathering, he was nervous. "I was pretty afraid," he says. "I was afraid they wouldn't accept it as a cowboy poem. And if I hadn't once upon a time earned money on horseback punching cows, maybe they wouldn't have embraced it. But it got a wonderful response. In truth, if there's been any criticism, it has been not in my hearing, and no one has told me about it."

Now *Anthem* has become the prologue of another non-traditional cowboy poem. *And as I Rode Out on the Morning*, recently published by Texas Tech University Press, is a sixty-three-page verse narrative about Billy Deaver, a fourteen-year-old who runs away from the drudgery of his family's farm to become a cowboy. The story of Billy's initiation into the cowboy life incorporates several earlier Ramsey poems and several characters from poetry and short fiction that he has written over the years. Mr. Ramsey sees the book as part of an eventually larger body of fiction and poetry focusing on various recurring characters — a sort of Faulknerian West Texas saga.

Whether prose or poetry, there's one strong thread that runs through all Mr. Ramsey's work. "Nearly everything I write," he says, "is out of a sense of loss and nostalgia. I don't intend it to be that way. But I put it down, and then I read it, and I see that it's a lament."

Loss and nostalgia have always been the underlying themes of cowboy poetry. The old cowboys who wrote around the turn of the twentieth century were remembering the end of the era in which they rode. The long trail drives were past. The open range was fenced. The cowboy no longer was a solitary voyager on a vast sea of grass. So Mr. Kiskaddon rode up and down his hotel elevator dreaming of the vanished past and composing verses about it.

"The boys could see their era comin' to an end," Mr. Allen says, "and that's where a lot of real good poetry came from. They could see it coming to a halt."

Now another century is about to turn, and many of today's cowboy poets feel the end of their era approaching. "Nobody has admitted it yet, but the West is comin' to be more like England," Mr. Allen says. "Li'l ol' small places. A lot of big ranches is sellin' off. Development, if that's what you want to call it. Take a 80- or 100,000-acre ranch, and they're sellin' it off to people who want 10 or 20 acres. Who knows what they'll use it for. And in these other western states where the guvmint owns nearly all the land, the feds are raisin' the grazin' fees so high that a lot of these boys is gonna have to turn it back to them. And all them boys have is 160 acres or 400 acres of deeded land, and they cain't make a livin' on it in this day and time. So it's comin' to a halt."

Millions have moved from rural places to urban places. Little ranch towns are drying up. "The pressures of the modern world — everything from politics to computers to bureaucracy and environmentalists — are closing in on the ranch country," says Mr. Cannon. "It's a very unstable time for people in the ranching West. There's a lot of people who want to reinforce some stabilities, who are looking for some sense of tradition, something that will give them a little bit of a touchstone, something to hang onto in a strange and uncertain world.

"When a culture is under a lot of pressure," he says, "often that's when art really flourishes."

December 1993

I've known some tough guys in my time, but I never knew a crowd of them at once until I met the Dallas Harlequins Rugby Football Club. After you've watched a rugby game, regular American football, with those helmets and pads and timeouts and all, seems kind of, well, sissy. Funny thing is, off the field and away from each other, most ruggers seem fairly normal.

I'm sorry to say the Quins didn't win the national championship they had hoped for.

The Mighty Quins

The sun has sunk early into the winter gloom. The north wind is blowing stronger, and the joggers head for home. The only lights in Glencoe Park are from a deserted tennis court and the softball field, where a skinny teenager still hammers lazy flies to a few friends, who pound their gloves and shout at him in Spanish.

On the darkling field between the lights, the Dallas Harlequins move through the evening like shadows. For two hours they run forth and back across the dying, brittle grass, from time to time falling to the ground for a quick bout of calesthenics, then up again, running, running, their breath still coming with no apparent labor.

One of them, Mickey McGuire, is wearing a white T-shirt with a big red cross and lettering on the back. "Give Blood," it says. "Play Rugby." The others are dressed much as he, in skimpy shirts and shorts and cleated shoes. But they seem impervious to the cold, while the few watchers standing bundled on the sideline are shivering.

"I'll bet at least half these guys are in better shape than the Dallas Cowboys," says Bill Smith, temporarily the Harlequins' coach. "Rugby is a very hard sport, a harsh sport, geared to endurance."

Nearly every Tuesday and Thursday evening from September through May the Harlequins gather in this park, most coming straight from their jobs as attorneys, construction workers, teachers, dentists, bartenders, sales-men, doctors. A few are unemployed at the moment. Some are native Texans. But years or only a few weeks ago many of them arrived in Dallas from faraway countries — Great Britain, South Africa, Canada, Tonga, Brazil, Australia, New Zealand — and from the other American states, each for his own reasons winding up on the North Texas prairie.

Mr. Smith says, "An Irish friend of mine was fond of remarking that rugby players constitute the world's largest fraternity. 'It's bigger than the bleeding Masons,' he would say, 'and you don't have to learn a funny handshake.' He was right. If a Martian were a rugby player, he would have no trouble being welcomed anywhere on Earth, even if he were purple and had a couple of extra heads. He would be asked two questions: 'What position do you play?' and 'Would you like a beer?' If any of those guys out there were to go to Hong Kong or Japan or New Zealand, Zimbabwe, France, Romania, or Russia, if they went to the local rugby club they would meet guys who are very simi-lar to the guys they know here. Rugby is a total ethos, a way of life. It's a worldwide club."

146

Beyond North America's borders the men running up and down Glencoe Park in the dark may be better known than any other Dallas athletic organization, including the city's beloved Cowboys. Many of the Quins, as they call themselves, have played in international competition, and for more than a decade the Harlequins have ranked among the best rugby teams in the United States. They've toured other countries. They've been written up in the international rugby publications. Ruggers everywhere know who and what and where they are.

Nelson Spencer, the Dallas real estate investor who started the club, says the Harlequins have benefited greatly from their fame within the fraternity. "We frequently get a call from some foreign rugby player at D/FW Airport who says, 'I'm on my way to Somewhere. Could you guys put me up for a few days?' Sometimes the 'few days' lasts for years. They become Harlequins, they marry American girls, they settle down and become fully integrated into Dallas."

The Quins won the Texas Rugby Union Championship for the first time in 1975, four years after they were organized. Since 1981 they've dominated Texas rugby, winning the championship every year except 1985, when they lost to their cross-town rival, the Dallas Reds. The Quins second side — or B team — has won the state championship in its division seven times during the same period.

The Harlequins are the only Texas club ever to win the Western Rugby Union Championship (the territory between the Mississippi River and the Rockies), and they've done it five times, including 1991 and 1992. "If we don't win at least the Western championship, that's a disastrous year for us," says their captain, Mark Gale. "We've been in the Western Union final nine of the last ten years."

In the Final Four competition for the National Club Championship, they've placed third three times, including 1991 and 1992, and won the championship in 1984. Followers of the sport say their chances of winning their second national cup this spring are good to excellent. Four of their players — Mr. Gale, Mike Waterman, Brannon Smoot, and Greg Goodman — also play for the Eagles, the United States all-star national team, which competes against other countries in international matches.

Yet, in a city noted for its love of sports and its adoration of winning teams, the Harlequins are almost a secret. For their regular cup games against their Texas Rugby Union opponents, maybe a couple of hundred fans turn out to Glencoe Park, the Harlequins' home pitch (as a rugby field is called), despite the free admission and as much action and violence as the bloodthirstiest spectator could want. And most of those are the wives and girlfriends of the players (the Harlettes, they call themselves), plus whatever entourage the visiting team brings, plus a few rugby groupies and a loyal collection of displaced Brits, Aussies, and Kiwis who roam the sidelines shouting, "Rubbish!" and "Shocking!" at the referee.

Sometimes, over their customary after-training beer (ruggers "train," they don't "practice") at the nearby Across the Street Bar, a Harlequin will express a whimsical wish that Dallas would devote more fan attention and press coverage to the city's most consistent winner. But then he'll shrug. This is America, after all, where sport is dominated by big-dollar professionalism and media hype, and the ruggers, following a different code, still are doing it for love. None of the players gets paid. Neither do their coaches nor their trainers nor their administrators nor even their referees.

"It's truly the last of the amateur games," Bill Smith says.

🐦   🐦   🐦

The sport was born one afternoon in 1823, when lads of England's venerable Rugby School were romping about the greensward in a ripping game of soccer and one William Webb Ellis committed a shocking transgression.

"Well, there I was with the line in front of me, and I thought to myself how *daft* to risk dribbling the ball with the foot, so I simply picked up the thing and ran over the line and touched down," Mr. Ellis is reputed to have written later.

His fine disregard of the rules earned his team a penalty and Mr. Ellis a rebuke from the headmaster. But it also made the lad a pioneer of sport. By the 1830s, boys at Eton, Harrow, Winchester, and the other English schools were running with the ball and passing it from one player to the next, disporting themselves in what was being called "the game of football as played at Rugby."

Despite the game's growing popularity, almost half a century would pass before representatives of the schools would sit down together and agree on a set of rugby rules. Until that meeting in London in 1871, each team devised its own rules, and the visiting team had to play the home team's version of the game.

It was during that period of anarchy — in 1859 — that Princeton and Rutgers played the first game of rugby in the United States. Indeed, they played two games that year, one by Rutgers' rules and the other by Princeton's. And by the time rugby's rules finally were established in Britain, Walter Camp and other American experimenters had turned the English game into "the game of football as played in America."

The similarities and differences between American football and its ancestor are as impossible to explain to someone who has never seen a rugby match as the variations between checkers and Chinese checkers would be to, say, a cocker spaniel. Suffice it to say that rugby is played on a field that looks something like a football field, but is larger, with a ball that looks something like a football, but is fatter, by two teams of fifteen players each who wear no helmets or pads. The ball may be passed from one player to another (but forward passes are illegal), dribbled with the feet, kicked, or carried.

The object, as in football, is to score points by carrying the ball over the goal line or by kicking it through goal posts. A "try," scored by carrying the ball across the goal line and touching it to the ground, is worth five points; a successful "conversion kick," awarded to the team that has just scored a "try," is two points; a "penalty kick," awarded to a team that has been fouled, is three points; and a "drop goal," a ball drop-kicked through the goal posts while it is in play, is three points. The opposing team tries to prevent the scoring of "tries" and "drop goals" by tackling whichever player has the ball. Play is continuous for two forty-minute halves, with only a five-minute break between them. There are no timeouts and no substitutions, except to replace badly injured players.

Sometimes rugby resembles American football. Sometimes, because of its speed and the tactics involved, it seems as close to basketball or even hockey. Other times, because of the tangle of bodies and the grunts and cries of the players and the grind of bone on bone, it resembles the roughhouse game called "dog pile" that small boys play. One Harlequin — a Brit named Geoff "Chesney" Hawkes — describes it as "a violent ballet," as apt a description as any.

While American football has evolved into a game played by specialists, rugby has not. "That's the beauty of it," says Harlequins club president Bob Latham. "Everybody on the field has to do a little bit of everything, unlike football, where one guy is just blocking and one guy is just kicking. In rugby, everybody has to be able to handle the ball, everybody has to be able to tackle, everybody has to be able to field the kick."

For Brannon Smoot, a Texan who played linebacker for Rice University before he entered University of Texas Southwestern Medical Center to learn orthopedic surgery, rugby is more fun to play than the American game. "In four years at Rice, I never got to touch the ball," he says. "But in rugby, *everybody* gets to run with it."

The pure form of rugby survived on the East and West Coasts and in a few isolated spots in the Midwest like Chicago and St. Louis, but there were only thirty or forty rugby clubs in the United States from 1871 until the 1960s, when the sport had a second American birth.

"It was a time when a lot of young people were questioning their parents' values," says Mr. Spencer. "It also was a time when people were examining athletics and questioning what recreation should mean. It was a time of a lot of football scandals, a lot of Olympic scandals and that sort of thing. People were saying, 'Recreation ought to be just for the fun of it. No commercialization, no money, no payoffs, no big-timing it. Let's just go out and have fun just for the sake of it.' College students began playing rugby, and after they graduated, they started their own clubs and kept playing. And it was purely recreational. Today there are between thirteen hundred and fourteen hundred rugby teams in the country, and the amateur code under which the game is played is *much* purer than the Olympic code now is."

In 1969, the Dallas Rugby Football Club, which fields the Reds, was formed and one of its members invited Mr. Spencer to drop by the band field at Southern Methodist University one afternoon and watch them practice. "I had a date with me," Mr. Spencer says, "but I decided to just drive by and take a look. I wanted to see what a rugby practice was like. After a few minutes, I said to my date, 'Excuse me, but I need to learn how to play this.' I raced home and changed clothes and came back. By then, practice was almost over. But at the end, the captain called us together and said, 'Anyone who can't go to Houston, raise your hand.' I didn't think I was included, so I just stood there. And I got selected to go to Houston with the Reds. I scored a try in my first game, and we won, and I was well and truly indoctrinated."

After the 1970 season, Mr. Spencer decided to leave the Reds and form his own team. "At the time, there was only one rugby club in North Texas, and to play any sort of match at all we had to drive two hundred miles to Austin or College Station or Norman, Oklahoma," he says. "Also, I had my own ideas about how a rugby club ought to be run, so I decided to set up a laboratory and try some of my ideas."

To recruit players, he took out an ad in *The Dallas Morning News* with the headline: "It Takes Leather Balls to Play Rugby." The line had been popular for years among college ruggers, but it was new to Dallas. "All the DJs picked it up and talked about it on their morning drive shows, as if they were the only ones in town who understood the *double entendre*," Mr. Spencer says. "It got a huge secondary effect. I managed to attract a number of guys who had played rugby before, and a great many more who hadn't."

He named his team the Dallas Harlequins Rugby Football Club after one of the oldest and finest clubs in London and dressed the players in distinctive four-checkered green-and-black jerseys and odd knee stockings — a black sock on the right leg and a green sock on the left — that have become one of the most recognizable, and often imitated, uniforms in American rugby.

"From the outset, the Harlequins were pretty good," Mr. Spencer says. "We managed to beat the Reds, 15-11, in the first season of our existence. We got stronger and stronger. In 1973, we played for the Texas Rugby Union championship for the first time. We got to the finals and were defeated by Texas A&M. Two years later, we won it."

Then the club split three ways. Several Southern Methodist University students left to form their own team at their university. Another group departed to form Our Gang, which today shares Lake Highlands Park with the Reds as their home pitch. "We had a very poor season in '76," Mr. Spencer says, "and it took us five years to get back to the top. But by '80, we were strong again and have been ever since."

While amassing their record, the Harlequins also were building something else that Mr. Spencer considers as important as their victories. Talking about it, he sounds like those old-fashioned coaches who made speeches about football as a builder of character.

"The Harlequins have a certain mystique in the rugby world," he says, "which I attribute to their first coach, the late Mike Allen, a Scotsman born in Argentina. Mike put an indelible stamp on the club, urging the guys to be first-rate at everything. He established a code of trying your best to be gentlemen on and off the field. His personality was very strong, and he created a bond that seems to be inheritable. As guys join the club from other clubs, they seem to know that the Harlequin mystique is something a little different. Other clubs accuse us of being too regimented, but if it is a regimentation, it's one the guys gladly submit to, and it doesn't diminish their *joie de vivre* and the fun they derive from playing. They're just very serious about their involvement in the game. They're serious when it's time to dig deep and pull out that something extra that it takes to win."

The Harlequins' seriousness about the game and their willingness to submit to the rigorous training demanded by their coaches over the years are the very attributes that have attracted some of their best players. "With a lot of clubs, the socializing is the main thing and the playing is kind of a second thought," says Mark Gale. "I used to play with another team, but I was getting beat up too much. I wanted to get into some *serious* rugby, so I joined the Quins. When you join the Harlequins," Mr. Spencer says, "you inherit a tradition, and you want to perpetuate what everybody else has worked so hard to build."

They are about to travel to Nevada for the Las Vegas Challenge, a tournament they lost in 1991 to James Bay, a Canadian team, by one point in the final match. If they win the Challenge this year, the Harlequins say, they'll know they're good enough to enjoy an undefeated spring and make a serious run for the national championship.

Meanwhile, their last cup game before their Christmas break is against the Dallas Reds, on the Reds' home pitch at Lake Highlands Park. So far, the Quins are unbeaten. A week earlier, their second side — B team — had defeated Our Gang, 28-7, and the first side — A team — had skunked them, 76-0. Indeed, the Quins haven't lost a cup match to any Texas team in eight years, but their rivalry with the Reds remains so intense that the Harlequins never take them for granted.

"We get along fine off the field, but on the field we still hate each other," says the Quins' 6-foot-4, 230-pound forward Norbert Mueller, taping his ears for the battle. "It's always a grudge match."

Lake Highlands Park is a mess. A driving rain has been falling for many hours. Large pools, some of them inches deep, dot the pitch. A handful of die-hard fans in slickers and rubber boots stand along the sideline. A few women wearing Reds jackets huddle under a soggy tarpaulin, hugging themselves. A few others watch from the windows of cars parked along the street. But the Harlequins and the Reds, covered with mud from head to toe, romp through the water like thirty huge Labrador retrievers.

The Quins second side wins its game, 11-0. As their exertion ends, they begin to shiver, too. Finally, as they stand along the sideline, they peel off their wet, muddy jerseys, strip to the buff, towel off and change into dry clothes. Nobody seems to notice.

As the first sides take the field the rain stops, but the wind grows immediately strong and raw. The ball sails crazily through the air, splashes into puddles, thuds dully on the drowned grass. Scoring is almost impossible. The Harlequins lead only 7-0 at halftime, and Mr. Gale, their bulldog-built captain, delivers a spirited and profane pep talk in a British accent that he believes, after his years in Dallas, holds a tinge of Texas twang.

"Let's not go to sleep now, all right?" he says. "We've got at least thirty or forty more points to put on these buggers! We are preparing for bloody Vegas right here, right now! I don't know about you guys, but I'm having fun out there! I'm having damn good fun!"

The Harlequins go on to win, 43-13. After they've scraped the mud off their bodies, they reconvene at the Stepladr Pub on McKinney Avenue, the Reds' regular watering hole, where the home team, in accordance with ancient rugby custom, picks up the tab for the beer.

At 6:15 a.m. the Quins are gathering in an out-of-the-way corner of the huge Las Vegas Hilton lobby to tape their wrists, hands, fingers, ankles, ears. Their hair is tousled, their eyes bleary. They scratch, blink, yawn, trying to clean cobwebs and hangovers from their minds. Mr. Gale is haranguing them to hurry. At 7:00 a.m. they pile into

two rental vans and head for Freedom Park on the out-
skirts of the city, where several soccer fields and softball
outfields have been refashioned into rugby pitches.

The previous night, snow fell most everywhere in the
West. Cajon Pass, on Interstate 15 between Los Angeles
and Las Vegas, has been closed by the weather, and in the
casinos newly arrived gamblers are telling horror stories
about their journeys. The surrounding mountains are covered with snow, but in Las Vegas it only has rained. Hard.
All night. More rain has been forecast for this Saturday
morning, too, but so far the sky is only overcast.

"I like this weather," says Geoff Hawkes. "The first
match I played in Texas, it was ninety-five degrees. I was
used to playing in sixty-degree weather in England. I
nearly died. I couldn't cope with it."

The Harlequins' first side is to open the tournament at
8:00 a.m. against the San Fernando Valley Rugby Football
Club in the first, or Aces, division. The second side will
follow immediately with its game against Olde Gael, from
North Oakland, California, in the second, or Kings, division. Each Harlequin side will play three games today. If
they keep winning, it will take a total of nine victories for
both to win their divisional trophies.

"Tournaments like this test your depth," says Bob
Latham. "You don't want to use all your best players in
any one game. You've got to pace yourself throughout the
day, so that all your best guys won't be too tired out and
will be available for the final."

As they warm up, the first-side players psyche themselves for the game. "Come on! We've got to bury these
guys right off the bat!" someone says to nobody in particular. "We can't give them room to breathe, they can get
fired up! We've got to stick it to them right away!"

And they do. The Harlequins demolish San Fernando
Valley, 43-0, and Olde Gael, 40-3. After their games, the

ruggers lounge about the grass, resting, mending wounds. "I have green blood running through my veins and black blood running through my arteries," Norbert Mueller muses, lying supine, eyes closed.

Within forty-five minutes of their victory over Olde Gael, the second side is on the pitch again, this time playing a team of Marines from Camp Pendleton, whom they beat, 32-7. The first side demolishes the Camelback Rugby Football Club from Phoenix, 42-0.

Throughout the day, the Las Vegas paramedics are busy, moving from field to field, examining fallen ruggers, hauling some away in ambulances. But none has been a Harlequin. As the shadows grow long and disappear, as the sun sinks over the western mountains, as the field lights come on and the temperature begins to slide, both Quins sides are still playing their third matches of the day. The only spectators left are a few Harlettes and players from some of the clubs the Harlequins have beaten. At last, well into the night, the second side squeaks by Fort Collins, Colorado, 18-17, and the first side defeats the host Las Vegas team, 20-10.

As the matches end, each team raises a cheer for its opponent, in accordance with rugby custom. Then, in keeping with Harlequins tradition, the men in black and green bellow their victory chant:

I was born on a mountaintop, raised by a bear!
Got two sets of jaw teeth, two coats of hair!
Swing a fist like a hammer, got a (unprintable unprintable)!
I'm a mean (unprintable), I'm a Harlequin, by God!

The first side must win only one more match now to win the championship trophy. The second side must win two. It opens the second day of the tournament in the semifinal match against Langley, British Columbia. It's a

157

low-scoring affair. The Harlequins lead, 6-3, with only a few seconds to go, when Kevin Phillipson, their young forward from South Africa, goes to the ground for the ball and is buried under a pile of bodies. When the pile is removed, Mr. Phillipson is flat on his back, lying unconscious and frighteningly still.

The paramedics are unable to revive him. The ruggers watch them work for a few minutes, then move to another field to play the game's remaining seconds. The score doesn't change, and the Harlequins win. An ambulance hauls Mr. Phillipson away.

The second-side captain, Keith "Flussen" Engelbrecht, tries to phone Mr. Phillipson's parents, but is unable to reach them. Rumor has it that they're somewhere in Wisconsin, travelling in a Winnebago.

The other Harlequins are worried about their fallen teammate, but take his injury stoically. "You get a lot of bumps and bruises in this game, but this still is quite rare," says Bill "Flounder" Bartok. "Yet, it does happen, you know."

And they must prepare for their final game, in which they soon will face the Mavericks from Arlington, Texas. "Go figure," says one of the Phoenix players, standing on the sideline. "These guys came halfway across the country to play in the finals against a team from across town."

It turns out to be *the* game of the tournament. At the end of the first half, the Mavericks lead, 14-12. For the first time all weekend, a Harlequins side is behind. In the second half, the Mavericks increase their lead to 24-12, but the Harlequins "dig deep and pull out that something extra," as Nelson Spencer has said. The game ends in a 27-27 tie. In the sudden-death tie-breaker, the Harlequins win, 32-27.

"A game like this takes about nine years off my life," says Mr. Engelbrecht. "I'm getting too old for it. I said last year and the year before: 'This is going to be my last year.' But you get so involved. You want to be part of the winning team. You want to help the tradition continue. So you come out every year, and you think: 'If I wasn't playing rugby, what *would* I be doing?'"

In the final game of the tournament, the Quins' first side is to play Belmont Shore, a club from the Bay Area of California, which has two huge visiting Australians in its lineup. "Look at that guy," one of the Harlequins says. "Each of his legs is as big as a man."

It doesn't matter. The Harlequins win, 22-0. In nine games, the Quins' two sides have outscored their opponents, 255-67.

I was born on a mountaintop, raised by a bear . . .

As the photographer for a rugby magazine is trying to line up the victors for a team picture, Kevin Phillipson appears as if by magic, groggy and wearing a neck brace, but alive.

"I went in to get the ball," he says. "Next thing I remember is looking up into the paramedic's sunglasses. They wanted to keep me in the hospital overnight and give me a bunch of tests, but I told them, "The hell with that. I have a plane to catch."

Later, the Harlequins learn that one of the casinos had a line on the Belmont Shore game, favoring the Quins by three. On the plane back to Dallas, the flight attendants run out of beer.

The Harlequins' 1984 national championship trophy, their Western championship trophies, and a few others are on display in a glass case at the Mucky Duck, a bar on Welborn Street where the Quins hang out. Still others sit on shelves at the home of Des Kirkwood, their vice president for operations and sometime coach. But while the two huge Las Vegas trophies rest snugly in his Porsche,

Bob Latham is driving out Garland Road to one of those rental storage companies.

He stops at the office for a key, then drives through the electronically controlled gate and around the maze of storage buildings. He stops, gets out of the car, and unlocks one of the bins.

It's piled with boxes filled with jerseys that have been presented to the Harlequins by visiting international stars, with framed antique rugby prints, and with trophies, dozens of them, lying in a jumble.

"We have more trophies in here than most clubs have won," Mr. Latham says. "Our dream is to have our own clubhouse someday, where we can display all this."

He lays the two big trophies on top of the pile. "So visitors can come and see, and immediately know who the Dallas Harlequins are."

February 1993

I met Ben Davis only once. We sat in his living room and had a quiet talk about his religious faith, his homosexuality, and his loneliness. I thought he was a very brave man.

A couple of weeks after this piece ran, he died of AIDS.

Fundamental Differences

One fall day in 1948, Ben Davis' mother taught Sunday school in the morning, made lunch for her pastor and a visiting evangelist, went into labor while doing the dishes, and gave birth to her son that afternoon. "By the next Sunday I'd already been in several services," Mr. Davis says.

One night when he was five, Ben was awakened by the voice of God calling him to be a Pentecostal preacher. "Go into all the world and preach the Gospel of salvation and temptation," God told him.

"It scared me so badly I almost wet the bed," Mr. Davis says now. But after discussing the incident with his mother, he abandoned his ambition to become an ambulance driver. "From that moment on, all I ever wanted to do was preach the Gospel," he says.

When he was about seven, the Reverend Oral Roberts held a meeting in Dallas, and Ben's father asked the evangelist to pray for God to give Ben — a sickly lad — an appetite. And God did. "Overnight my appetite became ravenous," Mr. Davis says, "and in no time I'd bloated up like a poisoned dog. I've been fat ever since."

These and other stories are in *Strange Angel: The Gospel According to Benny Joe*, Mr. Davis' memoir of the Assemblies of God congregations in which he spent his childhood and adolescence, singing, shouting, speaking in tongues, preaching, and praying seven nights a week and all day Sunday in meetings where "the power of God was so strong the entire area was literally held by the ankles over hell."

The book relates Mr. Davis' memories of Pentecostal Christianity in the pre-TV-evangelist days, when it was regarded as an across-the-tracks religion practiced only by the poor, and of his years spent studying for the ministry at Southwestern Assemblies of God College in Waxahachie, Texas. They are warm and often funny. "When you go to church seven nights a week," Mr. Davis says, "a lot of funny things happen." And any reader who grew up in the smaller congregations of any brimstone-preaching fundamentalist denomination will identify with many of them.

The real reason Mr. Davis wrote his book doesn't appear until page 172:

"I stood there, numb, staring at myself in the mirror, unable to move. Nothing would ever be the same again. What had gone wrong? I was fourth-generation Pentecostal. I was a licensed Assemblies of God minister, and I was to graduate from Southwestern in May. A lifetime of preparation, work, and dreams lay dead at my feet. How could it have happened? What would I do?"

He had come to realize that he was gay. And, because the Pentecostal churches consider homosexuality to be a sin, he says, he knew he would never be permitted to fulfill his lifelong dream. "I only knew two things for sure," he would write. "I couldn't be a preacher, and there was absolutely nothing else I wanted to be."

Mr. Davis says he still might have remained a member of his church if he had continued to hide his homosexuality, but his conscience wouldn't let him. "I decided I wouldn't be a hypocrite," he says.

At that point, the humor in the story assumes a tinge of bitterness. Mr. Davis dropped out of school ten weeks before he was to graduate. He confided in his pastor, seeking comfort. The preacher told him he would roast in hell. When Mr. Davis told his best friend that he was gay, the friend spread the news to the rest of the congregation.

The church members froze him out of their lives, turning their heads away whenever they would meet him. His mother went to her pastor, seeking guidance, and the minister told her: "Well, Sister Davis, as the mother of a queer you're not fit to teach Sunday school. I'll have to take that class away from you."

When Corona Publishing, a small house in San Antonio, brought out *Strange Angel* two years ago, Mr. Davis was amazed at the response it received. "People have called me from all over the country," he says. "Members of fundamentalist churches who have had divorces, who have had affairs, who have had abortions — who are sinners, in other words. They tell me of the ways those churches crucified them, tarred and feathered them, threw them out of town. They all say, 'I can identify with what you went through.' I've had calls from parents of gay children in fundamentalist churches. They say, 'You speak fundamentalist language. We know that you know what you're talking about.' Mothers tell me they were embarrassed to ask their children certain questions about gay life, and some of those are answered in the book, and it has made it a little easier for them to cope. My favorite was a mother who called and said she had lost her only son to AIDS, and that reading my book was the first time she had smiled since his death. I really love that."

On the other hand, he says, his former best friend "wrote me a letter saying I'm no better than Hitler, a child molester, an abortionist, or a murderer, then signed the letter, 'Your friend in Christ.'"

And at his grandfather's funeral, when Mr. Davis tried to shake hands with his uncle, a retired Assemblies of God missionary, "the man turned away," he says. "It's sad that the first twenty-one years of my life . . . it's like somebody has put a wall down, and the people I knew during that time won't even speak to me, when they used to be my family. I've felt more compassion from the people that the church has cast out than I have from people who think they're Christians."

For a while after his congregation shunned him, Mr. Davis visited a number of "mainstream" Protestant churches and a gay church in Dallas, hoping to find another congregation in which to worship. But, accustomed to the emotional fervor of Pentecostal worship, he found the services too cold and formal. "Besides, it doesn't appeal to me to go to a church that wouldn't want me there if they knew who I was," he says. "I've come to feel like there is no place for a homosexual in a regular church today. They're structured for families and for people who are looking to get married and start families."

As for the gay church, "It's extremely liberal," he says. "I couldn't be comfortable in a situation like that, either. I think I'll have a private relationship with God and just leave it at that."

He pauses. "I prayed to God, 'You know my heart, and you know how I've struggled.' In the Bible it says if you pray and pray and pray and there's no answer, you need to wait awhile. And that's where I am now, just sitting on the sideline, waiting . . . . "

He pauses again. "Deep down," he says, "I don't think I could ever be anything but Pentecostal."

November 1993

If Robert James Waller's name is mentioned in future histories of American literature, it's likely to be as one of the worst novelists ever to touch a keyboard — and one of the most successful, financially. The critics don't like him at all. But at this writing, his first novel, The Bridges of Madison County, *has been on* The New York Times *best-seller list for 142 weeks.*

He has published two more novels since. They're even worse than the first, the critics say, but not as successful.

When I heard that he had moved to my home country in the Trans-Pecos of Texas, I couldn't resist an inquiry.

The 'Last Cowboy' of Brewster County

This fellow walks into the Parsons Real Estate office in Alpine and says, "I want to buy a big ranch. Maybe a thousand acres."

Flop Parsons regards him with a sad blue eye. "Wellsir," he says. "Around here, a thousand acres is little."

The fellow looks like just a cowboy, says Flop's wife and business partner, Joy. "Of course, we don't know who he is."

He says he already has a place in mind. He has read about it in *The Alpine Avalanche*. He has flown over it in an airplane. He asks if he can drive out and have a look at it. Flop tells him sure, go ahead.

This was about a year ago, Flop says. A few months later, the fellow buys his thousand acres from Dr. John Pate, a local physician. The new owner and his wife haul in a Toyota full of gear from Iowa, and Brewster County acquires its most famous resident.

"He don't want people to know exactly where he's at, if you don't mind," Flop says. "He tries to keep a little privacy as best he can."

If privacy is what's craved, few places can provide it in larger supply than Brewster County, whose boundaries embrace more than six thousand square miles of rugged mountains and desert on the southern edge of Far West Texas, just a short wade across the Rio Grande from the equally harsh barrens of Chihuahua and Coahuila. It's a country where humans are scarce, and almost every form of plant and animal life scratches, bites, or stings, and "No Trespassing" signs mean what they say.

So Robert James Waller can be as alone as he wants to be.

"Most people in town have never met him," says Jean Hardy, proprietor of Books Plus. "They've never seen him. They just know he's here. He's just a presence." And no, he isn't available for interviews, his New York publicist has declared. Not now. Not ever. At least not before his third novel, *Border Music*, is in the stores.

If the name Robert James Waller doesn't ring a bell, you probably haven't looked at *The New York Times* best-seller list for more than two years, and you aren't among the 6 million-plus people who have bought a copy of *The Bridges of Madison County*. Nor one of the additional millions who have borrowed dog-eared copies from friends or libraries.

Mr. Waller wrote it. He's the creator of middle-aged-but-studly traveling photographer Robert Kinkaid and middle-aged-and-bored-but-still-sexy Iowa farm wife Francesca Johnson, who enjoy a torrid four-day love affair while farm husband and kids are away at the state fair, then spend the remainder of their years in unrequited longing for each other.

The story is a three-hanky paean to that apparently rare being, the sensitive-but-virile American male, of whom so many women are said to dream so hopelessly. And who can blame them? This is what goes through Mr. Kincaid's head when he stops at the Johnson farm to ask directions and claps eyes on Francesca for the first time:

"She was about five feet six, fortyish or a little older, pretty face, and a fine, warm body. But there were pretty women everywhere he traveled. Such physical matters were nice, yet, to him, intelligence and passion born of living, the ability to move and be moved by subtleties of the mind and spirit, were what really counted. That's why he found most young women unattractive, regardless of their exterior beauty. They had not lived long enough or hard enough to possess those qualities that interested him."

Mrs. Johnson, on the other hand, sees Mr. Kinkaid as "a leopardlike creature who rode in on the tail of a comet."

Like most first novels, *The Bridges of Madison County* was published without fanfare. But Oprah Winfrey read it and raved about it on her TV show. Thousands of her viewers went out and bought it, and word-of-mouth — the most valuable kind of publicity, publishers say — spread the book's fame like the proverbial wildfire.

It also changed the life of the surprised University of Northern Iowa business professor who had written it in the course of a few days, his daughter says, for the amusement of family and friends.

The book's astounding success — and the more modest success of Mr. Waller's second novel, *Slow Waltz in Cedar Bend* — has made the author a millionaire and a celebrity. The more than six million copies of *Bridges* that have been sold so far are all in hardcover. The sure-to-be-lucrative paperback edition is still to come, and soon the little book will become a major motion picture starring Clint Eastwood and Meryl Streep as the bucolic lovers.

"He did it for fun," says Rachael Waller-Young, the only child of Robert and his wife, Georgia. "He had this idea, and he wrote it. The original manuscript has a note he wrote on it: `This is something I did just for fun.' We have that in a lock box now."

Ms. Waller-Young moved to Brewster County from Brooklyn soon after her parents. She and her husband, Vincent Young, of the Bronx, were married last August in the Wallers' back yard, with Hallie Stillwell, the legendary ninety-four-year-old rancher, chili cookoff judge, and justice of the peace, performing the ceremony. The newlyweds live on a 350-acre spread that Ms. Waller-Young's parents bought for them.

An outgoing, energetic, quick-to-laugh fancier of dogs and horses, Ms. Waller-Young has become a favorite neighbor in her part of the county. "Everybody likes Rachael," Joy Parsons says. "How could you not?"

The daughter, twenty-seven years old, is still amazed at her father's success. "I can't believe he wrote the best-selling novel in history," she says. "My dad?"

But the published reports that the author and his wife had to abandon their home in rural Iowa because too many tourists were crowding up to their door for autographs and snapshots just aren't true, Ms. Waller-Young says.

"He enjoys his fans," she says. "He's a very personal guy. But a writer has to have privacy to do his work. He

170

wanted what he called `an artist's retreat,' a place where he and my mom could go and get away. They wanted a place that was warm. My mom's tired of Iowa winters. They were looking around the South. They've gone there a lot. My mother has really embraced Mexico. She goes there every year. But my dad has always loved West Texas and everything about West Texas. To see him here is to see the little boy in him. Here he has everything he dreamed about when he was little. He has always been a cowboy. He couldn't show it so much where he was, but there has always been that cowboy inside him. And it fits. I look at him with that Stetson on, and it's just killer. He wore a black tux and a Stetson at my wedding. He looked so cool."

The snapshots of the man in the black Stetson that Ms. Waller-Young displays on her coffee table are the spitting image of Robert Kinkaid, the studly photographer, who calls himself "one of the last cowboys" in Mr. Waller's novel. Like Mr. Kinkaid, Mr. Waller also shoots pictures, plays the guitar — as well as the banjo, the saxophone, the flute and the mandolin — and sings.

"Kinkaid *is* Dad in lots of ways," Ms. Waller-Young says. "I read the book and went, `This is my mom and dad.' But in a different lifetime, know what I mean? Not in this lifetime, because none of the things in the book really happened. The description of Francesca is my mother exactly. She's stunning. Everybody thinks she's my dad's second marriage. She doesn't look like a woman in her fifties, I tell you."

Her parents aren't at home right now, Ms. Waller-Young says. They're off somewhere on a "swamp crawl."

"Destination unknown," she says. "Even I don't know where they are. They do this a couple of times a year at least. They call them 'swamp crawls' because the first time they did one they went down through like Florida and

Louisiana, through swamps," she says. "They don't make any plans. They reach an intersection and flip a coin to decide which way they should go. Dad finds some of his characters that way. That's also how they found Alpine."

When the Wallers bought their ranch, Flop Parsons says, their plan was to live part of the year in Brewster County and part on their Iowa farm. But when they began extensive remodeling and expansion of the ranch house and drew up plans for a huge art studio for Mrs. Waller's pottery- and jewelry-making, they began to think differently.

"He told me he was going home to Iowa for a few days," Flop says. "But later he said that while he was on the road, something happened. It suddenly hit him: 'Naw. I'm not *going* home; I'm *leaving* home. I'm just going to Iowa to get some stuff to bring *back* home."

And the rumors that floated out of Far West Texas that the newly arrived famous author was putting on airs — wearing leather pants and gold chains, driving around in a Mercedes and acting stuck-up — just aren't true, they say in Alpine.

"No, no, no, that was Tommy Lee Jones, when he was out here filming *The Good Old Boys*," says Barbara Kellim, manager of Ocotillo Enterprises, which sells, according to its sign, "Books and Rocks, Crafts Supplies and a Little Bit of Music."

"Robert and Georgia are down-to-earth, neat people," she says. "This town is pretty funny. If you want to be isolated, you can be isolated. If you want to be popular, you can be popular. You can be your own person."

Indeed, Brewster Countians say, the Wallers have fitted themselves so neatly into their loose-knit community that they're not using nearly all the privacy they have at their disposal.

"They love country and Western music," says Joy Parsons. "They go to all the dances."

"He came to the Fourth of July celebration at Camp Peña Colorado, down near Marathon," says Jean Hardy, "and sang some songs and played on the guitar. He has a real sweet voice."

"He doesn't want people to see him as a celebrity," says Mindy Young, who works at *The Alpine Avalanche*. "And, really, not many do. They fit in pretty well about here. Especially his wife. She loves to gossip."

"He hangs out with the cowboys at the Crystal Bar," says Rachael Waller-Young. "He's just a good old boy."

"He fits in real good," says Flop Parsons. "He likes beer."

November 1994

If any topic of conversation can dissolve into argument faster than politics or religion, it's UFOs — whether they're real, what they are and where they come from. And there's no place in the country — possibly the world — where UFOs are a hotter topic than in Roswell, New Mexico, because in 1947 a UFO either did or didn't crash near there.

In 1993, Congressman Steven Schiff of Albuquerque sicced the General Accounting Office — the investigative arm of Congress — on the Pentagon in an attempt to find out what really happened in the high desert on that dark and stormy night nearly fifty years ago.

As of this writing, in February 1995, Mr. Schiff still hasn't received his answer.

The Incident at Roswell

On the morning of July 3, 1947, Mac Brazel and Dee Proctor saddled their horses and rode into the wide nowhere of Lincoln County, New Mexico. Mr. Brazel was the foreman of the scrubby high-desert sheep ranch upon which they rode. Like ranchers in all times and places, he was alert to the weather, and earlier, in the black wee hours of this day, while a ferocious thunderstorm was slashing across his land, he had heard a roar that didn't sound like thunder. Maybe lightning had struck a windmill. Maybe some of his sheep — not the smartest of nature's creatures — had managed to drown themselves in a flash-flooded arroyo. Now that the sun was up, he had better take a look. Anyway, he wanted to see which parts of the range had received the welcome moisture.

His companion, age seven, was the son of Floyd and Loretta Proctor, Mr. Brazel's nearest neighbors, who lived on another ranch about ten miles away. Dee loved riding horseback and tagging along with Mr. Brazel, and sometimes he would come and stay overnight at the foreman's headquarters and ride out with him in the morning.

July 3, 1947, must have been a fine morning for riding, for such a storm washes the desert clean. It settles the dust, cools the air, brightens and purifies the sky. The beauty and fragrance of the damp sage and cactus and buffalo grass on such a morning fills the senses with intimations of liberty and joy.

But a few miles south of the house, the riders happened upon something strange. A huge section of pasture was strewn with debris that must have fallen from the sky. Some of the wreckage apparently was dull-finished metal, some was shiny and very thin, resembling aluminum foil. Some looked like transparent plastic string or wire. There were thin sticks, shaped like I-beams, made of some material that Mr. Brazel didn't recognize.

The debris — large and small pieces of it — covered an area estimated by Mr. Brazel to be about three-quarters of a mile long and two hundred to three hundred feet wide, as if something had exploded in the air and its pieces had rained to earth. But it didn't look like the wreckage of an airplane, and there was no sign of a crew.

Mr. Brazel dismounted and picked up some of the fragments. They were extraordinarily lightweight. He put a few of the smaller ones in the pockets of his chaps and remounted. Then he and Dee Proctor continued on their way.

If Mr. Brazel was excited by their discovery, he apparently didn't show it. Young Dee, his mother says, soon forgot it. But Loretta Proctor, now eighty years old, still remembers Mr. Brazel's story and the strange object that he showed her and Floyd later that day when he brought Dee home.

"He had a piece of stuff about five or six inches long that looked like wood or plastic," she says. "It was a little bit bigger than a pencil and kind of tannish color. I remember Mac and my husband trying to whittle it with a knife and trying to burn it. It wouldn't burn and it wouldn't whittle."

Mr. Brazel hadn't brought a sample of the foil-like material that he had found, but he told the Proctors about it. "He said you could crunch it in your hand and it would just straighten back out by itself. No creases or wrinkles would stay in it. It wasn't like anything he had ever seen."

He invited the Proctors to come to his place and see the field of debris, but they declined. "The war hadn't been over long," Mrs. Proctor says. "Gas and tires was still hard to get. And it was way out in the pasture, away from the roads. About that time, we was hearing a lot about UFOs, and we told Mac, 'Maybe if you take it in, you might get a reward.' We had heard there would be a ten thousand dollar reward for anybody who brought in a flying saucer."

The nearest settlement to Mr. Brazel's place was the ranch village of Corona, about thirty miles away. But the nearest authorities to whom Mr. Brazel might report his find were in Roswell, about seventy rough, hot miles to the southeast in neighboring Chaves County. He had no telephone and plenty of work to do, so the reward, if there was one, would have to wait.

On July 6, a Sunday, Mr. Brazel finally drove into Roswell and showed a few pieces of the wreckage to the Chaves County sheriff, George Wilcox. He described what he had seen in his pasture and whispered — "kind of confidential like," he told reporters later — that he might have found a flying saucer. The sheriff suggested they phone the military authorities at Roswell Army Air Field.

The base, at the south end of Main Street, was the home of the 509th Bomb Group (Atomic), the unit that had devastated Hiroshima and Nagasaki two years earlier. It was the only atomic bomber group in the world, and its base was just one of several top-secret military installations in the area. Not far to the west, near Alamogordo, was the White Sands Missile Range, where scientists were experimenting with German V-2 rockets captured during the war, and Trinity Site, where the first atomic bomb had been tested.

Sheriff Wilcox barely hung up the phone before the base commander, his intelligence officer, and a plain-clothes counterintelligence agent drove up to his door.

Congressman Steven Schiff, a Republican from Albuquerque, thought he was making a routine request on March 11, 1993, when he wrote his letter about the Roswell Incident, as it came to be called, to Secretary of Defense Les Aspin.

"Last fall," the letter began, "I became aware of a strange series of events beginning in New Mexico over forty-five years ago and involving personnel of what was then the Army Air Force. I have since reviewed the facts in some detail, and I am writing to request your assistance in arriving at a definitive explanation of what transpired and why . . . . "

The congressman asked for "a full and honest review and reporting of the facts" and a personal briefing about the wreckage that Mac Brazel found in the desert and the widespread belief in New Mexico and elsewhere that the U.S. government had lied to the public about what it was.

"I had received a number of letters from New Mexico and other states alleging cover-up," Mr. Schiff says. "People who wrote me said that the evidence appears, on its face, to contradict the Department of Defense's official explanation. So wouldn't it be in the interest of the Department of Defense to demonstrate that there was no cover-up? I was really writing from a favorable point of view for the Department of Defense. I was trying to lay out for the secretary: 'Look what people are saying. Aren't you, the Defense Department, interested in setting the record straight? That you, in fact, did everything as you said you did it? Don't you want to put this to rest?'"

Even if it was necessary for national security reasons to conceal the truth in 1947, Mr. Schiff reasoned, surely it could be told now, almost a half-century later.

"Instead," he says, "I got a run-around."

Secretary Aspin, who since has resigned, never answered the letter. But about three weeks later, Mr. Schiff received a reply from an Air Force colonel in the Pentagon:

"I have received your letter of March 11, requesting information on alleged events which occurred in Roswell, New Mexico.

"In order to be of service to you, I have referred this matter to the National Archives and Record Administration for direct reply to you.

"If I can be of further assistance to you, please do not hesitate to let me know."

"It was that simple," Mr. Schiff says. "With the implied words, 'Go look it up yourself.'"

The letter stung the third-term congressman, who numbers among his House committee assignments both Government Operations and Science, Space and Technology, and who serves as a colonel in the New Mexico Air National Guard. "I'm not hung up on protocol," he says, "but that was a bit terse, I thought. So I contacted the Department of Defense again and got a more protocol-oriented letter from a special assistant to the secretary that said basically the same thing: 'Go to the National Archives and look it up yourself.' So OK, if that's the way it is. I went to the National Archives. And someone there wrote to me and said: 'We don't have anything on the Roswell Incident.' And then he went on to say, kind of humorously, I think: 'We've gotten a lot of requests for information here on that.' And I'm thinking, 'I'm not terribly surprised. The Department of Defense is sending the whole world to you.' "

The congressman wondered: "Why was the Department of Defense sending me to an agency for my request, when they ought to have known that agency didn't have any information?"

So in October 1993 he asked the General Accounting Office, the investigative arm of Congress, to help him. "What I asked them was: Can we account for the records that I'm sure would have existed at the time? And if the records no longer exist, what happened to them? I'm positive that at the very least there had to be some kind of 'Oh my gosh' memorandum from one Army Air Force headquarters to another when they found out that they had put out a press release saying they had picked up a flying disc."

Sometimes they were called "flying discs," sometimes "platters," sometimes "flying saucers." In late June and early July of 1947, they seemed to be everywhere.

180

By July 7, newspapers were headlining sightings in thirty-nine states, Mexico, and Canada.

"Folks sitting on front porches or out driving see them dash teasingly across the sky," the Associated Press reported in Texas. "'There one goes,' the delighted witness cries. But in a twinkling of an unbelieving eye the disc is spinning out of sight, leaving a bewildering puzzle in its wake."

Rewards of one thousand dollars — not the ten thousand dollars that Mrs. Proctor thought — were being offered in Chicago, Los Angeles, and Spokane to anyone finding a genuine flying saucer.

On July 6, after examining what Mac Brazel had brought to town and hearing the story of his find, the Roswell Army Air Field commander, Col. William Blanchard, ordered his intelligence officer, Maj. Jesse Marcel, to accompany the rancher back to the debris field. According to several authors who have written about the Roswell Incident, the major drove his own car, a Buick convertible. A counterintelligence agent followed in a jeep carry-all. By the time they reached the ranch house, it was too dark to continue on to the wreckage site, so they spent the night. The next morning, Mr. Brazel led them into the pasture, showed them the wreckage, and left them.

Major Marcel and the counterintelligence agent spent most of the day examining the debris and loading pieces of it into their vehicles. Near nightfall, they told Mr. Brazel they were returning to Roswell, but that someone would come later to gather the rest of the wreckage.

The next morning, July 8, two counterintelligence agents and a contingent of military police arrived and cordoned off the debris area. While the MPs were gathering the rest of the wreckage, the agents asked Mr. Brazel to accompany them back to Roswell, which he did.

"They kept him down there right close to a week," says his neighbor, Mrs. Proctor, who remembers that Mr. Brazel was morose and uncommunicative when he returned home. "He was real unhappy about that. He never did say why they did it. He never would talk about it after he come back."

Sometime around noon on July 8, the Roswell Army Air Base public information officer, 1st Lt. Walter Haut, began making his rounds of the town's two newspapers and two radio stations, distributing one of the most extraordinary news releases in the history of the armed forces. It was only three paragraphs long:

"The many rumors regarding the flying disc became a reality yesterday when the intelligence office of the 509th Bomb Group of the 8th Air Force, Roswell Army Air Field, was fortunate enough to gain possession of a disc through the cooperation of one of the local ranchers and the sheriff's office of Chaves County.

"The flying object landed on a ranch near Roswell sometime last week. Not having phone facilities, the rancher stored the disc until such time as he was able to contact the sheriff's office, who in turn notified Maj. Jesse A. Marcel of the 509th Bomb Group intelligence office.

"Action was immediately taken and the disc was picked up at the rancher's home. It was inspected at the Roswell Army Air Field and subsequently loaned by Major Marcel to higher headquarters."

Mr. Haut, who still lives in Roswell, says he doesn't remember exactly how Colonel Blanchard broke this extraordinary news to him. "I can't say specifically, 'This is the way it happened,'" he says. "But if Colonel Blanchard said a flying disc crashed out there, then as far as I was concerned, a flying disc crashed out there. He was a colonel. I was a first lieutenant. First lieutenants weren't paid to think, They were paid to do. And I did what the colonel told me to do."

The colonel's news didn't particularly amaze him, he remembers. "It wasn't that big a shock. There had been I don't know how many reports of flying saucers prior to that time. And when you're following orders, you don't ask a lot of questions."

After he delivered his release to the news media, Mr. Haut says, he went home for lunch. That afternoon, the *Roswell Daily Record* and several other evening newspapers in the western United States ran the story on their front pages, and several radio stations put it on the air.

"I didn't return to the office until about two o'clock," Mr. Haut says. "The phone was ringing. I picked it up. It was a call from London. They wanted to know more about the disc. I didn't have anything more to tell them. I got a lot of calls that afternoon. I got home at 5:30 or six o'clock. I sat down and ate, played with my daughter for a while, then started doing things around the house. We had moved to that house only a couple of months before, and there were lots of things that needed to be done. We didn't turn the radio on that night. The next morning, I went out and picked up the morning newspaper. That's when I saw the story that it wasn't a flying saucer. It was a mere weather balloon."

The pieces of wreckage that Mac Brazel brought to the sheriff and the pieces that Major Marcel and the counter-intelligence agent hauled to town had been boxed up and flown to Fort Worth Army Air Field (later Carswell Air Force Base), headquarters of the 8th Air Force. On the evening of July 8, only a few hours after Lieutenant Haut distributed his press release, Brig. Gen. Roger Ramey, commander of the 8th, showed reporters the pieces of a weather balloon and the radar reflector that it had carried. This, he said, was the wreckage that Mr. Brazel had found.

The next day, Mr. Brazel, who had been in the custody of the army since the MPs arrived at his ranch, changed his description of what he had found. The huge field of wreckage that he had described to the Proctors and Sheriff Wilcox shrank dramatically. He told the local press that he had gathered all the debris he found into two bundles less than three feet long and eight inches thick, weighing maybe five pounds. It consisted, he said, of tinfoil, paper, cellophane tape, sticks, and rubber. He said he thought the object might have been "about the size of a table top" before it was wrecked.

Had this been so, he could have brought the bundles with him to the sheriff's office and saved Major Marcel and the counterintelligence agent the long trip to his ranch, and the following day's journey there by the counterintelligence agents and military police.

Then, in what may have been a veiled hint that his new story wasn't true, Mr. Brazel added that he had found weather balloons on his ranch twice before, and that this new wreckage didn't in any way resemble the others. "I am sure what I found was not any weather observation balloon," he told the *Record* and the Associated Press. "But," he added in disgust, "if I find anything else besides a bomb, they are going to have a hard time getting me to say anything about it."

"General Ramey's retraction [of the press release] was in the morning papers of July 9," Mr. Haut says. "Within a week there was very, very little, if any, interest shown in the incident. It was over. It died real quick."

But Mr. Haut — and many others — remain convinced that General Ramey's weather balloon and Mr. Brazel's revised description were the beginning of a cover-up designed by higher-ups in Washington.

This is Mr. Haut's outline of the events:

"Proctor told Mac Brazel to come in to the sheriff of Chaves County. He did, on the sixth of July. The sheriff sees what he's got, and he calls the base commander. The base commander calls his intelligence agent and his CIC [counterintelligence] agent to meet him at the sheriff's office. Blanchard sees what it is, he takes it back to the base and tells both his intelligence agent and his CIC agent, 'Go out with this guy and bring back everything you can bring back.' That's all [taking place] on the sixth. He then calls General Ramey and tells him about this material. Not much happens on the seventh of July until Jesse Marcel and the CIC boy return with more of the wreckage, which also is sent to Fort Worth. Not much happens on the eighth of July until around noontime, when Haut comes into the foreground and lets his press release go. Then General Ramey, five or six hours later, comes back and says, 'Oh no. It's a weather balloon.' Why didn't he know it was a weather balloon on the sixth of July, when he saw it? He knew what a weather balloon looked like. So did Blanchard. So did Marcel. So did Mac Brazel, for that matter. The brass had that material in their hands for two days. My feeling is that someone — I wouldn't want to guess who — starts thinking, 'We've got to cover this up.' And how better a way to cover it up than to have a colonel say, 'Yes, we do have a flying saucer,' and then to have a general come out and say, 'Oh no, that was a weather balloon'? It was a pretty good cover. The whole thing died almost immediately."

If he and Colonel Blanchard goofed up by distributing the news release, Mr. Haut says, none of their commanders ever reprimanded them. Colonel Blanchard eventually became a four-star general and served as deputy chief of staff of the Air Force. Mr. Haut resigned from the Air Force less than a year after the Roswell Incident. He stayed in Roswell and went into the insurance business.

Twenty-eight years later, he gave up insurance and for ten years ran a gallery and frame shop.

His resignation, he says, was in no way connected to the press release. General Ramey was about to be promoted, and Colonel Blanchard was going to take over command of the 8th Air Force. "He told me, 'You're going to Fort Worth with me, and you're going to be the public information officer for the 8th Air Force,'" Mr. Haut says. "But I had made up my mind to stay here. Blanchard and I were extremely close. If we were at the Officers' Club, my wife and I sat at his table all the time. If someone was dancing too close with his wife, I would have to go and cut in."

When General Blanchard died in 1965, the Air Force sent a lieutenant colonel from the Roswell base to notify Mr. Haut. "He introduces himself," Mr. Haut remembers, "and he says, 'I have some very sad news for you. General Blanchard passed away at 8:10 this morning at the Pentagon in a staff meeting. Nothing could be released to the press until you personally were notified.' I still get choked up when I think about it."

In 1992, Mr. Haut and some of his friends opened the International UFO Museum and Research Center across Main Street from the Chaves County Courthouse in a building they rent from the city for a dollar a year. It contains 118 UFO books, shelves of reports and papers from the Center for UFO Research in suburban Washington, photographs, newspaper clippings, a reading room, a TV room for viewing more than twenty UFO videotapes, and a shop selling UFO T-shirts, videos, books, coffee mugs, refrigerator magnets, and reproductions of the Roswell newspapers headlining Mr. Haut's press release: "RAAF Captures Flying Saucer On Ranch in Roswell Region" and General Ramey's retraction: "Gen. Ramey Empties Roswell Saucer."

There also is a huge painting depicting a flying-saucer crash, and a statue of a small alien from outer space called RALF (Roswell Alien Life Form). More than twenty thousand people have visited the museum since it opened.

"Why do I feel so strongly that it *was* a flying saucer?" Mr. Haut asks. "Because of Major Marcel, who was the base intelligence officer. I spent several hours with him on two different occasions, and he was so *adamant* about the materials. Foil that you could take in your hand and crumple it up as tight as you could, and it would spring back to its original shape after you released it, without any creases. Nothing! Even to this day, I don't think we have a metal that has a memory built into it like that. He talked about a thirty-inch I-beam that they hit with a nineteen-pound sledge hammer, and it bounced off of it. And transparent wires that resembled today's fiber optics. I have no reason to doubt Marcel's honesty. He had no ax to grind. He was *adamant* about the fact that these materials were not of this planet."

Stanton Friedman, a nuclear physicist who used to work on government projects for General Electric, Westinghouse, and other companies, became interested in flying saucers back in the 1950s. For the past twelve years, he says, he has lectured full time about them, at more than six hundred colleges and to more than one hundred other audiences in all fifty states, nine Canadian provinces, and Germany and Finland.

"And I've done a lot of radio and TV," he says. "Everything from *Nightline* to *Unsolved Mysteries* to *Sally Jesse Raphael*."

One day in 1978, while waiting to be interviewed at a television station in Baton Rouge, Louisiana, he was having coffee with the station manager. "And the manager, out of the blue, says, 'You know, the guy you ought to talk to is Jesse Marcel.' and I said, 'Who's he?' And he said, 'Well, he handled pieces of one of those saucers you're interested in when he was in the military.'"

Mr. Marcel, long since retired from the Air Force, was living in Houma, Louisiana. Mr. Friedman called him and heard, for the first time, the story of the Roswell Incident. But, says Mr. Friedman, Mr. Marcel couldn't remember when it had happened.

"Not long thereafter, I was giving a lecture at Bemidji State College in Minnesota, and two people came up to me and asked if I had heard of a crashed saucer in New Mexico. There was a third story early on about a woman who tried to put a story about the crashed saucer, which had been called in from Roswell, on the wire, and her transmission was interrupted on the teletype by the message: 'Do not continue this transmission. FBI.' Then a fellow told me about an English actor named Dewey Greene who was driving from the West Coast to the East Coast. The actor claimed in his autobiography that he heard on his radio in New Mexico about a crashed flying saucer, but when he got to the East Coast, there was nothing."

Mr. Friedman, who lives in Canada, and a partner, William Moore, began investigating the origins of the stories about the crash. General Blanchard, Mac Brazel, Floyd Proctor, Sheriff Wilcox and many of the servicemen who participated in the events had since died, but friends, associates, and relatives told second- and third-hand stories about what had been discovered in the desert in 1947.

Mr. Friedman and Mr. Moore concluded that the wreckage Mr. Brazel found was part of a flying saucer that was struck by lightning or experienced some malfunction during that stormy night over Lincoln County. According to their theory, an explosion blew a hole in the saucer and sent debris falling onto Mr. Brazel's pasture. The saucer itself crashed several miles farther on. An army pilot, perhaps with Mr. Brazel aboard his plane, spotted the wreckage. Soldiers recovered the craft and the dead bodies of its crew of extraterrestrial aliens. Mr. Friedman, Mr. Moore, and other UFO believers contend that the bodies and the pieces of the saucer then were packed up and flown to Fort Worth and/or to Washington and/or to secret facilities at what is now Wright-Patterson Air Force Base in Ohio.

The stories of these theories and investigations — and others — have been published in at least three books: *The Roswell Incident* by Charles Berlitz and William Moore, *UFO Crash at Roswell* by Kevin Randle and Donald Schmitt, and Mr. Friedman's own *Crash at Corona*, which he wrote with Don Berliner.

In their book, Mr. Friedman and Mr. Berliner claim a second saucer crashed on the Plains of San Agustin, near Magdalena, New Mexico, about 150 miles west of Mr. Brazel's ranch, and that the army recovered that craft, too, along with several bodies and at least one live space alien.

In Roswell, stories are still told about autopsies performed at the base hospital on small alien corpses with large heads and gray skin, of soldiers catching unauthorized glimpses of the strange bodies, of a frightened nurse drawing pictures of them for a friend.

When John Tilley came to Roswell as a young GI in December 1947, about six months after the Roswell Incident, he heard a disturbing tale which he still passes on.

"The scuttlebutt at the base," he says, "was that something had escaped from the military, and that whatever had escaped had left the base and was peering through windows and scaring the heck out of people. That didn't mean anything to an eighteen-year-old kid from West Virginia. But four or five years ago, I met a UFO historian who told me that in UFO circles there has always been a whispered rumor that one of the four aliens that crashed at Corona was alive and that it escaped. And when the military located it near the base gate, they killed it. They were afraid of it. So you take that and put it together with what I heard, and what have you got?"

Mr. Tilley and his friend John Price operate the Outa Limits UFO Enigma Museum at the south end of Main Street, not far from the gate of the old air base, which is now an industrial park. A slightly older rival of sorts to Mr. Haut's downtown International UFO Museum and Research Center, the Enigma Museum walls are covered with newspaper clippings about UFO sightings, people who claim to have been abducted by aliens, and the filming of a Showtime cable TV movie about the incident, starring country singer Dwight Yoakam as Mac Brazel.

But the centerpiece of the museum is a diorama of a crashed saucer, made of two eight-foot TV satellite dishes welded together and painted silver, with real smoke wafting from the wreckage. Dead aliens, made by Mr. Price's sister, are scattered about. A store-window mannequin dressed as an army MP stands guard over them.

"We have reason to believe that some people still have parts of the saucer and photographs of it," Mr. Tilley says. "They just won't come out because the government would take these things away from them. So we have got ourselves a bona fide UFO phenomenon mystery."

"The biggest story of the millennium," Mr. Friedman, the author, calls it. "Visits to Planet Earth by alien spacecraft," he says. "A successful cover-up of the best data for almost forty-seven years. Quite a remarkable achievement. A cosmic Watergate."

That's what bothers Congressman Schiff: the possibility that the government hid — and maybe continues to hide — the truth about the Roswell Incident from the people.

"On the issue of UFOs, I fall more closely into the group that are called skeptics," he says, "in the sense that an extraterrestrial explanation is not what pops into my mind. My first two possibilities would be as follows:

"1. It really was a weather balloon. It has just been a public relations fiasco for the Defense Department from back in 1947 until today.

"2. And now I'm into sheer conjecture — that it was some kind of military experiment from White Sands, a Cold War experiment of some kind, that went awry.

"But I don't think the bottom-line belief is what's important here. That's not why I got into this. The *real* issue is: Are people entitled to an accounting of the records of their government? I knew when I started this that, because the issue of flying saucers was involved, I possibly would be subject to some ridicule. 'Why are you helping people who believe flying saucers crashed and alien bodies are being hidden?' And the answer to that is, it doesn't matter what they believe. The people who have come to me have said, 'We are interested in knowing what the government did with its files.' I think that's a reasonable request by any citizen of this country. And I don't think it matters whether the subject of their inquiry is extraterrestrial creatures or radiation experiments or any other subject. The people are entitled to know what their government did. And that should not be, if you'll pardon the expression, a federal case. I'm intent on seeing that the people who want to see these records can see whatever's available, or get an explanation of what happened to them if they don't exist anymore. What they choose to believe or not believe is their business."

The Government Accounting Office is working on it, he says. He has given no deadline. Whenever and whatever the GAO reports back to him, he will report to the people.

And he will leave it to others to answer the question that Loretta Proctor poses to the skeptics:

"If we're here, why can't somebody be somewhere else?"

May 1994

My earliest memories are of a farm in Comanche County, Texas, near the Hamilton County line, and Carlton, a tiny community on the Hamilton side of the line. In those places, I spent the first eight years of my life. The farm is the one described in "Generations," the first piece in this book. The town is the one mentioned in "Mrs. Miller."

A great sadness comes over me whenever I remember those places.

A Memoir of Hamilton and Comanche Counties

They tell me of a home where my friends have gone,
O they tell me of that land far away,
Where the tree of life in eternal bloom
Sheds its fragrance thro' the unclouded day.
                                        — hymn

The Baptist Church stood on one side of the square, and the Methodist Church on the other. The Church of Christ was just across the road. In the middle of the square stood a large shed with a shingle roof. All the sides of the shed were open. Under it were rows of crude wooden benches with an aisle down the middle, and at one end of the shed was a platform for the choir and a pulpit for the evangelist. The shed was called "the Tabernacle," and it was used by the churches for their revivals in the summertime.

The main purpose of the revivals was to save souls — to persuade us to desert the deadly pathways of sin, accept the Lord Jesus Christ as our personal Savior, be baptized into whichever of the households of faith was occupying the Tabernacle at the moment, and live thenceforth in the knowledge that death would not be our end, but the beginning of our eternal life of joy with God in his heaven. For those whose souls already had been saved, the revivals offered a chance to revive the spirit, to shore up a rickety determination, to suck in the gut of faith and persevere with the righteous life. And for everybody they were a chance to get together and talk about the weather and the children and the war — World War II — in which many young men from the town and the farms were fighting, in Europe and Asia and Africa and the South Pacific, half a world away from Carlton, Texas, and everything they had ever known.

There were two preaching services a day during the revivals — one in the morning, which was supposed to end about noon, and one in the evening.

In the evening, when the young men had finished their work for the day, and the young mothers had washed and put away the supper dishes and dressed their sons in clean shirts and overalls and their daughters in pinafores, and the families were arriving in the square in their old Fords and Chevrolets, there was a festive air about the revivals. Before the service, the men would lean against the cars and talk, their cigarettes glowing like orange lightning bugs in the darkness. The young women would hustle

their babies and toddlers into the Tabernacle and arrange
them along the benches, and visit with the mothers on
the bench ahead and the mothers on the bench behind.
We school-age kids — six to ten or so years old — would
play tag or hide-and-seek among the cars until a father or
mother came to herd us to the Tabernacle.

Sometimes we children would stand in front of the congregation and sing a song that we sang only at revivals:

> *I've got that Baptist booster spizerinctum*
> *Down in my heart,*
> *Down in my heart,*
> *Down in my heart!*
> *I've got that Baptist booster spizerinctum*
> *Down in my heart,*
> *Down in my heart to stay!*

The morning service was attended mostly by the older
women and men of the town and whatever children could
be dragged to it. I was about six years old when my grandmother began taking me along.

The word that comes into my mind as I remember
those interminable hours of squirming on the hard
wooden benches is "hot" — the perspiring faces of the
women and the faint *whit, whit* of their cardboard funeral-
home fans trying to stir a breeze into the sticky air; the
torrid white sunlight just beyond the edge of the
Tabernacle roof; the sweating evangelist, coatless, his neck-
tie loosened, leaning over the pulpit, and his detailed
description of the eternal fires of hell and the everlasting
agonies of those doomed to dwell therein; the fervent
tears of the repentant as they plodded down the aisle,
hunched under the weight of their sins.

Outside the Tabernacle, beyond the edges of the town,
under the pale, blinding sky, locusts were whirring in the

creek bottoms, milk cows were grazing, and the crops that gave us our livelihood and were Carlton's only reason for being — the corn, the maize, the oats, the hay, the wheat, the cotton — were creeping silently upward from the dark earth.

One of the farms belonged to us. Our hogs were grunting in their pen, wallowing in their mud, seeking coolness. Our chickens — white Plymouth Rocks and a few bantams — were strutting about the barnyard, pecking at the ground, their yellow eyes blinking. On the front porch, my father's hounds — asleep and perhaps dreaming — were thumping the floorboards with their tails. Whenever a puff of breeze came up, the windmill wheel would groan and turn a time or two, and the sucker rod would move slowly up the pipe and drop a dollop of cool water into the tank.

Except on the days when my father cranked up our old Farmall and drove it out of its shed to work the fields, and the days when my mother or my father started the car for a trip into the town, there were no noises of engines or motors on our place. The only other machinery sounds I remember were the *thunk, thunk* of the windmill sucker rod and the clatter of the old Singer sewing machine on which my mother made nearly all our clothes. It was powered by her feet on the treadle.

Pres. Franklin D. Roosevelt hadn't yet brought electricity to our house, nor to any farmhouse in our part of Comanche County. My mother washed our clothes in a big iron pot that was sitting on a wood fire in the yard. She scrubbed them on a washboard with soap home-made of lye and the fat of our butchered hog, and ironed them with heavy irons heated on the burners of her kerosene cook stove. I sounded out the words of my first-grade Dick and Jane reader by the light of the coal-oil lamp on the round oak dining table. In winter, the only heat in the house was provided by a wood stove in the living room. When my father would pile in the logs and the kindling and douse them with kerosene and throw in a match in the chilly morning, we would huddle shivering around it, holding out our hands to catch the first waves of warmth, watching the walls of the stove slowly brighten to a rosy glow. Our milk and perishables were kept in a washtub with a big block of ice on the back porch. We brought the ice from town once a week, and covered the tub with an old blanket to hold in the cold. We owned a radio, but it was powered by car batteries, and our batteries were old and wouldn't hold a charge. Since the war made it impossible to buy new ones, we didn't hear the radio often. There was no telephone.

We had a cold-water faucet in the kitchen. It was the only plumbing in the house, but it was more than many of our neighbors had. We bathed in a washtub in water heated on the kitchen stove, and went to an outdoor toilet that stood some distance from the house. In the winter, our visits there were infrequent and brief, especially at night and when a norther was blowing. In the summer, copperheads sometimes would be attracted to the toilet's shade, and there were always spiders.

I was born during the Great Depression, the eldest of five. Ours wasn't the most prosperous farm in the county, but it wasn't the poorest, either. My mother says the country people didn't feel the Depression as acutely as the people in the town. Being a child, I didn't feel it at all. Only years later would I learn I had been born during hard times.

We were almost self-sufficient. Our cows provided all our milk and butter. Our chickens provided our eggs and part of our meat, especially for our Sunday dinners. My mother raised a large garden. The vegetables we didn't eat fresh, she canned in Mason jars and stored in the cellar.

We knocked pecans out of the trees in the creek bottoms. My father shot squirrels and rabbits and doves and quail and brought them home for us to eat. He raised most of the feed that our animals ate. Every winter, we butchered a hog, which provided not only bacon, ham, sausage, and pork chops, but lard and soap as well.

Hog-killing day was one of the days it was fun to be a child on the farm. Despite the terrible scream the animal would make as it died on that cold morning, it was a day of laughter and good feeling.

The neighbors — two or three families of them — would come. The men would kill the animal, scald its bristles off in a barrel of hot water, and butcher it. The women would salt the bacon and ham, sew the cloth sacks in which the meat would be hung in the smokehouse, grind and season the sausage, build a fire in the yard, throw the fat into my mother's iron wash pot, and render it into lard. While the fat was boiling, they would toss strips of the hog's skin into it and dip them out a few minutes later as golden, hot "cracklings," a delicacy only faintly akin to the dry, cellophaned "pork skins" sold now in supermarkets.

A lot of the work was done that way — neighbors helping each other out. The neighbors would help us butcher our hog or pick our cotton or reap and shock our oats or wheat, and we would help them with theirs. The women worked together on their canning and quilting. Everybody brought his own tools to whatever job needed doing. No money was offered or accepted among neighbors, but sometimes, when cash was needed, we would hire out to others. I remember dragging a cotton sack down the rows of Walker Bingham's field with my parents one long, hot day, and when the work was over, Mr. Bingham — one of the more well-to-do farmers of the county — gave me a shiny quarter. It was the first wages I ever was paid. I

remember how hard and sharp the cotton bolls were.
I remember how tired my mother was that night.

Threshing the grain was more fun than cotton picking.
My family and the neighbors would reap the crop with a
horse-drawn reaper not much changed from Cyrus
McCormick's original design. The machine would move
around the field, cutting the plants, binding them into
sheaves with twine, and spitting them onto the ground.
Or was there another machine that bound the sheaves?
I was very young. The rest of us would walk behind the
reaper, stacking the sheaves into neat shocks. After the
shocks had dried in the sun for a few days, the thresher
would come.

A truck pulled the huge machine from farm to farm. Its
crew came with it. The thresher, our mothers warned us
every year, was dangerous, full of pulleys and gears and
belts and teeth. It took special knowledge to avoid its
perils and, even so, many men lost arms in threshers. Each
farmer paid the owner of the thresher in cash or in a share
of the crop for the services of his machine, and the owner
paid his crew.

They would park the thresher in the middle of the field,
and the neighbors would come with their pitchforks and
help my father haul the sheaves to the thresher and the
threshed grain to the barn in mule-drawn wagons, and
help my mother cook the huge meal that the thresher
crew and the field hands would consume under the live
oak trees beside the windmill at noon.

I was too young to know it then, but the work was brutal. Having so many people on the farm — normally a
lonely place — was what made the day so full of laughter.

Now all the work that was done by all those people can
be done by one man on a combine. He can bring his
lunch to the field with him and eat it alone in his air-conditioned cab and listen to his radio for company.

The combine and other machines — huge, costly contraptions that have replaced the brawn of humans and animals with steel and internal combustion engines and fossil fuels — are part of the reason the countryside of Hamilton and Comanche counties has changed so much since I lived there. It doesn't take as many heads and hands and shoulders and backs to run a farm now as it did then. Many families have lost their lands to markets and weather and banks, too. And many fields — those where King Cotton reigned too long — are worn out and good only for grazing now.

So there are fewer farms than there used to be, and fewer farmers, and fewer neighbors. The fading remains of abandoned farm homes — leaning piles of rotting lumber, lone chimneys pointing skyward like work-worn fingers, groves of shade trees marking the home sites of long-departed families — dot the hills and prairies.

But the dwindling few who still live on the land don't have to do their laundry in the yard or read by lamplight or keep their food in washtubs or go to outdoor toilets. President Roosevelt's electric lines reached their houses long ago. They own stereos and VCRs and computers. Television comes to them by satellite. They buy most of their food in supermarkets and most of their clothing at shopping centers and discount stores, like the people in the cities. Their cars and trucks take them as far away as they want to go, and all or most of the way is paved.

Nearly all the young people ride those roads into the cities now, to schools and jobs that will divorce them from the land forever. There's neither room nor livelihood for them anymore on the land of their ancestors.

No one who lived through the old times and has a good memory would say all the changes in the rural places are bad. Most of the people who left have no serious yearning to go back. Not to stay. Not to work there as their parents and grandparents did. Not to try to wrestle a living from the stubborn soil in the old way. To build a little weekend retreat in the country someday, maybe. To go hunting or fishing. To try to find old landmarks that still live in memory. To visit the graves of their forebears.

I don't know how long ago my ancestors — the DeVolins, the Gibsons, the Whites, the Woolleys — settled in Hamilton and Comanche counties. Some of them, I know, moved there while the Comanches still roamed the land. All my great-grandparents and grandparents but one — my maternal grandmother, Clora DeVolin Gibson — are buried there. But no living member of any of my ancestral families is there now.

There are thousands of families like us from many parts of rural America. Our exodus from the countryside happened all of a sudden, during the life span of a single, still-not-old generation — we who were the children in the Tabernacle during the great war that changed everything. And as our land has emptied, the little towns that lived to serve us have shriveled.

The Carlton of my childhood had a cotton gin and a feed mill, two grocery stores, a blacksmith shop, three gas stations, a laundry, a feed store, a barber shop, a Masonic lodge, a beauty shop, a telephone office, a variety store, a post office, a doctor, and a drugstore. On a hill on the edge of the town stood the two-story stone schoolhouse where I went to first grade and my grandmother Gibson taught for many years. My great-grandfather's name — I. J. Gibson — was on the cornerstone.

But the school is shut down now. Its last class graduated in 1969. Of downtown Carlton, only one business — the grocery store that belonged to Hob Thompson — survives. The Tabernacle no longer stands amidst the churches. One of the churches — the Methodist — is dead. The others are fading shadows of the robust congregations they used to

201

be. Their *spizerinctum* is gone. If the Tabernacle still stood, and if there were to be a revival, no mothers with babies would be there, and no children playing hide-and-seek among the cars. No young sinners would be moving down the aisle toward their salvation.

Only a few dozen people remain in the town that used to be home to hundreds. Nearly all of them are old. As they depart, their places won't be filled by newcomers or new generations. Soon Carlton — like Sunshine and Honey Grove and Fairy and Altman and Alexander and the other rural communities that time already has wiped from the countryside — will live only in the memories of a few old people, and then they'll die, too.

In 1986, the sesquicentennial year of the Republic of Texas, the remaining citizens of Carlton collected the memories of many families who used to live there and in the countryside around, and compiled them into a book. In it, Betty Jo Fine McKenney, a woman of my mother's generation, wrote of her grandson, who lives in a city: "I have taken him to Carlton and shown him the names on the graves at the cemetery and explained to him how it was at one time, in the hope that we can pass it on to another generation."

My own sons were born in 1969 and 1971. They've always lived in cities. One day when they were small, I was telling them some of the things that I've told here, and one of them said: "You sound like you lived in pioneer days." To children born after men had walked on the moon, boys who flew in airplanes when they were infants and studied computers along with their spelling and multiplication tables, these memories *are* of "pioneer days" — a time when Texas and America were younger, fresher, simpler, and less crowded than they are now. Even so, those days aren't yet past memory, and the bitter words of the Old Testament's Preacher needn't be let to come true:

"There is no remembrance of former things, nor will there be any remembrance of later things yet to happen among those who come after."

Those who come after should at least hear the echoes and see the shadows.

1992

To those who view life in a slightly skewed way — which, in my opinion, is the only sane way to look at it — the retirement of Gary Larson and the end of his daily newspaper cartoon, The Far Side, *is a major calamity. So the guy is tired and also filthy rich. Big deal. He had no business leaving us to the likes of* Nancy *and* Peanuts *and* Family Circus.

After this piece ran, I spent weeks listening to long stories about other people's nightmares.

A Far-Gone Conclusion

For years I suffer a recurring nightmare: I'm sitting in a college classroom, about to take a final exam in organic chemistry. Suddenly I realize: I haven't attended a single lecture in this course! I've never opened the textbook! I know nothing about the subject of this exam! And it's *too late to drop the course*!

Then I wake up in a sweat.

So one morning I see a cartoon in my newspaper: A classroom full of academic-looking people — professors, apparently — each holding a duck in his lap. Another professor, standing before them on a stage, is holding a duck under his arm. But in the midst of the crowd of duck-holders is a man with large, panic-filled eyes.

The caption reads: "Suddenly, Professor Liebowitz realizes he has come to the seminar without his duck."

A cartoon about my nightmare!

I laugh and laugh. Seeing my subconscious deep-night terror taken to such absurdity places the world and my life into a refreshingly bearable new perspective.

Does the cartoon cure me of my recurring nightmare? Of course not. I still dream the thing about once a month. But now, when I wake up, I think of ducks.

And there's that other cartoon, captioned "The Elephant's Nightmare": An elephant is seated at a grand piano on a stage before a large audience, his eyes bulging with fear. He's thinking: "What am I doing here? I can't play this thing! I'm a *flutist*, for crying out loud!"

I have that dream, too. I'm sitting at a piano on the stage at Ed Landreth Auditorium at Texas Christian University, a contestant in the Van Cliburn International Piano Competition. Jackie Kennedy Onassis is in the audience. And *I don't know how to play the piano*!

I wake up thinking of elephants.

These are common nightmares. Many people have them. They're about the world we live in.

The world — the American part of it — is divided into two parts: Those who attach clippings of *Family Circus* and *Peanuts* to their bulletin boards and refrigerator doors, and those who hang up *The Far Side*.

The former group lives in the delusion that the world is a warm, fuzzy, safe, sweet-smelling place that makes sense; that people are good; that dogs and children are cute and harmless; that love conquers all; that right will prevail.

The latter group knows better. Our world — the real world — is full of terror and night sweats. Danger lurks just outside our peripheral vision, ready to pounce, and we're unprepared and helpless. It's a world not far from *The Far Side*, inhabited by scoundrels, bunglers, monsters, nerds, insects, and cows, where evil and incompetence (an innocuous-looking form of evil) are determined to do us in. We know that, eventually, they will.

The only sane thing to do in the face of such a world is laugh.

Gary Larson has been helping us do that since January 1, 1980, when *The Far Side* made its debut in the *San Francisco Chronicle*. A few months later, it was offered to other newspapers through syndication. Since then, *The Far Side* has run every day in as many as nineteen hundred newspapers. It has been translated into seventeen languages. Mr. Larson's small cluster of followers has grown to multitudes. He has amassed a fortune from the sale of nineteen *Far Side* books (twenty-eight million copies in print so far) and calendars, greeting cards, T-shirts, and coffee mugs bearing imprints of his cartoons.

Oddly, he didn't grow up dreaming of being a cartoonist. He was clerking in a music store, he writes in *The PreHistory of The Far Side*, a sort of autobiography and *apologia*, when one day "the sky seemed to suddenly open up over my head and a throng of beautiful angels came flying down and swirled around me. In glorious, lilting tones, their voices rang out, 'You haaaaate your job, you haaaaaate your job. . . . ' And then they left."

Mr. Larson took a couple of days off. Sitting at the kitchen table, pondering the angelic visitation, he began to draw. "I never studied art other than the required classes in grade school and junior high," he writes. "My love was science — specifically biology and, more specifically, when placed in a common jar, which of two organisms would devour the other."

From Mr. Larson's love of biology came the snakes, spiders, insects, crocodiles, gorillas, wolves, lions, deer, gazelles, rhinoceroses, fish, fleas, zebras, dinosaurs, amoebas, bears, penguins, slugs, elephants, sharks, whales, buffalo, aardvarks, butterflies, buzzards, earthworms, mammoths, porcupines, and squids that inhabit *The Far Side*. And scientists have acknowledged him as one of their own. Mr. Larson's drawings of these uncute, uncuddly creatures have been exhibited at such scientific places as the Denver Museum of Natural History, Shedd Aquarium in Chicago, the Smithsonian Museum of Natural History and the Washington Park Zoo in Portland, Oregon. *Strigiphilus garylarsoni*, a biting louse, was named in his honor.

There are domestic fauna in Mr. Larson's cartoons, too — dogs, cats, sheep, horses, ducks, chickens. And his trademark cows, which entered Mr. Larson's life in 1980, only a few months after *The Far Side* began. One day he drew a cartoon of a cow trying to pole vault, clotheslining herself on the bar. Nearby, a cat is playing a fiddle and saying to an onlooker: "We've still got a couple of years before we're ready for the moon."

"When I finished [drawing the cartoon]," Mr. Larson writes, "I sat back and stared at my little creation. Something moved me. This was *more* than just a cow — this was an entire *career* I was looking at."

People inhabit *The Far Side*, too — Neanderthals, Indians, cowboys, Tarzan, farmers, fishermen, nagging housewives, the Lone Ranger, nerdy children, Eskimos, Dr. Frankenstein, hunters, medieval torturers and their victims, Captain Ahab, explorers in pith helmets, and, of course, scientists in lab coats, one of whom is Albert Einstein. Satan appears from time to time. Also, space aliens and, occasionally, God.

Whatever their genus, species, or planet of origin, all *Far Side* creatures behave pretty much alike. Whether as predator or as prey, their thoughts and actions are reprehensible, disgusting, incompetent, or stupid.

A family of Holsteins poses for a picture at the Grand Canyon. One calf holds up its hoof behind the head of the other.

A bespectacled female gorilla (*Far Side* wives always wear ugly eyeglasses) is grooming her mate and accuses him: "Well, well — another blond hair. . . . Conducting a little more 'research' with that Jane Goodall tramp?" The guilty look on the male's face suggests he is.

A dog, sitting in front of his doghouse, reads a book titled *1001 Ways to Skin a Cat*. A cat, perched in a nearby tree, reads a book titled *Why Every Dog Should be Euthanized*.

A steer, sitting with a group of cowboys around a campfire, betrays his fellow kine, saying: "A few cattle are going to stray off in the morning, and tomorrow night a stampede is planned around midnight. Look, I gotta get back. . . . Remember, when we reach Santa Fe, I ain't slaughtered."

The brave defenders of the Alamo are lined along the top of the wall, firing at the enemy. Below, a nerdish vendor peddles T-shirts imprinted: "I kicked Santa Anna's butt at the Alamo." On his sign, the price has been slashed from $3.95 to $2.95 to $1.00.

Such a vision offends some people. Some call it bizarre. Some call it macabre. Some believe *The Far Side* warps the minds of our tender young. But for fifteen years, millions of clear-eyed realists who know we really *do* live in a boa-constrictor-swallows-pig world have counted on Mr. Larson to provide us a prophylactic laugh before we take that dangerous step outside our doors each morning.

Now it's over. After a-cartoon-every-day deadlines for all those years, Mr. Larson says he's tired. He's hanging up his pen and ink while he's still at the top of his form.

But he's only forty-four. What will he do with the rest of his life? Being a recluse, Mr. Larson isn't saying. His syndicate says everybody wanted an interview with him, so he decided not to talk to anybody. Maybe he'll just watch TV. Maybe he'll go on drawing his creatures in secret and stash them in a cave for some future generation to find, like the Dead Sea Scrolls. Maybe he'll open the restaurant that he once told a reporter he wanted to start. One that would serve nothing but cereal, and "You'd, like, have the special of the day be Rice Chex or something. And you'd offer a variety of milk from whole to 2 percent to skim."

Well, Mr. Larson, whatever you're up to, happy new year. You've really screwed up ours.

I feel a nightmare coming on.

HE CAME FROM A SEEMINGLY NORMAL FAMILY

On August 15, 1950, in Tacoma, Washington, Vern and Doris Larson became the parents of a baby named Gary. Vern, a car salesman, and Doris, a secretary, seemed average, middle-class American folks. But before long, their baby was harboring a monkey, several lizards, and a number of snakes, including a boa constrictor, on the Larson homestead and was recruiting his brother Dan to help him turn the back yard into a swamp. Vern and Doris apparently encouraged, or at least tolerated, this.

After high school, Gary enrolled in Washington State University at Pullman, majoring in communications, inexplicably preparing himself for a career in advertising. He graduated in 1972, but never did a lick of advertising. He became half of a jazz banjo duet and, later, got a job clerking at a music store. It was there that he received the visitation of angels described in the accompanying article. After he quit the music store, he got a job as an investigator for the Society for Prevention of Cruelty to Animals. Driving to work his first day on the job, he ran over a dog.

One day, Gary dashed off six cartoons, took them to a wilderness magazine in Seattle and sold them for ninety dollars. Encouraged by the promise of great wealth, he kept drawing and soon was publishing a daily cartoon called *Nature's Way* in the *Seattle Times*. The newspaper canceled him after a year because of reader complaints about his weirdness. Gary didn't mind, because he had just returned from a vacation in San Francisco, during which he had sold his cartoon to the *San Francisco Chronicle*, which soon syndicated it.

The rest is, as they say, history.

Although readers around the world will miss their daily visit to *The Far Side*, another, smaller group isn't at all unhappy to see Gary retire. In secret, they're clicking heels and slapping high fives. They're other cartoonists, who hope to fill the newspaper space Gary's vacating.

Especially jubilant are two syndicated Dallas cartoonists — Dan Piraro and Buddy Hickerson — whose work teeters with *The Far Side* at the top of the weird-o-meter.

"People like me are going to be the least upset by Larson's retirement," says Mr. Piraro, who draws *Bizarro*. "It saves us from having to wish he would go down in a plane.

"On the other hand," he acknowledges reluctantly, "Gary's a terrific guy, and he's awfully darn good at what he does."

Mr. Hickerson, who draws *The Quigmans*, calls Gary "the grand titan of cartooning," and says *The Far Side* was an important influence on his own early work.

"But he was hanging around too long!" he mutters. "Let him go! Bon Voyage! Don't let the door hit him in the butt on the way out!"

A few years ago, Gary declared himself burnt out and took a sabbatical, traveling to Africa and the Amazon to look at strange animals and to Greenwich Village for jazz guitar lessons. Then he returned to work. Is it possible that his present retirement will turn out to be temporary as well, that at some future time he might bring back *The Far Side*?

"Over my dead body," says Mr. Piraro with a curious chortle.

January 1995

I'll never understand the thinking of the rodeo cowboy. I can understand rolling around in the dirt with a steer if a cowboy's job requires it — if the beast has to be branded or doctored for worms or something. But to do it for fun? Naw.

So how can I explain men who lay down hard-earned cash to learn how *to roll around in the dirt with a steer? I can't. All I can do is describe them.*

A School of Hard Knocks

The men are standing in a semicircle in the shade of the 7/F Arena, a metal-roofed, open-sided rodeo ground that stands next to the 7/F Ranch Supply store beside Interstate 45 in Madisonville, Texas. In the sun-warmed trees along the south side of the arena, a chorus of birds sings of springtime, but the men in the shade — about forty of them — are silent. Although they're standing together, each man seems isolated from the others in that way that men have of seeming alone when they're in a crowd of male strangers. Some seem wary, their eyes shifting, squinting. Some gaze downward into the soft brown dirt, kicking lazily at clods. Some stare intently at the tall young man standing before them, who is talking.

They've found their way to this small courthouse town from every part of Texas, from Louisiana, New Mexico, Colorado, and Nevada, from North Dakota, Nebraska, Tennessee, and Mississippi, from Indiana, Alabama, Oklahoma, Virginia, Wisconsin, and California and paid $250 apiece to hear what the tall young man and his father can teach them.

The young man — Rope Myers is his name — is demonstrating a machine that looks like something a bunch of kids might have put together from junk they found behind the barn. Its identifiable parts are a shock absorber and a coil spring from an automobile, several slabs of iron, a couple of hinges, a number of nuts and bolts of various sizes, about half a roll of duct tape, some foam-rubber padding and a fake steer head made of fiberglass. The machine is attached to a steel frame with two rubber-tired wheels on it, which is hitched to a pickup truck.

This machine, Rope tells the men, is a "Steer Saver."

Then he shows them another machine which, he says, is a "Sure Catch." It's a four-wheel-drive off-road vehicle — a sort of four-wheel dirt bike — with a framework of two-by-four lumber attached to its back. An old saddle is cinched to the top of the frame.

The machines are inventions of Rope's father, Butch Myers of Athens, Texas, world champion steer wrestler of 1980 and nine-time qualifier to compete in the National Finals Rodeo. Butch is to steer wrestling what Arnold Palmer is to golf, say, or Jimmy Connors is to tennis. And he's the inventor not only of these odd machines, but also of his own method of steer wrestling, or as many of its practitioners still call it, bulldogging.

"There's so many things you've got to do to make bull-dogging work," says Ron Wilkinson, a thirty-seven-year

214

veteran of the rodeo circuit who is watching the quiet men listen. "It's the most complicated event in rodeo. It involves five living things — two men, two horses, and a steer. This makes it pretty unpredictable. But Butch's philosophy of steer wrestling is that there's a reason and an explanation for every move you make, and every move is teachable."

Those moves go something like this: 1. Release a steer from a chute; 2. Chase him on horseback; 3. Jump off the horse onto the steer, landing with your weight on the steer's shoulders; 4. Grab the steer's right horn in the crook of your right elbow; 5. Grab the steer's left horn with your left hand, holding the elbow high; 6. Lift your feet off the ground and fall on your butt, simultaneously turning the steer's head; 7. Allow the steer's momentum to pull you back to your feet, but continue to hold the steer's head down; 8. Place your butt against the steer's side and twist his head to the left; 9. Grab the steer's nose with your right hand and turn his head until he falls; 10. Do all this within about thirty yards and in as few seconds as you can. (During all this commotion, a second rider and horse are "hazing" the steer from his other side, trying to keep him running in a straight line.)

Since 1969, Butch has conducted at least two and as many as fourteen schools a year to teach men how to make these moves. Now, at forty-eight years old, he has turned over much of the teaching to twenty-four-year-old Rope, who in 1992 followed his father's training to win the Professional Rodeo Cowboys Association's overall Rookie of the Year Award.

It's Friday, the first session of the three-day school. Rope shows the men the proper way to deal with the Steer Saver. "You don't have to be big," he says. "A hundred and sixty pounds is enough weight to throw a five hundred-pound steer if it's applied in the right place. Where's a steer's head going to go with 160 pounds on it? Down. But if we stick our feet in the ground, how much of the 160 pounds is on the steer? Very little. You can go anywhere in the world but here to learn how to bulldog, and everybody will tell you to do what? To stay on your feet, stay on your feet, stay on your feet. But if you're going to learn this method of bulldogging, you've got to learn how to fall on your butt."

With the Steer Saver he shows them how. He makes it look simple.

Butch, sitting on the arena fence, says, "If we started these boys out on steers, in thirty minutes they would be through for the day. They would be wore out. But starting them out on the Steer Saver, they should all be here Sunday night. We're going to have a guy with a sore ankle Sunday, a guy whose ribs are hurting, maybe a hurt shoulder and some sore spots. But generally speaking, we hurt very, very few. Since I started these schools in 1969, we've had only two broken legs, one broken arm, and knocked out only one boy."

Since this is the first session, most of the students aren't yet ready for the Sure Catch. They must learn to walk before they can ride. As the pickup tows the Steer Saver slowly around the arena, the students trudge silently behind it, taking turns at grabbing and twisting the fiberglass head. The machine simulates all the movements of a steer except the falling. Some of the men already understand the basics, some show a natural aptitude and are learning quickly, a few obviously are near hopeless. But no matter how ridiculous they look or how badly they fail, nobody laughs.

"I won't let them," Butch says. "I won't let anybody hurt somebody else's confidence. I've thrown people out of the arena for laughing."

Bulldogging was invented by a black cowboy named Bill
Pickett in the 1870s, when he was working on ranches in
the Brush Country of South Texas. Sometimes the brush
was so dense that roping was impossible, and the cowboys
would have to catch a cow by wrapping her tail around
the saddle horn or haphazardly wrestling her to the
ground by her horns. One day Mr. Pickett was having a
hard time with a particularly tough cow when he remembered seeing a cow dog bring an animal down by grabbing
her nose with his teeth. So Mr. Pickett twisted the cow's
head around, gripped her lip or nose with his own teeth,
and pulled her down.

This method of catching wild cattle in the brush was so
effective that Mr. Pickett began using it regularly, and
exhibiting his peculiar skill at various Texas stock yards.
Sometime in the 1880s he began performing at county
fairs, and, as his fame grew, he was booked by circuses and
Wild West shows and staged bulldogging exhibitions at
rodeos in which he was competing as a bronc and bull
rider. During his forty-year career as a performer, he toured
North and South America and Europe with the Miller
Brothers' famous 101 Ranch Wild West Show and
appeared in several motion pictures.

Many years after his death in 1932, he was inducted
into the National Cowboy Hall of Fame and the Pro Rodeo
Hall of Champions. A statue of him bulldogging a longhorn stands in front of the Cowtown Coliseum in the Fort
Worth Stock Yards where he often performed.

Mr. Pickett's popularity attracted imitators, of course,
and bulldogging eventually became a regular event in
rodeo competition. But few of the imitators were willing
or able to use his lip-biting technique to throw the animals. Most bulldoggers simply wrestled down the steer or
bull in any way they could devise at the moment. In the
1970s, when the rules of professional rodeo specified that

only steers, and no bulls, would be used in competition, the official name of the event became "steer wrestling."

"I started steer wrestling in 1957 or '58," says Ron Wilkinson. He's one of several rodeo hands who assist Butch and Rope with their schools. "And I had to learn the hard way. I got on a horse that had never been used for bulldogging, and a steer that had never been got down on. I had a guy hazing who had never hazed a steer before, and he was on a horse that had never hazed. I started from scratch. I started picking things up from other steer wrestlers, but I never had anyone who could sit down and explain every move to me: Practice doing this. Do that. This is why you keep your feet in front of you. This is why you keep your elbow up. This is how you get up off the ground. This is how you keep from getting hurt. This is when you want to go for the nose."

Then Butch Myers taught him the right way. "But by that time, I was too old."

Was he any good?

He laughs. "I don't remember. The older I get, it seems, the better I was."

Butch's system of bulldogging and the ways he and Rope now teach it to others have evolved together over the past twenty-five years.

"When I started with the schools, it frustrated me that I couldn't get the kids to do certain things just out there talking about it or by showing them on the steer," Butch says. "I couldn't get them to get down on the steer. So I built a stiff dummy and got them so they could catch that. But I still couldn't help them with what we call the 'curl' or the 'circle.' So I invented a dummy that would bend. I took movies on Super 8 film of people doing it the right way. I studied good runs real hard, because if you watch somebody doing something wrong, you'll start doing it wrong, too. You give your muscle memory bad vibes, bad images. But I burned up the film, running it back and forth. So about '82, I made my first video. Then when my kids were little, I turned off the cartoons, kicked in the video, and they watched it. Now, my little boy, Cash, who's fourteen now, is oriented to know where his body is supposed to be and what it's supposed to do. Any kid can do it. I think I could take any kid out of the city at eight or nine years old and start him with this process, and he would learn what his body needs to do. It's harder for some of these boys here, who have some experience, to change and do it right. They have their own wrong mental picture of what to do."

The wrestling style that he developed amounts to a kind of steer physics involving speed, weight, balance, and leverage, using the animal's weight against itself. A kind of man-vs.-bovine judo. "Our total system is *our* system," Butch says. "I developed it by studying the people who were better than me. That's how you get better, by studying the people who are beating you."

He has had some unusual students over the years, such as a weight lifter from Las Vegas, who could pick up a steer, but couldn't figure out how to wrestle one to the ground, and a corporate jet pilot from Norway, who had never even seen steer wrestling before. "It was really fun to teach somebody who had no earthly concept of what it was all about," Butch says. "But he was a good athlete. He picked it up real fast. He came to the school three times. The third time, he brought another Norwegian with him. But he never competed. I think that's a shame. To this day, I'm not sure he has ever seen a rodeo."

There are no exotics in the Madisonville class. All the students are average-looking cowboy types, ranging from seventeen to thirty-five years old. "The oldest guy I ever started was fifty-seven," Butch says. "He was from the East.

The youngest I ever want to start is fourteen, and I really don't encourage that. Fifteen or sixteen is better."

All the while he's talking, he's studying the boys' work on the Steer Saver. Now he sees something he doesn't like. He pounces with the fervor of an in-debt evangelist: "You're going to spend most of your life on your butt if you don't figure out that your butt has to go . . . where?"

Silence.

"Where's it got to go?"

Silence.

"Over your feet! If it goes over your feet, then what happens?"

Silence.

"You can stand up! If your butt *doesn't* go over your feet, what never happens?"

Silence.

"*You never get up!* Lots of guys bulldog their entire life on the ground, trying to *get up*! If you learn nothing else here, *learn this*!"

Then, resuming his interrupted conversation, he says, "I get a lot of kids whose dads I had in school. If I get any grandkids, I'm quitting."

By late morning, some students already have advanced to the Sure Catch. The four-wheel off-road vehicle roars about the arena, bearing a would-be bulldogger perched fourteen and one half hands high (the height of the perfect bulldogging horse) in the saddle attached to the wooden framework. On his bizarre mount he chases the Steer Saver, which is towed behind a pickup. He catches up, leans from the saddle, then falls onto what would be the shoulders of a real steer. But he fails to fall on his butt. This displeases Rope.

"We're not going to teach you how to be world champions in three days," Rope says. "We're going to teach you how to practice. Learning how to practice is how we end up learning how to bulldog, because *I'm* not going to be able to be your coach. *Dad* isn't going to be able to be your coach. *You're* going to have to be your coach. And when you go home, and a steer gets you down underneath him, you're going to have to be able to say to yourself: 'OK. Now what did I do wrong?'"

At 3:00 p.m. the machines are put away, and the students are introduced to real steers. They're Mexican cattle, called *corriente* — common, cheap, inferior — in their homeland. Hernán Cortés landed their ancestors on the eastern shore of Mexico, and their breed has been improved not at all in the past four hundred years. Their lean, lanky bodies and bony, homely faces betray their kinship to the old Texas longhorns, although their own horns aren't unusually long.

"They're tough, tough, tough cattle," Ron Wilkinson says. "They're tough little cattle from a tough country."

A student gets into the chute with a steer and gets a hold on his horns. When the gate opens, the steer and his would-be dogger take off together down the arena. Another student grabs the animal's tail and hangs on as a sort of brake. Some of these encounters turn into wrestling matches, often with the steer on top.

Jim Wilton, another ex-student of Butch's, who has come down from Toronto to help with the school, hollers Canadian-accented encouragement to the boys.

Why does a fellow willingly submit himself to this sort of ruction?

Jim grins. "You'd think a lot of them would say, 'Naw, this isn't for me,' but once you try it, it's hard to keep from doing it. I would say conservatively that 75 percent of the guys at this school will keep going. It's the macho event of the rodeo, you see. The big guys, the guys who are too big to ride bucking horses and bulls, they do well in it. And even if you lose, you get to go to the dance with mud on your clothes."

Rope is a patient teacher. He concentrates his attention on each student and vividly explains what he's doing wrong. He remembers what each one has done earlier in the day, and addresses each by name without having to consult notes. By 5:00 p.m. his charges are filthy and dragging, but Rope sends them back to the Steer Saver for more practice. He rides on the tailgate of the pickup, closely watching each take his last exhausted turn.

"They'll be better in the morning than they are now," Butch says. "They improve overnight. I've never figured out how. They'll go in tonight and they'll take a shower and eat and sit on the bed, and they'll talk. And they'll come in tomorrow, and we'll warm them up a little bit, and they'll all do better."

Saturday morning, everybody's wearing clean shirts and jeans. Several of the young men are inserting a pinch of Skoal or Copenhagen between cheek and gum. Rope asks: "Is anybody sore?"

Silence.

They resume their crazy game, chasing the Steer Saver around the arena on the Sure Catch. The students are more talkative today, though not much.

"Morning."

"Morning."

"How's it going?"

"Pretty good."

"You done bulldogging before?"

"Yeah. But I'm used to a whole different style, you know. When I get hold of the head, I just want to crank it in, and I'm getting the hell beat out of me. But it's going OK. Maybe I can come to a happy medium between the two styles, know what I mean? It's a good school."

He's Tim Moorhead. He drove eleven hours from Montgomery, Alabama, to attend the school. He says he has thrown steers in practice, but hasn't yet competed in a rodeo. "I was running with a PRC [professional rodeo cowboy] named Terry Kelly for a while. He got me interested. I didn't touch my first steer until last year. At thirty years old. I went to another school in Alabama, and that was brutal. Oooh, man! That was steer-wrestling boot camp there. They started out with fifteen students and wound up with six on Sunday. I was black and blue all up my legs. I had a steer horn rip my pants and cut my leg. I got kicked right here. I had a big cut over here. I was bleeding. I went through hell. I didn't get that kind of brutal treatment in the Marine Corps."

"Why do you want to do this?"

"I just got bored. I grew up playing football from the time I was seven years old, then I went into the Marines. I missed the physical contact. I've had two lower-back surgeries. I've broken just about every major bone in my body. But I can't stay away from something like this, know what I mean? I got to running with Terry, and he asked me if I wanted to throw a few on the ground, and I just loved it. The first time that steer hit the ground, I was hooked. And coming off the horse! That's like a high!"

Among bulldoggers, coming off the horse is called "going in the hole." Later on this day, some of the students will "go in the hole" for the first time in their lives. "A lot of these boys out here are scared," Tim says. "You can see a lot of bad crashes among beginners. But the ground doesn't hurt that bad."

He lights a cigarette. "You have to sort of like pain to do this. Plus the women. That's another point entirely. Women like anything that's physical, I think. Know what I mean?"

223

While the beginners continue to work with the Steer Saver and the Sure Catch, Rope divides the advanced students into teams of two to work with the steers again. When the first steer bursts from the chute and the guys grab him, Rope yells: "Yeah! Yeah! I like it! We're getting things done this morning!"

Butch was right. The boys *are* better than they were yesterday. "You thought I was fibbing to you yesterday, didn't you?" he says. "It's a little amazing."

Rope is bright-eyed and cheerful. "Get your elbow up and drop down to your butt one time for me, Pecos!" he yells, as Pecos is being steer-handled about the arena. "Good job! Good job! There you go!"

At the other end of the arena, Ron is supervising the work of the beginners on the Steer Saver. One of them jumps from the Sure Catch, misses the Steer Saver, and hits the ground on his shoulder. Ron runs to him.

"You OK?"

The boy jumps up. "Yep." He walks away and goes back to work.

"Ah, that thing called youth," Ron says.

After lunch, the school moves on to the acid test: bull-dogging from horseback. It's a different story entirely from everything they've done so far. When the steers and the horses leave their chutes, they'll be running thirty to thirty-five miles per hour. The boys must jump from the back of one to the back of the other.

The *corriente* steers run like coyotes, so fast that the first five or six riders can't "go in the hole."

"We either need slower cattle or faster horses," one of the students says. Finally, Steve Brady from Liberty, Mississippi, throws one, and a cheer goes up. But the next boy almost falls off the horse when it bolts from the chute. The boy's so busy trying to stay aboard that he can't begin to think about "going in the hole." Then he falls in front of the steer, and the steer runs over him.

Rope hollers: "You've got to tell me if you've never ridden a horse before! I can't tell that just by looking a you!"

The boy is slow getting up. He walks stoically back to the fence. Rope says: "Pardner, you didn't tell me you don't know how to ride. Riding is part of this bulldogging, OK?"

The boy nods.

By 2:15 p.m., more and more of the students are requiring help to get off the ground, and the steers are strutting about as if they're in charge. Some are bucking like jackrabbits. You can almost hear them thinking, "I'm *bad*! I'm *bad*!"

Some of the riders can't bring themselves to leave the horse and make a try for the steer. "We got to move out of that saddle, folks, from Point A to Point B!" Rope yells. "That's what it's all about!" Are you willing to make a commitment to me to drop in that hole and go from Point A to Point B? You been kind of weakening on me, and right now's the time to get that squared around! On the next steer I want Jeff! You ready, Jeff?"

"I . . . I . . . I guess."

"I don't want to hear 'I guess.' Are you ready?"

"Yeah."

As the boys each throw their first steer, the only sign of pride that they allow themselves is a big grin. But there's much camaraderie among them now. They're no longer strangers. Rope grins, too. "Every guy today who was a virgin, I broke him in," he says.

At the end of the day, he names several whom he wants to appear at 9:30 Sunday morning to work some more on the Steer Saver. The others don't have to come until ten.

"Get some sleep," he tells them. "Don't stay out in the bars too late."

Two guys don't show up for the third day. "They had enough," Ron says. "It was not what they thought it was going to be. It was a little bit too much. A little bit scary. They make it through the Steer Saver and do OK going off of the Sure Catch, but when they back those horses in there and start running those live cattle, that's a whole different game. One boy yesterday, he just told me, 'Ronnie, I'm just scared to death.' And I said, 'Well, let me tell you something. Nobody here is going to *make* you get down. And if you don't like it, if you don't want to, you just get a good night's sleep and see how you feel in the morning. If you decide you want to run cattle in the morning, come back.' But he didn't show up."

A third student's back is hurting too much for him to continue. But the others are on horseback. Several show marked improvement, but by 2:30, some haven't yet brought themselves to "go in the hole."

Tim Moorhead, who has had the two back surgeries, goes, but misses his steer. He lands on his head and turns a flip. He doesn't get up. He lies very still. Several of the guys group around him, asking questions. Finally, he rises and walks over to the stands and sits down. The others applaud in relief.

"How you doing?"

"All right, I guess."

"Did you hurt your back?"

"Yeah. Upper back, though. Right between the shoulder blades."

"You turned a flip out there."

"I did something. I sure didn't bulldog right, that's for sure. Man. It felt like a dream when I was first laying out there."

"Can I get you anything?"

"No, sir. I'm fine. Thanks." He sighs. "Oh. My back hurts. Damn. Wooo! I feel kind of disoriented. I've got to drive home tonight. That's going to be a looong eleven hours. I hope it's just the muscles. I can't stand another surgery. I've broken every bone in my body. Oh! Damn! I'm in pain! I think I'm done for the day. But I'll be back. I ain't going to quit. That's what it's all about, you know? It was my fault totally. I didn't come out of the saddle the way I was supposed to. Man, I'm going to be sore tomorrow. Damn it! Wooo!"

"You got a right to hurt, I tell you."

"I did it the wrong way, you know? I don't think I'll do it wrong again. Oh. Man. I wish I was home right now. I've got to drive eleven hours." He gets up. "I'm going to walk this off, sir. And have myself a cigarette."

As the afternoon wears on, the weariness of the students and the horses and the Mexican cattle begins to show. Rope decides it's time to shut down. "Everybody wants to go more," he says, "but everybody's so tired that their bodies can't take any more."

Tim Moorland pleads for one more try. Rope reluctantly assigns him the next-to-last steer of the school. It's a good steer, and Tim gets a good ride and a good haze, but he doesn't "go into the hole."

Should he have gone?

"Maybe," Ron says. "But he had a lot on his mind."

"Go and do good," Rope tells his students. "Take care of yourselves. And practice, practice, practice right."

One by one, the young men solemnly shake his hand, then walk stiffly, some limping, to their pickups and vans for the long drive home. They'll meet again, "on down the road," as rodeo hands say. Some of them will, anyway.

June 1994

Almost every little town in Texas, it seems, throws a party
sometime during the year to celebrate some local glory. One of
the reasons, of course, is to raise money for civic clubs, schools,
churches, or other doers of good works. Another reason is just to
have a good time.

I love these small-town festivals and the sense of community
I feel when I attend them. They make me think that
humankind were meant to live in small towns, and that big
cities are a huge mistake.

A Time to Reap

Cheerleaders shiver in the bright morning chill, mothers herd excited children to their places on the floats, Miss
Teen Texas arrives in a stretch limousine, waving, waving.
A white kitten with black ears saunters down the street,
pauses, glances incuriously at the hullabaloo, then continues on toward the courthouse.

At last the drum major's whistle shrills, the Brownfield
High School band steps out, its music golden as the
October morning, and the big parade is on its way.

"It's the cotton," says Sunny Martinez, who's taping a
hand-lettered sign to the door of his 1954 Chevy pickup.
"This is our way of celebrating the cotton harvest."

"Vote for Sunny's Ugliest Truck," his sign says. His truck *is* ugly. An unclassifiable green in color, not washed or waxed for forty years. "But it still runs beautiful," he says.

Mr. Martinez and his truck are waiting in line, waiting their turn to join the parade. If noise and confusion are a gauge, half the ninety-five hundred residents of this West Texas town, it seems, will march down the street. But a big crowd is standing along the route down Broadway, too, waiting to cheer. "Isn't it a beautiful day?" Mr. Martinez says.

He has lived in Brownfield forty of his sixty years. "Brownfield is getting better and better," he says. "Brownfield is better than any other town I have surveyed."

Everything has turned out beautiful, it seems, for the Brownfield Harvest Festival and Terry County Fair, one of dozens of such festivals that Texans have thrown throughout October, celebrating the harvest of everything from peanuts in Aubrey and Whitesboro and Grapeland to yams in Gilmer and rice in Winnie and Katy and Bay City. In Cameron, they celebrate pumpkins. In Center, poultry.

In Brownfield and throughout the Texas South Plains — the largest agricultural area in one of the largest agricultural states — it's cotton that's celebrated, as Mr. Martinez says. Although the town received its name from an early settler, it could as easily have been named for the flat brown fields that surround it to the horizon and beyond, full of cotton ready for the picker. And grain sorghum. Also cattle. Corn. And, yes, peanuts. But mainly cotton, the region's big cash crop.

"The Fabulous Fifties" is the theme of this year's whoop-de-do, and most of the float-builders have come up with pretty much the same idea — the old malt shop with soda fountain and jukebox playing do-wop songs. On each, smiling, waving, is one of the candidates for harvest

queen: Patricia Thomas, sponsored by the Optimist Club;
Stacy Flores, by Amigos Travajando Unidos; Cara Burran,
by the Noon Lions; Misty Day, by the Evening Lions; April
Moore, by Rotary.

Interspersed among the floats are pickup loads of cheerleaders, trailers full of 4-H Clubbers, Girl Scouts, the trucks
of the Brownfield Electric Department and the Fire
Department, cop cars with sirens wailing, fancy motorcy-
cles, the latest thing in cotton pickers, the district governor of the Lions, beautifully restored Fords and Chevys
driven by members of the Nifty Fifties Car Club and the
Lubbock Mustang Club, Sunny Martinez's ugly truck, a
few horseback riders, and enough tractors for an Aggie
funeral procession.

"Our festival is pretty much your typical homemade
small-town affair," says Rodney Keeton, president of the
Chamber of Commerce. "Everybody in the community
pitches in. Everybody comes. Everybody has a good time."

The parade leads the crowd down to Coleman Park, just
beyond the fringe of downtown, where all the civic and
church groups of Brownfield have set up booths — nearly
one hundred of them — to sell homemade food and soft
drinks (no beer, Terry being a dry county), crafts, and the
chance to play games and win prizes.

The booths surround the American Legion
Amphitheater, where a stream of local singers — both solo
and in groups — takes the stage throughout the day. Some
are professional in a small way, some semipro, most thoroughly amateur, their earnestness compensating for lack
of finesse.

"About two weeks before, people start calling and
telling us they want to entertain," says Ann Hearn, festival
chairwoman and entertainment coordinator. "Everybody
just likes to show off their talent. A lot of them don't get
an opportunity to do that very often."

Across the way and up the hill at the National Guard Armory, the Terry County Fair — a separate but related event — is under way.

"The Harvest Festival is one of the big fund-raisers every year for the service clubs and the Chamber of Commerce," says Greg Dellinger, president of the Terry County Fair Association. "We tie the fair in with it. They started the fair in 1904, and when World War II came around in the '40s, they shut it down for a while, and it stayed shut down until about 1973. Then they started it up again, and it's been going strong ever since."

In the huge, barnlike building, large tables are laden with more than three thousand entries in baking, canning, quilting, arts and crafts, floral arrangements, and antiques. Samples of all the winning crops of Terry County are on display: cotton, several kinds of beans, hay, pumpkins, walnuts, peanuts, pecans, peas, cantaloupes, cucumbers, honeydew melons, watermelons, okra, onions, jalapeno and bell peppers, tomatoes, turnips.

More than twelve hundred ribbons were awarded this year. "It's for everybody in the county," Mr. Dellinger says. "We're an agricultural community, and this is a celebration of what we do. Every year, it seems to get bigger and bigger."

Except for an annual five hundred dollar grant from the Terry County Commissioners Court, the fair is self-supporting. "It doesn't hurt that the staff sergeant in charge of this building happened to go to high school with my son," Mr. Dellinger says.

Outside, the antique tractor pull — an event added to the fair just last year — is beginning. One by one, the old tractors — some of them nearly sixty years old, many as beautifully restored as the old Fords and Chevys in the parade — are hitched to a weighted sled. As the tractor pulls the sled, the huge weight slowly shifts forward, making the sled harder and harder to pull until the tractor can go no farther. The tractor in each class that pulls the sled farthest is the winner. The audience is almost entirely men and teen-age boys, clad in gimme caps and jeans, admiring the old machines as some men admire fine horses.

On the other side of the armory, at the pet show, the crowd is smaller, almost entirely women and small children.

"You never know how many pets will show up," says Edreann Jones, one of the fair volunteers. "Sometimes we only have two. We had a dog and a turkey one year."

This year, five dogs and a goat are entered. Every one is awarded a blue ribbon.

Peanut, the goat, wins "most original pet"; Princess, a Chihuahua, is "shiniest pet"; Coco, a scruffy puppy with "mutt" written all over him, wins "friendliest pet"; Noel, a toy dachshund, is "longest pet"; Daisy and Perky, toy poodles, are "fluffiest" and "curliest" pets respectively.

The Fowler children — Stephanie, Louis, and Jordan — smother Coco with hugs. Coco, as the "friendliest" pet should, turns into one big wag from nose to tail.

"He's two months old," says Leslie, the Fowler mother. "We got him from the SPCA. He's going to be a fine dog."

As the afternoon shadows lengthen, kids get cranky, mothers herd them home for naps, crafts exhibitors start packing their unsold wares, food booths run out of things. The Harvest Festival is winding down. But one last duty remains: The queen must be crowned.

Since April, when the civic clubs named them candidates, the five girls have looked forward to this moment. They've performed in a talent show. They've helped build, then ridden on, their floats. They and their families and sponsors have sold tickets relentlessly.

Now they've marched to the stage dressed in beautiful gowns and new hairdos, escorted by bathed and curried boyfriends. And the winner is ...

Cara Burran, sponsored by the Noon Lions.

Miss Burran puts hands to face in the traditional I-can't-believe-it's-me way. Rodney Keeton places the crown on her head. Snapshot cameras flash. Camcorders turn. The other contestants continue smiling, some through tears.

"She worked so hard," says Gail Burran, the queen's mother. "The club worked so hard. We worked on the float daily for a month. The whole town pulled together. That's how Brownfield is."

October 1994

From time immemorial, people have believed that water can cure whatever ails you — if it smells and tastes foul enough and deals in a purgative way with your bowels. In recent times, the regulations of the Federal Food and Drug Administration have dampened the enthusiasm of this belief in this country, but it still has its adherents.

In the past, Texas was blessed with a number of mineral water health spas, but none other as magnificent as Mineral Wells, which now stands as a monument to a wacky time in America's medical history.

Crazy Water Days

This is the story as they still tell it around Mineral Wells:

It all started in 1877, when James Lynch sold his farm near Denison, hitched a team of oxen to his wagon, and headed west with his wife, Armanda, their nine kids, and fifty head of livestock. They were in search of a higher and drier clime because the whole family, the story goes, was feeling poorly. Tired, listless, feverish. Kind of malarial, you know. No spizerinctum at all. Armanda's rheumatism had been acting up something fierce. Sometimes she couldn't raise her hands to her head. And James was nigh as rheumatic as Armanda, stiff and creaky even for a man of his age, which was fifty, and way too skinny.

Leaving behind the dank, heavy air of the Red River bottoms seemed the thing to do. Go west to some unknown spot where the air was drier, where a body's joints could function with greater ease and the kids could grow up strong.

They wandered out beyond the Brazos River with no apparent destination in mind, turned back eastward when they heard rumors of Comanche raiders, had one ox collapse and die after a rough recrossing of the Brazos, had the other ox get struck by lightning while Mr. Lynch and his boys were skinning the first one, and wound up in a pretty little valley in the hills of Palo Pinto County on Christmas Eve.

They built a fire, cooked their Yuletide dinner, and decided they liked the place. The ground looked fertile. There was plenty of wood about. The scenery was nice. Besides, the rigors of their journey were debilitating the ailing Armanda and the remaining oxen. So for $240, Mr. Lynch bought eighty acres from the Franco-Texan Land Co., which owned a big swatch of that part of Texas, and settled down.

Trouble was, the Lynch place didn't have any water on it. Mr. Lynch and his boys dug down forty-one feet and still didn't find any, so they had to haul water from the Brazos, four miles away.

Then in July of 1880, a fellow named Johnny Adams was traveling through the country with a well-drilling outfit. Mr. Lynch traded him a yoke of oxen to drill a well. One of the Lynch boys, Charley, who was about eighteen at the time, claimed many years later that he was the first to draw a bucket of water from it.

"It tasted funny and everybody was afraid to drink much of it, because they thought it might be poison,"

236

Charley would tell a historian. "But after sampling, we found it did not harm us. Mother was suffering from rheumatism, and after drinking the water for some time she was not bothered with it anymore."

The Lynch children, following their mother's example, drank the water and perked up. And father James, reluctant at first, finally joined in the imbibitions, got rid of his rheumatism, and started putting on weight.

As news of the rejuvenated Lynch family spread across the countryside, neighbors began arriving to try the water for their own ailments. Within a month, strangers were showing up, too, and were more than willing to pay the nickel a quart that Mr. Lynch now was charging for the water.

"There are several hundred people there for the benefit of their health," J.H. Baker of Palo Pinto wrote in his diary a few weeks after Charley raised the first bucket. Mr. Baker had sent his own wife and children to the well. In February 1881, they were still there, living in a tent, apparently growing healthier by the day. During one of his periodic visits with them Mr. Baker wrote, "It seems that the waters here are performing wonderful cures of cancer, neuralgia, nervousness, rheumatism, and other various ills that the human flesh is heir to."

Soon a town was growing up. James Lynch had taken to calling himself "Judge" and would be its first mayor. The town would acquire a name: Mineral Wells.

"Selling water! Whoa! What a business it was!" says Ron Walker, the present owner of the Crazy Well and the Crazy Hotel in the city that embraces the word "crazy" with pride.

Uncle Billy Wiggins was the one who drilled the Crazy Well at what's now the corner of First avenue and Fourth street. That was in 1881. He was among the first of the entrepreneurs who flocked to Mineral Wells after the Lynches and bought land and drilled, hoping to strike miracle water. Uncle Billy did.

How his well got its name depends on whom you ask. The simplest version says a woman suffering with a "nervous breakdown" came to the well. She hung around for weeks, imbibing copious amounts of the elixir, resting under the shade trees. The pupils at the nearby school took to calling her the "crazy woman," and when she finally departed, apparently whole and healthy again, Uncle Billy's well became known as the "Crazy Woman Well," and then simply as the "Crazy Well." It's the well that made Mineral Wells worldwide famous.

It's still there, under a steel plate that covers a square hole in the sidewalk near the Crazy Hotel. Asked nicely, its owner, Mr. Walker, will raise the plate and let you look at it. "There it is," he says. "First it was just a hole in the ground, then they built a pavilion, then they built the first hotel, which burned down, and then they built this hotel, which is fireproof. And everything else just grew up around the water in this well. Bathing in it, drinking it, rubbing it."

The "crazy woman" might have been "cured" by the substantial amount of lithium contained in the water of the Crazy Well. The chemical, which was found in several but not all the one hundred or so wells that eventually were drilled in Mineral Wells, is used even today to regulate the moods of manic-depressive patients.

Hundreds others who came to Mineral Wells in a sickly condition testified that they were cured of cancer, rheumatism, arthritis, neuritis, addictions to alcohol and cocaine and morphine, high and low blood pressure, goiter, St. Vitus' dance, gout, diabetes, Bright's disease, female complaints, various stomach disorders, dropsy, malaria, insomnia, and any number of other ailments, simply by drinking the water and bathing in it for periods of weeks or months. And, in that prescientific age of medicine, the doctors who sent their patients to "take the waters" were equally lavish in their praise.

There was no scientific evidence that the chemicals most commonly found in the water — calcium, magnesium, and sulfates in the form of Glauber's and Epsom salts — were capable of working such wonders. But there's no denying that the Crazy Water, as it came to be called, and its competitor brands from other wells worked powerfully well as diuretics and laxatives.

An early ad for the Crazy Water Pavilion hawks various strengths of the stuff ranging from No. 1, the mildest, to No. 4, the most potent. Near the pavilion where the waters were served up to the puny stood a staircase of some one thousand wooden steps leading to the top of a hill. Many of the patients, after drinking a few glasses, would climb the stairs for their exercise.

The locals still swear that spectators could tell whether a patient had indulged in No. 1, 2, 3, or 4 water by noting how far up the stairway he got before having to turn around and run back down.

The pavilions — gazebo-like affairs built around the wells — became centers of social life as well as treatment centers. Chairs and tables were provided, so the patients could drink and visit in comfort. Sometimes they played dominoes or checkers or cards. The fancier pavilions even offered orchestra music and dancing. Bath houses, hotels, and rooming houses grew up around them.

By the 1910s and '20s, the socializing had become almost as important as the therapeutics, and folks were making a good living figuring out things for the patients to do between their drinking and bathing and restroom sessions. When a rich widower rancher wanted to meet a lonely widow, he was likely to come to Mineral Wells, for it was easy to meet people and strike up courtships there.

Widows knew this, too.

Those couples who were only moderately sickly could rent donkeys and ride them about the Palo Pinto hills and loll in romantic nooks among the rocks and trees. The less hearty or more sedate could ride a streetcar to Lake Pinto or Elmhurst Park for boating and picnicking. The little town of some 4,000 or 5,000 people was attracting 100,000 to 150,000 visitors a year, and most of them were staying a few weeks or several months at a time.

In 1925 a fire destroyed the Crazy Hotel, Mineral Wells' most famous landmark, dealing the town a discouraging blow. But a year later, Dallas financier Carr P. Collins — a fervent believer in Crazy Water's curative powers — and his brother Hal bought the well and the burned-out hotel and began construction of a new, million-dollar, two hundred-room, fireproof Crazy with a beautiful roof garden for dancing, a huge bath house and massage parlor in the basement, and a drinking pavilion featuring a row of doctors' offices and a long, elaborate, Moorish-looking bar at which patients could order a tall glass of No. 1, 2, 3, or 4.

"The doctors would prescribe the water," says Ron Walker. "They'd say, 'Take twelve twelve-ounce glasses of No. 3 a day.' It was a helluva deal. They were all in on selling the hype — the doctors, the Collins brothers, everybody."

For sufferers who were too far away to seek relief at the Crazy Hotel, or couldn't afford the trip, the Collins brothers had a factory that evaporated Crazy Water and packaged the mineral residue. Crazy Water Crystals were purveyed over drugstore counters throughout the country and several foreign realms, so that the puny could mix a spoonful of the crystals into a glass of ordinary water at home and enjoy the same blessed result as those who were bellying up to the Crazy's water bar.

"I heard that even back during the Depression the Collins Brothers were doing eleven million dollars in business a year from the hotel, the bath house and selling the water and the crystals," Mr. Walker says. "Eleven million dollars a year during the Depression!"

By the time the new Crazy opened in 1927, another, even larger hotel was under construction only a couple of blocks away. And it would be T.B. Baker, owner of the Baker Hotel in Dallas, the Gunter and the St. Anthony in San Antonio, and several other of Texas' finest hostelries, who would usher little Mineral Wells into its truly Golden Age.

Charles Pool is sitting on a counter stool at Murray's Grill, which he owns, looking through the plate-glass window at the Baker Hotel across the street. "People came from all over the world," he says. "Some of them would stay six, eight months, a year at a time, drinking that mineral water, taking those baths and massages. They said it really got them back on their feet. They said they would limp in and walk out."

Mr. Pool went to work at the Baker in 1949, when he was fifteen. He started as a hall boy, or janitor, then was promoted to bus boy, then waiter, then bartender, then cook. When he quit in 1970 he was manager of the hotel's food department.

"It has 450 rooms," he says, "but you'd have to make reservations six weeks ahead of time to get in. Once you were in there, you never had to leave. Anything you wanted was right there in that hotel."

The Baker, fourteen stories and almost as wide as it is high, looms over Mineral Wells like a cathedral over a European village. Even now that the population has

grown to some fifteen thousand, it's still the town's domi-
nant landmark, and in its heyday was the center of the
way of life that gave Mineral Wells its origin and reason
for being.

The hotel opened in 1929, two weeks after the Black
Friday crash of the stock market drove the country into
the Great Depression. But while most of the country was
suffering, Mineral Wells was enjoying not only prosperity,
but glamour.

The Collins brothers set up a radio station in the lobby
of the Crazy and broadcast live music and comedy daily
over the Texas Quality Network and weekly over the
nationwide NBC hookup, hawking their Crazy Water
Crystals and making the whole nation aware of Mineral
Wells and its amazing water.

"The Baker packaged its own brand of water crystals,
called Pronto-Lax. It was powerful stuff," says Vernon
Daniels, who worked at the Baker from 1935 until 1962
and was its general manager for the last ten years of his
stay. "But we didn't get into shipping it all over the United
States as the Crazy did. We didn't want to sell the water to
people in other places. We wanted them to come to the
Baker and drink it."

Well, come they did. The Baker quickly became an "in"
spot for the rich and famous to see and be seen in. "The
leading doctors were all in the Baker Hotel," Mr. Daniels
says, "and they had a great clientele from all over the
United States. People would come to the Baker, mostly on
the recommendation of their doctors back home, and they
all would stay at least a week — some for several weeks at
a time — and would drink the water. We had it flowing
through a fountain in the lobby, and they could have all
they wanted, and they would go up to the bath department on the second floor every day for their baths and
massages."

242

Will Rogers was a frequent visitor to the Baker. Tom Mix signed its register, too, and Clark Gable, Marlene Dietrich, Jack Dempsey, Helen Keller, Roy Rogers, Ronald Reagan, Gen. John J. Pershing, Pres. Franklin Roosevelt's son Elliot, Pres. Harry Truman's vice president, Alben Barkley, Sam Goldwyn, Lyndon Johnson, Sam Rayburn, Minnie Pearl, Judy Garland, Joan Blondell, Harpo Marx, *Our Gang's* Spanky McFarland, and even the Three Stooges. Charles Pool remembers serving breakfast to Wild Bill Elliott, the cowboy star, every morning. "He had a ranch out west of town here," Mr. Pool says, "but he lived at the hotel."

Most of the celebrities came by train from Hollywood and New York. "We picked them up at Millsap, nine miles from here," says Mr. Daniels. "That was our railroad station. We would send a car and drive them to the hotel. They were very ordinary people. So down-to-earth. They liked to sit around and talk, and they just mingled with the other guests."

The Baker had a social hostess who greeted them as they arrived. She would ask if they liked to play bridge or other card games, and would arrange for like-minded people to get together. There was bingo every night on the West Terrace, dancing in the ballroom, sunbathing in the garden and swimming in the large outdoor pool. The locals say the Baker was the second hotel in the United States to have a swimming pool.

"But people stayed for long periods of time," says Ninfa Daniels, Vernon's wife. "In a little town like Mineral Wells, where there's really nothing going on — we had one movie theater and that was it — what in the world did they do with themselves? But they never complained. And of course a lot of their time was taken up with their massages, their baths, their facials. And they loved sitting on the veranda. I can still see them, in their rocking chairs."

For twenty-five years, Jack Amlung and his Orchestra —
which had been hired away from the Crazy — played in
the lobby and ballroom and, later, in the hotel's swanky
Brazos Club. Sometimes entertainers would be hired from
outside as well. Some, like Paul Whiteman's orchestra,
already were famous. Others soon would be. A young
accordion player named Lawrence Welk, "whose English
was really atrocious," says Mrs. Daniels, played the Baker
when he was starting out. So did a young North Texas
State College student named Pat Boone and a young
dancer from Weatherford named Mary Martin.

For the less-affluent guests, the Baker offered a weekly
package plan that included a room, three meals a day, a
daily bath and massage, and all the mineral water the
guest could drink. "The baths consisted of steam heat or
dry heat, either one you wanted or both, the tub bath, a
massage and shower," says Mr. Daniels. "Other things, like
facials, were optional. In the late '30s, the package plan
was thirty-five dollars a week."

From the time it opened, the opulent Baker, built in the
Spanish Colonial Commercial style so popular in the '20s,
was the hub of the town's social life as well. "Everything
revolved around the hotel," Mrs. Daniels says. "I was so
surprised that so many, many people — I mean all the
ones that were invited — would not miss the big eggnog
party that the hotel management gave every year on
Christmas morning. You'd think they would want to stay
at home with their families on Christmas of all mornings,
but, listen, they all came. It was by invitation only, and
they wanted everyone to know that they were in the
'in' crowd. If you weren't there, people might think you
hadn't gotten an invitation. And they were all decked out
to the hilt with furs and hats and gloves. The whole
shebang."

244

"But the baths were what the Baker was all about," says Mr. Daniels. "They really did seem to help the health of the people who came. I've often wondered if it wasn't the rest and relaxation that helped them more than anything else. You take it easy and get a massage every day, you're bound to feel better. But they just *knew* the water did it."

"Oh, yes," Mrs. Daniels says. "They were so positive. They would say, 'I could hardly walk when I got here. Now look at me!'"

"The water didn't taste very good," Mr. Daniels says. "But everybody loved it. I guess if it had tasted real good, it wouldn't have had the medicinal value."

As early as 1933, the federal Food and Drug Administration had been hounding the Collins brothers about the medical claims they made in their advertising of Crazy Water Crystals. And as Franklin Roosevelt's administration stepped up its efforts to reform and regulate the over-the-counter medicine business, the promises that the Collinses made on their packages became more and more modest.

"The crystals were simply a mild laxative," says A.F. Weaver, Jr., whose father had been the auditor and purchasing agent for the Collins brothers and later bought the Crazy Water Crystals side of their business.

The younger Weaver peddled the crystals in the Houston and New Orleans markets for his father, pulling up to the drugstores in a Mercury with a big Crazy Water Crystals box on its roof. When Mr. Weaver, Sr. died in 1949, his widow and son sold their stock and got out of the business.

"A lot of people came here to drink their way to health, and I think a lot of them did," Mr. Weaver says. "I've seen people brought in on stretchers from ambulances. I've seen them come in on crutches, and later you'd see them walking around just fine. They'd drink the water with the mild laxative and take the baths and get the rubdowns and work their bodies and walk — things we should do in this day and time — and they'd get cured. Then the war came along, and there went the mineral water."

World War II would change Mineral Wells more than it realized at the time. In 1941 the Army opened Camp Wolters — which later was renamed Fort Wolters — as an infantry replacement training center, outside the town. When, after Pearl Harbor, the rationing of gasoline made travel for pleasure or even for health impossible for most Americans, the Crazy and the Baker became dependent on the GIs and their families to keep their doors open. But the new customers had neither the money nor the leisure to indulge in mineral baths and massages. And most of the celebrities who visited Mineral Wells during the war years came to entertain the troops. They didn't stay long.

What really ended the town's Golden Age, however, were the medical advances made during the war. "Suddenly you had sulfa drugs and penicillin and other antibiotics, and you didn't see the doctors recommending that their patients go to health resorts," Mr. Daniels says. "They kept them home and gave them shots. So for ten bucks or whatever, the patient could get well without coming and spending a week at the Baker."

After the magic of the waters faded, the Crazy, and especially the Baker, looked to small conventions and non-medicinal vacation packages for their survival. "The Democratic State Convention was held at the Baker several times," Mr. Daniels says, "and so was the Republican State Convention of 1952, where the groundswell to nominate Eisenhower is said to have begun. And we would promote such packages as the Indian Summer Vacation between Labor Day and Thanksgiving. We would have as many as one hundred rooms every week on that package. It was very popular, mostly with prominent Dallas and Fort Worth people — the Murchisons, the Hunt family, the Bass family from Fort Worth, Sid Richardson, their uncle. They all came for baths and massages. The bath department always remained busy. The mineral water was the thing that dropped off in demand. People didn't drink it as much anymore. They switched to scotch and soda."

In the 1950s, the Baker advertised its baths both as a remedy — for arthritis, rheumatism, neuritis, bursitis, high blood pressure, and the like — and as a general aid in "promoting health, vitality and a more attractive personality." Its ads suggested that a bath and a massage were just the ticket for the overworked, stressed-out executive, and about 80 percent of the Baker's nonconvention business was Dallas and Fort Worth businessmen and their families just getting away from the city for a few days. In those days when liquor-by-the-drink was illegal in Texas, a big attraction of the Baker was the private Brazos Club, where guests' room keys made them members and the Texas rich could dress to the nines and have a good martini in an elegant, pink-mirrored setting.

"Back in the early days of the Dallas Cowboys, when they would black out the games on TV in Dallas, people would rent rooms at the Baker to watch them on Channel 6, out of Wichita Falls," remembers Charles Pool, who was in charge of the hotel's food department in those days. "They would just pile over here. It was one big party."

But as jet travel made more distant and exotic resorts quickly accessible to the Baker's customers, Earl Baker, nephew of the founder and the hotel's owner, saw the handwriting on the wall for his big-time hotel in the small-time town. He told his manager, Vernon Daniels, that he intended to get rid of the Baker when he turned seventy. In 1963, when he was about to reach that milestone and had found no buyer, he closed its doors.

A group of Mineral Wells businessmen bought the Baker in 1965 and reopened it. But the magic was gone. And when the government shut down Fort Wolters, where it had been training helicopter pilots during the Vietnam War, the hotel's fate was sealed. The doors shut again in 1972.

Since then, a number of dreamers have bought the building and announced grandiose plans, the most interesting being a scheme to turn the Baker into a vertical theme park, with a different era of Texas history portrayed on each floor. But none of the dreams has come true.

"It hurts to look at it now, knowing how it once was," says Charles Pool, gazing out the window of his diner. "They say they can't tear it down, it's built so strong. I wish they could. Why leave it? Its time is over."

Motorists on U.S. 180 can see the Baker looming for eight miles before they reach Mineral Wells. So it's natural that, when they reach the town, many of them get out of their cars, climb the wide flight of steps to the main entrance, cup their hands around their eyes and peer through the windows. "What was this?" they ask. "Why is it here?"

Jayne Catrett keeps the keys for the present owner, Harlow Jones, who lives in Arizona. And she pays the bills and collects the rent for the three small shops that remain in business on the hotel's street level. If she happens to be around when the curious are poking around, she'll unlock the door and let them have a look at the lobby, which she and another volunteer, Margaret Maxwell, keep clean for the occasional wedding receptions or town meetings that still are held there. And she opened it to the public during the town's annual Crazy Festival last June. "I just do it because I enjoy it," she says.

If Ms. Catrett's fifteen-year-old grandson, Kyle Charles, happens to be around, he'll guide a tour for two dollars a person. He knows how to operate the old elevators, and zooms the visitors up to the old rooftop ballroom, where traces of glitter still stick to the plaster behind the bandstand where Jack Amlung and his Orchestra used to play. The wooden dance floor is buckling. Water is dripping through the ceiling from last night's rain. A dead pigeon lies near a broken window.

In the Baker Suite, where the owner stayed, Kyle conducts the visitors through the three bedrooms and five baths, the living room with its hand-painted pillars and ceiling, its fireplace and Moorish arches, and the study with its bookcases, all empty now. He points out the secret door in the back of the china closet, which hides the compartment where Mr. Baker stashed his liquor during the Prohibition era.

And on the second floor, in the fabled white-tiled bath house, moving among the rows of empty doctors' offices and the bathtub and shower stalls, and the massage stalls with their thick marble slabs, he retells the old Mineral Wells story.

But all is empty and dusty and ruined beyond hope. It takes a powerful imagination to place Marlene Dietrich or Clark Gable or Judy Garland in such a place.

The Baker's smaller rival, the Crazy, has fared better. It's now the Crazy Water Retirement Hotel, a clean, well-lighted place where some 180 senior citizens are living pleasantly. It's owned and run by Ron Walker, a Dallas stockbroker who got tired of the rat race.

"When I saw the ad in the *Wall Street Journal* that this place was for sale, I had never been this far west," says Mr. Walker, who grew up in Boston. "I had never heard of this town. I didn't know why anybody would call a hotel `the Crazy.' But I kept hearing the stories and reading the

249

books, and I said, 'Holy cow, man! This is history!' And
I've decided that there's a lot worse things in the world I
could do than own an old folks' home in Mineral Wells,
Texas. This is a retirement town now. Half of Palo Pinto
County is retired folks."

A few blocks away, Charles Hickey is filling a water jug
for one of his customers in the last of the great water
pavilions. The Famous Water Co., which Mr. Hickey owns,
is the only place in Mineral Wells where visitors still can
sample the liquid that made the town renowned throughout the world, and can buy a jugful to take home.

Mr. Hickey, who keeps the place open only three days a
week, says most of his customers are locals and people
from Dallas and Fort Worth, but a few from as far away as
Michigan still order Famous Water through the mail. They
pay more in postage than they do for the water, which
sells for eighty-five cents a gallon, but they don't seem to
mind, he says. You can't get water like Famous Water just
anywhere.

"I've got a customer that comes in, he was using a
walker," Mr. Hickey says. "And he started drinking the
mineral water, and he went from a walker to a cane. Now
he doesn't use anything. He swears he'd be dead without
this mineral water. And I have another customer who
swears that this water solved his kidney problems. He
doesn't take any medications anymore. And I myself drink
the mineral water all the time because it stopped my
heartburn and acid indigestion. I was eating Rolaids every
day. I just carried a package with me. I've always had a bad
stomach. Then I got into this business, and I said, 'This is
supposed to be great stuff. I'll just try it.' So I just laid the
Rolaids down and started drinking the mineral water. I
probably drink a gallon a day. No more acid indigestion.
No more upset stomach."

Somewhere the ghosts of Judge Lynch and the crazy woman must be smiling. Or laughing.

November 1992

One of the great privileges of my life was getting to watch
Nolan Ryan pitch for the Texas Rangers during the last years of
his amazing career. That career didn't end as gloriously as
Ryan and his fans hoped. His last season was cut short by
injuries.

Nevertheless, he is one for the ages — an immortal hero of
America's best game. We'll not see his likes again.

How He Played the Game

The largest crowd ever to witness a baseball game in
Texas assembled in the Houston Astrodome on the
evening of April 3, 1993. And it was only an exhibition
game.

A record 53,557 fans streamed in, all that the stadium
could hold. But it wasn't the Astros that drew them there.
They went less to see one team win than to see one man
play. They had come to pay tribute to the pitcher of the
opposing team, Nolan Ryan of the Texas Rangers.

In a time when so many Americans consider winning to
be the only thing in sports that matters, Ryan is living tes-
timony to the truth in a paraphrase of Grantland Rice's

trite old verse: What Nolan Ryan will be remembered for is not whether he won or lost, but how he played the game.

Ryan. A former Astro. For many Houston fans, *the* Astro, the man who lifted the team out of the mediocrity in which it had wallowed during most of its history. He was their hometown boy, born and raised just down the road in the little town of Alvin. He and his wife Ruth, who was his high school sweetheart, still lived in Alvin. They reared two sons and a daughter there, and Ryan taught the children the proper way to raise calves, as he had learned in Alvin when he was young.

Ryan loved playing in Houston for "his" people. He pitched there for nine seasons with never a thought of leaving. Even back then, everybody knew he was headed for the Hall of Fame. What team would allow such a player to get away? But at the end of the 1988 season, during which Ryan won twelve games and turned forty-one years old, his contract expired. Astros owner John McMullen, apparently thinking his star pitcher was over the hill, offered to re-sign Nolan, but at a reduced salary.

This was seen — by Houston fans, at least — as the dumbest contract move since the Red Sox traded Babe Ruth to the Yankees. Ryan, a free agent, immediately put himself on the market. He received better offers from three teams and chose the Texas Rangers, mainly because Arlington is the second-closest stadium to Alvin.

"Also," he told the press, "I'm a die-hard Texan."

Five years later, Ryan announced that the 1993 season would be his last. At age forty-six, older than any other active player in baseball, older than the president of the United States, he would hang up his glove and wait for an invitation to Cooperstown. But he would come to pitch in the Astrodome one last time.

Of the five thousand people who live in Alvin, three thousand were in the crowd that night.

The evening didn't turn out the way such evenings are supposed to. The hero pitched six innings, gave up ten hits and four runs, and struck out only one batter. He and the Rangers lost, 4-3. But the crowd gave him a standing ovation anyway.

That evening was an omen of Nolan Ryan's last year on the mound. In his first three outings of the regular season, he won only one game, then went on the disabled list for knee surgery. In his first inning after returning to the lineup, he gave up six runs, and two more before he was yanked from the game in the fourth. A few days later, he was on the disabled list again, this time with a hip injury. On Memorial Day, a few days before he was to return to the lineup, he cut his foot in a boating accident, took seven stitches and returned to the disabled list.

So it has gone. Ryan's last season won't go into the books as one of his best, or even as a good one. But it doesn't matter. Wherever he has made even a brief appearance on the mound, however good or bad his performance has been, the fans have risen to their feet to cheer him. And the mere rumor that he may pitch has been enough to pack old Arlington Stadium, where fathers admonish their sons, "Watch and remember. You'll never see the likes of him again."

The fathers are probably right. In a sport now populated with whining, self-absorbed millionaires with egos larger than California, Ryan reminds us of the players of another age — of Lou Gehrig, Joe DiMaggio, Jackie Robinson, Stan Musial, and Hank Aaron, who wore the mantles of greatness with dignity and grace. In an era when the stories of baseball games compete on the sports pages with accounts of athletes' addictions to drugs, alcohol, gambling, and greed, Ryan stands as the all-American boy grown into the all-American man. The shy, laid-back, small-town Texan who grew up dreaming of becoming a veterinarian just became one of history's greatest ballplayers instead.

His lifetime won-lost record won't be among the best on the plaques at Cooperstown. Neither will his earned run average. His detractors — there used to be many; they seem to have thinned out lately — claimed over the years that he's just an average pitcher with a good fastball and a career spent on average teams.

But the Hall of Fame has begun collecting Nolan Ryan memorabilia. And no one — not even his old detractors — believes he'll have to wait longer than the minimum five years to take his place among the immortals, even though the part about Ryan's teams is true.

In twenty-six years in the majors, he has pitched in the World Series only once, coming out of the bullpen to save the third game for the "Miracle Mets" of 1969, the high point of his third full season. After two more years with the Mets, he was traded to the California Angels. He labored for eight years before making the playoffs again. In 1980, he went to the Astros as the first one million dollar-per-year pitcher in baseball. He stayed for nine seasons and helped lead them into two playoffs, but never into a Series.

In December 1988, when McMullen drove Ryan to the Rangers, a team that never has appeared in a postseason game, he signed a single-year contract. Everyone thought he would play it out and retire. But every year, the Rangers were just good enough to keep alive the hope that the next year could be the one to drive North Texas crazy — their first playoff and maybe Ryan's second crack at the World Series.

He's the only member of the "Miracle Mets" still playing and one of the oldest men ever to play in the big leagues. He has endured to stay in the majors longer than any other player. But he hasn't spent these waning years of his career simply occupying an occasional spot in the Rangers' pitching rotation between ailments.

During his prime in Houston in 1981, Ryan pitched his fifth no-hitter, breaking Sandy Koufax's record of four. With the Rangers in 1990, at age forty-three, he pitched his sixth. At age forty-four, on May 1, 1991, he pitched his seventh, giving him three more no-hitters than Koufax and four more than Bob Feller, the only other pitcher to throw as many as three. Ryan's fastball averaged ninety-three miles per hour that night. He struck out sixteen batters.

Back in 1983, in Houston, Ryan broke Walter Johnson's ancient record of 3,508 strikeouts, a record that was expected never to be broken. Only two years later, he became the first pitcher to strike out four thousand batters. And on August 22, 1989, at Arlington Stadium, in the fifth inning against Oakland, Ryan threw a ninety-six-mile-per-hour fastball over the plate and fanned Rickey Henderson for his five thousandth — 864 more than any other pitcher's career total at the time.

Baseball Commissioner Bart Giamatti witnessed the event, calling it "one of the great achievements in the history of the game."

But what sticks in the mind about that night is what Ryan did after he fanned Henderson. He just gave a little pump with his fist and doffed his hat to the 42,369 screaming fans. After his teammates ran to the mound and shook his hand, after allowing only a minute and twenty-five seconds of roaring ovation, he raised his glove to the umpire and called for another ball. It was time to get back to work.

That's how he has played the game.

September 1993

Back in the 1950s, when I was a teen-age cub reporter for
The El Paso Times, *I was sent down to Ysleta to write a story about the dances the Tigua Indians were doing there. I didn't know anything about the Tiguas then, and I'm sure my story reflected my ignorance, but I enjoyed the dances.*

The Tigua community has changed a lot since those days, but it's still struggling to hang onto its identity, as it was then.

As of this writing, the Tiguas are fighting the State of Texas in the courts to assert their right to operate a gambling casino on their reservation.

Bloodline

Marty Silvas, war chief of the Tiguas, is in a warlike mood this morning. "There's no respect," he says. "There's no respect for the living or the dead. They keep it hush because they're afraid of losing their jobs. But the only thing they had to do is come up to us and tell us, 'Look. We found this and this. What do you want to do about it?'"

The previous evening, Mr. Silvas received a disturbing phone call. A Tigua had fallen into conversation with a security guard at a construction site just a couple of blocks from the tribe's administration building. The guard told the man that workers had uncovered human bones and pottery shards during their excavation.

"It's on land that used to belong to the tribe," Mr. Silvas says. "They found the parts of a spinal column, a shoulder blade, a femur, and a jawbone. But they didn't inform the tribe. They did not contact the tribe in any way. They wanted to keep it hush."

While he fumes, he waits for one of the tribe's lawyers to return his phone call. "I need to talk to them to see what we should do," he says, "whether we should get a court order or just go down there and stop this damn thing. If it were me, I would just go down there and stop the damn project by any means necessary. But we want to go through proper channels. These days, we have to go through the courts like everybody else. That's the only way to win battles nowadays."

Mr. Silvas is only thirty years old. Unlike his ancient predecessors, he isn't expected to lead his tribe into battle against its foes, but his duties still are important and heavy for one so young. The war chief of the Tiguas is the right-hand assistant of the *cacique*, the chief spiritual leader of the tribe. "I'm the keeper of tradition and cul-ture," Mr. Silvas says, "keeper of the sacred drum and the grandfathers. I guess you could say I'm the medicine man."

It's his job as keeper of the grandfathers that occupies him this morning. Someone knocks on his office door and hands him a plastic bag containing a shard of red pottery and a sliver of bone, which he removes from the bag and holds up to the light.

"This is the bone of a human being," he says. "Everybody in El Paso knows our people are buried around here. We even have an agreement with Fort Bliss that if the army takes remains out of the ground, we work with them to rebury them. Companies that build things around here know that our people are in this ground. It gets me very, very angry that people can take my grandfathers out of their graves and not even care about it."

His phone rings. It's the lawyer. After a brief conversation, Mr. Silvas hangs up and begins phoning the other members of the tribal council. They must meet right away, he tells them.

Soon a half-dozen men arrive together. They retire to the meeting room and shut the door. An hour later, they emerge and walk together toward the site of the desecrated grave. They're going to confront the construction crew.

A white visitor wants to go with them, but Mr. Silvas waves him back. "You can't come," he says. "This is tribal business."

Being a Tigua has never been easy. In 1680 a chief named Pope led the Pueblo tribes of northern New Mexico in a revolt against their Spanish conquerors. In a series of bloody battles, the badly outnumbered Spaniards retreated southward along the Rio Grande. On the way, 317 Tigua Indians from the pueblo of Isleta, near the present city of Albuquerque, joined them on their march. When the rebellious tribes finally stopped their pursuit, the weary refugees halted beside the river a few miles below the spot where it becomes the border between present-day Texas and Mexico.

They built a village, and in 1682 the Franciscan friars who had fled with them established a new mission for the Tiguas and called it La Misión de Corpus Christi de Ysleta del Sur, to distinguish it from Isleta del Norte, the home that they had left in New Mexico.

"We didn't want to be Christians," says Miguel Pedraza, a former governor and the present lieutenant governor of the tribe. "The Spaniards' attempt to force Christianity on us was what made the pueblos revolt against them. There was a time when our people were killed for speaking our language and dancing our dances, and even for the way they dressed. Our people were afraid to teach their children, thinking that their kids would be punished or killed by the Spanish missionaries." His ancestors accompanied the Spaniards on their march, he says, only because they were forced to.

Spanish records, on the other hand, say the Tiguas were Christian converts who voluntarily threw in their lot with the Spaniards.

In 1693, Diego de Vargas reconquered the northern pueblos. Some of the southern Tiguas returned to New Mexico and reoccupied the old Isleta pueblo, but most remained in the south. They had established farms and vineyards around the mission and made it their home, and the Franciscans allowed them to perform their ancient dances and religious rituals along with their new Catholicism.

"We went into the practice of Christianity, but not the way the Spaniards wanted us to," Mr. Pedraza says. "We fooled them when we accepted Christianity by having our own way of doing our dances in front of the churches. They thought we were practicing their religion, and at the same time we were having our own religion going on without them knowing it. They were happy and we were happy at the same time."

Despite attacks by Apaches and other hostile tribes, the mission and the village around it survived and eventually became the oldest settlement in the new state of Texas. In the nineteenth century, the newer village of Franklin, just upstream, would grow much faster and become the city of El Paso, but Ysleta remained an independent town until the 1950s, when El Paso annexed it.

For more than three hundred years, the Tiguas have lived beside the old mission that the Spaniards established.

262

But the geographical accident that put their pueblo in Texas instead of New Mexico or Mexico almost ended their existence as a tribe. In the 1860s, while the Civil War was raging, President Lincoln recognized the sovereignty of the pueblo tribes in New Mexico and presented the *cacique* of each tribe an engraved walking cane symbolizing that sovereignty. The canes are still prized by the pueblos and sometimes are displayed during their ceremonials. Mr. Lincoln's action also confirmed the tribes' titles to their lands and gave them the protection of the federal government.

But the Tiguas lived in Texas, a Confederate state. Their sovereignty wasn't recognized. And when Texas rejoined the Union after the war, nobody bothered to rectify the injustice. The Tiguas were swindled out of much of their land and lost more of it because of taxes they had no money to pay. Many of them married into the growing Hispanic population around them.

"We were a forgotten tribe," says Mr. Pedraza, who has lived all his sixty-three years in Ysleta.

Then in 1966, at the urging of El Paso attorney Tom Diamond and anthropologist Nicholas Houser, the Texas State Historical Survey Committee passed a resolution finally recognizing the Tiguas as a tribe. An act of the legislature the following year placed them under the care of the state Commission on Indian Affairs, which had been established in 1965. And in 1968, Congress passed Public Law 90-287, acknowledging that the Tiguas are, indeed, an Indian tribe in the eyes of the federal government.

The law declared that "the Indians now living in El Paso County, Texas, who are descendants of the Tiwa Indians of the Ysleta del Sur Pueblo, settling in Texas at Ysleta in 1682, shall from and after the ratification of this act be known and designated as the Tiwa Indians of Ysleta, Texas."

The remnants of their tribal lands — forty-seven acres amid El Paso's urban sprawl between Interstate 10 and the Rio Grande, and about twenty acres elsewhere — are now their tiny reservation. And the 1,463 people on the tribal membership roll — some of them, anyway — are trying desperately to preserve what is left of their ancient traditions and culture and are trying to recover what they can of what has been lost.

They also want to change the federal definition of what a Tigua is, and bring about a major change in the state that has been their inhospitable home for three centuries.

They want to build the first legal gambling casino in Texas.

"We have lost a lot of our tradition on account of we live in the city," Mr. Pedraza says. "But we still have our burial ceremony. We still do the same dances we did back before we came from Isleta, the same processions. We still elect our officers the same way. We still remain a pueblo without a constitution or bylaws. We still have the traditional way of voting for members of the council."

But the Tigua culture suffered during his lifetime, he says, because the tribe had to endure the worse of two worlds: The U.S. government didn't recognize them as a tribe, which deprived them of the federal benefits that went to other Indians, but at the same time, the non-Indian people they lived among thought of them as Indians and discriminated against them.

Years later, when Mr. Silvas — a much younger man — was growing up, the situation still hadn't improved much. "It was rough being an Indian," he says. "People didn't like you because you had long hair, because you followed your way, because you wanted to learn about your grandfathers and traditions. We were always being called witches because we followed our own way of prayer, because we pray different from the people surrounding us. We were called 'dirty Indians.'"

Elias Torrez, the Tiguas' thirty-four-year-old governor, also remembers some of his school friends treating him "differently" when they found out he's an Indian. "I went to Ysleta High School," he says. "The mascot there is an Indian. But when all of a sudden *real* Indians surfaced, problems occurred. There was a time when people didn't want to be Indians anymore. It wasn't cool, if I may use that word, to be an Indian."

During those years, many Tiguas intermarried with their Hispanic neighbors, and many claimed to be Hispanics themselves. "But now a lot of people want to be Indian," Governor Torrez says. "If we could bottle our Indianness and sell it, we would be rich."

Mr. Pedraza gets letters and phone calls from people all over the El Paso area who want to become members of the tribe. "*Everybody* wants to be part of it," he says. "They think we're rich or about to become rich, which is not the case. Nowadays, there are two kinds of Indians. We have our traditional Indians, and we have our program Indians. The traditional Indians are the ones who have always kept the traditions and the feasts and do all this work for the tribe during the year. The program Indians are those who are just interested in what kind of benefits they can get by being Indians. They want to exploit the tribe for what they can get out of it — medical attention, education, whatever. There's a little town called Tigua five or six miles from here, and some people believe that because they were born in that town they're members of this tribe. Some people think that because they went to Ysleta High School they're members of the tribe. They try all kinds of ways to get onto the tribal rolls. But our tribal rolls were closed in 1987."

Under federal law, in order to be a member of the tribe, one must be of at least one-eighth Tigua blood and a member of one of the families registered before the rolls were closed. Because they're such a small tribe, the one-eighth "blood quantum," as it's called, is becoming a problem for the Tiguas. Of the 1,463 people on the tribal rolls, only six — all of them women — are full-blood Tigua. Another 582 are one-eighth. The rest are in between. But only about eight hundred of the tribal members live in El Paso, and most of them are related.

"We can either marry our cousins, or we can marry outside the tribe," says Governor Torrez, whose blood quantum is one-eighth. "I think marrying cousins is dangerous. It could cause a lot of problems. But if we marry outside the tribe, the blood quantum of our children or grandchildren won't qualify them to be Tiguas. I myself am married to a non-Indian. My children's blood quantum is one-sixteenth. The government doesn't consider them members of the tribe. But Indian people amongst ourselves don't discriminate. We don't see each other as a quarter, an eighth, a full blood. We're all Indians. Period. Look at me. If you saw me in downtown El Paso, I would be just another Hispanic. But it's what we have in our hearts — the tradition that was planted in our hearts and in our souls and in our minds — that matters."

Blood-quantum qualifications vary from tribe to tribe among American Indians. Some large tribes require high quantums — as high as one-half blood — to encourage members to marry within the tribe. Other tribes require only a small amount of Indian blood to qualify. Each tribe's blood quantum has been determined through negotiations with the federal government, then made law through an act of Congress.

"Implementation of the blood quantum was done by the U.S. government as a means of getting rid of the

Indian people," says Mr. Pedraza. "Just like they tried to starve the people by killing the buffalo. The U.S. government gave us a blood quantum in order to diminish us."

The Tiguas' tribal council has petitioned Congress to reduce the blood-quantum requirement from one-eighth to one-sixteenth and to change the official name of the tribe from "Ysleta del Sur Pueblo" to "Tigua Indians of Texas," which is what they have always called themselves. They also request that "Tigua" become the official spelling of their name, rather than "Tiwa," as it is in the 1968 law.

Lowering the blood quantum would more than double the size of the tribe, but all the new Tiguas would be children or other relatives of present members.

"It's sad to have to tell a family, 'Yes, I can help you, ma'am, but not your husband or your children. They don't qualify,'" says Governor Torrez. "We don't tell them they're not Indians. We just say they don't qualify."

"Often the one-sixteenth knows more about tradition and follows his heart better than the full-blooded Indian," says Mr. Silvas. He's also one-eighth Tigua blood, and his children are one-sixteenth. "It all depends on the family you're in. I've lived here all my life. I've been dancing since I was four years old. I started singing when I was three. That's the reason I'm the war chief right now. Everything that is supposed to be learned, I learned it. I might have a low blood quantum, but in my heart, it don't get more Indian than I am. A young lady from our reservation has said, 'It's not the Indian blood that runs through our veins, it's the Indian in our hearts.' And nowadays that's all that matters."

Although Mr. Silvas' children aren't eligible for medical and other benefits that the federal government grants to Indians, they're being brought up Indian. "My son goes to Tigua language classes at school," he says. "And then he comes home and teaches me. In the old days, the older people would teach the kids. But now the kids teach the older people."

Whether or not Congress lowers the blood quantum, he says, the one-sixteenth people are true Tiguas, and the tribe has an obligation to them. That's why the Tiguas must build a casino.

The complex of pueblo-architecture buildings that the Tiguas have built on their tiny reservation includes a popular restaurant, a shop where Tigua-made Indian souvenirs are sold, outdoor ovens where delicious Tigua bread is baked for the restaurant and for sale to the public, and a courtyard where dancers entertain tourists during the summer. But the part of the reservation that draws the biggest crowds is a huge bingo hall with expensive carpets, brass rails, and chandeliers.

It looks too fancy to be a mere bingo parlor. And indeed, the Tiguas hope that someday soon it will become a full-fledged casino, offering blackjack, craps, slot machines, and any other diversion that a Las Vegas casino might offer.

Then, if business is good, the tribe hopes to build a Las Vegas-style entertainment center including a large casino and hotel, perhaps at the intersection of Interstate 10 and Avenue of the Americas, a major thoroughfare between El Paso and Ciudad Juárez across the river in Mexico.

In the two years since the Tiguas first proposed the casino, however, the state has refused to sign the required compact, or treaty, that would allow the establishment of such a gaming facility on Texas soil. Gov. Ann Richards and Attorney Gen. Dan Morales contend that state law prohibiting casino gambling in Texas applies to the Tiguas as well as everybody else.

The Tiguas, on the other hand, claim their status as a sovereign Indian tribe entitles them to go into the gaming business as Indians in other states have.

"The gambling is our white buffalo," says Mr. Silvas. "In the old days, the buffalo was the Indians' housing, it was our clothing, it was our food, everything we needed. We need something to hold the future. We need something to take care of our children. The gaming money will bring education, housing, health, job placement to our people, whether they qualify under the blood quantum or not. Everything that our people need will be there for them."

"It's not for one person to get rich," says Governor Torrez. "It's not like Donald Trump, becoming rich for his pocket by gaming. The money generated by gaming is going to the pueblo, to give us everything that's required for us to become better citizens. And the city of El Paso wants the gaming because we're going to generate a lot of jobs."

The fight between the Tiguas and the state is in the federal courts now. To Miguel Pedraza, the drawn-out battle is just another example of the state's long indifference to the plight of his tribe.

"The state wanted to get out of the Indian business a long time ago," he says. "The Sunset Commission shut down the Indian Commission. That was bad, because the Indian Commission was a mediator between the Indians and the state. It could negotiate a lot of problems that Indian people have, but now it's costing the state a lot more to go to court and fight us.

"It's like Hueco Tanks," he says, referring to a huge jumble of boulders in the desert northeast of the reservation. Hollows in the rocks catch rainwater, and various tribes of Indians and their ancestors camped or lived there over the millennia. "We consider Hueco Tanks sacred ground," he says. "We do a lot of our praying out there. We go there to

give names to children. I've done it to my grandchildren.
A lot of our grandfathers that we talk about and remember
are associated with Hueco Tanks. There's a place we call
the Grandfathers' Cave where we see names of our people
who are here no more. It's sacred ground to us. We have
begged the state many times that Hueco Tanks should be
in our hands. But Hueco Tanks has been made a state
park. And since that happened, vandals have destroyed a
lot of the pictographs there, and the state has allowed
mountain climbers to climb the rocks. They have drilled
holes in the rocks.

"When people go and desecrate something that's part of
you . . . it's like digging up graves."

After half an hour, the governor, the lieutenant governor, the war chief, and the other members of the council
walk back from the construction site where the bones of
their ancestor were uncovered.

"What happened?" their white visitor asks.

"No comment," comes the reply.

"No comment."

"No comment."

"We have a lot to be angry about," Governor Torrez
finally says. "But so be it. It was our destiny to be placed
here. This is where the Life Giver intended for us to be.
And he's a tough guy to go against."

July 1994

No place is dearer to me than Fort Davis and the Davis Mountains, where I grew up in a hidden, isolated heaven during the 1940s and '50s. I can't imagine a better time and place in which to have been a child and an adolescent than then and there. Almost as dear to me are the Big Bend to the south, the Guadalupes to the north, and the desert flats that connect the mountain ranges. My favorite city is El Paso, the only city I saw when I was growing up, and the city where I began my manhood and my career.

It's all changing now. Some of the changes are good, some downright evil. In the long run, I believe it's a bad thing that the world has discovered my country.

Trouble Across the Pecos

One night David Finfrock was delivering his Texas weather report on Channel 5 in Dallas/Fort Worth and mentioned that some meteorological thing was happening "in the Trans-Pecos." At the conclusion of his forecast, he returned to the anchor desk to exchange the usual TV happy talk with his colleagues.

"David," said anchorman Mike Snyder. "What the heck *is* the Trans-Pecos, anyway?"

The somewhat bemused Mr. Finfrock replied that the Trans-Pecos is "the part of Texas that's on the other side of the Pecos."

It's the fat arm that juts westward between the two Mexicos. It's 31,478 square miles, slightly larger than South Carolina and shaped much like it, drooping southward into Chihuahua and Coahuila as South Carolina droops into Georgia and the Atlantic.

Some 673,000 people live there. Of those, 615,000 live in El Paso County, the smallest of the nine Trans-Pecos counties, at the western tip of the state. If El Paso were to secede from Texas and join New Mexico, as it sometimes threatens to do, there would be only 58,000 people in the region, and its largest city would be Pecos — about twelve thousand population.

The Trans-Pecos used to be a secret place. Its several magnificent mountain ranges are isolated in a kind of western Shangri-La, surrounded by desert flats, many of which are covered with greasewood, mesquite, and cactus. Its towns are small and far apart, connected by narrow two-lane roads.

The only major highway — Interstate 10 — hugs the flat places wherever it can and bypasses the little towns. On much of it, the mountains are only pale shadows on the horizon, and driving it is a long and tedious ordeal. Those doing it usually are in a hurry to get from Dallas or San Antonio to El Paso or some point beyond, or from California to some place east. Not many drop off the interstate to follow the lonely two-lanes southward to the beautiful grasslands and oak and piñon groves of the Davis Mountains or the rugged ranges of the Big Bend, or northward to the looming Guadalupes.

The Trans-Pecos is a place where not much has changed over the years except nature's cycle of rain and drought, the rising and falling of livestock prices, and the model years of the cars and trucks. The region is almost as empty and isolated today as it was more than a century ago, when the army and the Texas Rangers removed the last Indians and cattlemen moved their herds across the Pecos to settle the last Texas frontier.

Most who have lived there for the past century haven't minded their isolation. Many have cherished it. They're self-reliant people, independent, individualistic, conservative, distrustful of all government in which they aren't personally involved. Fort Davis, the seat of Jeff Davis County, has never even bothered to incorporate and become a real town, because its people haven't wanted a mayor and city council making rules for them.

Few outside the Trans-Pecos have known about it, or cared. Those who live there like it that way. The freedom they value most is the freedom to be left alone.

In a Texas rapidly becoming urban, the Trans-Pecos is one of the few remnants of what the state used to be, the last patch of almost pristine wilderness.

But the world has discovered the Trans-Pecos. Change is arriving, and with it, dread.

As the old ranch patriarchs and matriarchs have passed on, many of their holdings have been divided among heirs. Some have sold out to buyers from outside. Developers have bought parts of ranches and subdivided them into "ranchettes" of five or ten acres. They've cut roads into the canyons and up mountainsides and sold the land to retired people and fed-up urbanites as sites for small houses and mobile homes.

The City of El Paso has bought a twenty-five thousand-acre ranch on the edge of the Davis Mountains, not to raise cattle, but to suck its water from under the earth someday and pipeline it to that always water-needful city. Neighboring ranchers fear the water under their land will be sucked into the pipeline, too, leaving them literally high and dry.

"If six hundred thousand people in El Paso need water, who are we to stand in their way?" asks Bob Dillard, Jeff Davis County judge and editor of the county's weekly newspaper, *The Mountain Dispatch.* "From a political standpoint, we're nobody. We have no clout."

An Oklahoma company has purchased a ranch in the Sierra Diablo of Hudspeth County, not to raise cattle, but to move in daily trainloads of human waste from New York City and spread it over the land.

"If they want to put sludge on their property, that's all right with me," says Topper Frank, who ranches eight miles from the site. "But nobody knows what it contains, or where it goes."

About twelve miles from Topper Frank's place, a nuclear waste storage site is in the planning stage. It will receive waste from Vermont and Maine. And cities and states all over the country are casting glances at the wide-open spaces for possible dumping grounds for their own urban poisons.

Near Van Horn, a consortium of utilities companies is about to erect 150 wind turbines — one hundred-foot-tall towers with huge propellers on them — to generate electricity. "There's talk in Fort Davis, too," Judge Dillard says, "of putting a wind farm on top of Star Mountain."

The tall cliffs of Star Mountain are one of the spectacular sights along the road through Limpia Canyon, one of the most scenic highways in the state. "Can you imagine it with one hundred-foot-tall windmills on top?" Judge Dillard asks.

A group of businessmen in Pecos, on I-10, seventy-five miles north of Fort Davis, has proposed that an interstate be built through that same Limpia Canyon to Fort Davis and on southward through Marfa to Presidio and the Rio Grande. Its chances of approval are nil, but other highway construction already under way has people wondering.

"Suddenly the state is widening the highway between Fort Davis and Marfa," says Judge Dillard. "Suddenly they're widening all the bridges in Limpia Canyon. Suddenly they're widening the road from Kent to Nunn Hill, one of the least-traveled roads in this country."

Kent is a gas station-store on I-10 at the northern end of the Davis Mountains. Nunn Hill is near the McDonald Observatory of the University of Texas at Austin, in the highest, most pristine reaches of the range.

"Suddenly we've been noticed," Judge Dillard says. "I can't help thinking there's some kind of movement to . . . I don't know what. There are pressures that this part of the world has never seen before. They're pressures that are going to be really stressful for the people of this area, from a lot of different directions. And they're all land-use issues. What is going to happen to this place?"

The alarm that warned the rural Trans-Pecos that its way of life is threatened was an item in a newsletter from Congressman Ron Coleman to his constituents in 1989. The El Paso Democrat, who represented most of the Trans-Pecos then (he since has been redistricted out of some of it), announced that Congress, at his request, had authorized one hundred thousand dollars for a study of a portion of the Trans-Pecos to determine the feasibility of adding it to the National Park system.

"I received Coleman's newsletter regularly," Judge Dillard says, "but it usually was about Fort Bliss and the *colonias* at El Paso, so I didn't pay much attention to it.

When I saw the mention of the study, though, I called the congressman's office and asked a few questions."

He learned that the area under study included nearly all of Jeff Davis County and parts of Presidio, Brewster, Pecos, and Reeves counties. He published an article about it in *The Alpine Avalanche*, which he edited at the time.

Word of the study spread across the Trans-Pecos like a grass fire on a windy day. Angry citizens demanded and got a public hearing. About four hundred people — almost a quarter of the Jeff Davis County population — gathered at the parish hall of St. Joseph's Catholic Church in Fort Davis. "The hall was packed," Judge Dillard says. "People were standing outside, listening at the windows. The Park Service sent people from Santa Fe, Denver, and Washington to say, 'We're not as evil as you think we are.'"

Mr. Coleman didn't attend, but sent an aide to read a statement. "Let me make one thing perfectly clear," he read. "There is no proposal on the table, here or in Washington, to create a national park in the Fort Davis area. The team from the National Park Service is here only to survey the area's resources. Nothing more. The reason I ordered a study instead of introducing legislation was to determine first the feelings of the greater Fort Davis mountain community about the idea. And I can tell you another thing, too: If the community does not want a park, there won't be a park. It's that simple."

The locals weren't bashful in making their feelings known. To put such a huge area under federal ownership, they said, would destroy the tax base of Jeff Davis County and harm the tax base of neighboring counties, all of which already are among the poorer counties in the state.

Furthermore, the federal government already owns two large national parks — the Guadalupe Mountains and the Big Bend — in the Trans-Pecos, and a national historic site right there in Fort Davis. And a quarter of the acreage in the Texas state park system also is in the Trans-Pecos.

Furthermore, the landowners weren't about to give up their ranches to the feds.

"Our ancestors bought our property over one hundred years ago with their blood and their sweat and their tears," said Andrea Allen, president of the Borracho Cattle Co. at Kent. "Our ancestors preserved very ably the land that we now live on, paving the way for what is now the fourth generation. We were taught to love the land and to love our freedom. We were also taught to hold on to the land and hold on to our freedom. That is our mandate, and that we shall surely do."

"People were enraged," Judge Dillard remembers. "Folks were screaming at the park people. But there were others who *quietly* said, 'It's the best thing that could happen to the area.' A lot of people were saying, 'The only way this country will ever be preserved and kept from going the way of those five-acre ranchettes is the federal government stepping in and taking control of it.' But will anyone say that on the record? No."

Mr. Coleman quickly killed the study and washed his hands of the park idea. But the national park scare had one important result: It led to the creation of the Davis Mountains Heritage Association, which, as its membership and sphere of influence grew, became the Davis Mountains Trans-Pecos Heritage Association. Now it's metamorphosing again into the Trans-Texas Heritage Association.

Whatever its name, its message and mission have remained unchanged. "Preserving Land & Its Natural Resources," its bumper stickers declare, "Through Private Ownership."

"We thought they were talking about maybe one or two particular parcels within the Davis Mountains," Topper Frank says. "You can imagine the look on everybody's face when they drew a line around 4 million acres, virtually all of it privately owned. That was the beginning of the association. We went to work and got the funding cut and stopped the [national park] study. Then after that, the Endangered Species Act came into the picture, and since then it has been just one thing right after the other."

Mr. Frank, of Van Horn, is current president of the Heritage Association. Ben Love, of Marathon, is a rancher and lawyer who helped organize the group and served as its first president. They're sitting in the association's office in Alpine, explaining the work that's taking so much of their time.

"A lot of people think the association is just the big ranchers of West Texas, but we're quite diversified," Mr. Frank says. "We have teachers, lawyers, doctors. What's at jeopardy here is not just large ranches in West Texas, but private property in general. We do represent a lot of people who own a lot of land. We represent over thirteen million acres in Texas — almost 10 percent of the state. But we have members as far away as Connecticut and California. The same thing that's going on in West Texas is going on in New York, New Hampshire, Maine, places where there are not large land holdings. Private property is in jeopardy everywhere."

And, Mr. Love adds, the big villain is the federal bureaucracy. "There are so many regulatory regimes at both the federal and state levels. And most of them are in the name of some sort of environmental protection, either under the Clean Water Act, the Wetlands Act, the Coastal Zone Management Act, the Endangered Species Act. The bureaucrats have found that they can exercise more land-use control under the guise of environmental quality protection than any other way."

If government bureaucrats can keep writing regulations for the land, the association members say, they can restrict use of it so severely that its market value will plummet, and its only willing buyer then will be the government.

So the Heritage Association serves as a sort of Minuteman organization, to monitor the doings of government agencies and warn landowners of possible threats to their autonomy.

"Don't misunderstand me," Mr. Love says. "The members of this association are probably the stoutest believers in a good-quality environment, and we've done a pretty good job of keeping it that way. We're very careful about where we build roads. We don't create eyesores. We don't use herbicides and pesticides. We don't pollute the water or the air. This is the reason the bureaucrats are interested in the Trans-Pecos — because we've kept it the most pristine part of Texas."

Even though the federal government dropped the idea of another Trans-Pecos national park, the Heritage Association believes it has resorted to other means to try to gain control of as much of the area as it can. And its favorite weapon in its back-door attack is the Endangered Species Act.

"When it was passed in 1973, nobody thought twice about it," Mr. Frank says. "Who's in favor of killing off a species? The problem is the rules and regulations that followed. What the feds couldn't get done through law, they accomplished through rules and regulations. And that's where the real danger is. There's no input from the public on rules and regulations. They start setting these things up, and then all of a sudden you find yourself included in it, and you find out you can't erect a windmill or a tank or a barn on your own private property because it affects the migratory flight of something. You get sucked into it."

"And the Trans-Pecos has the greatest share of endangered species per square mile of any area of Texas," adds Mr. Love.

In August 1988, not long after her husband died, Kack Espy got a letter from the Department of the Interior. "This letter," it read, "is to inform you that the U.S. Fish and Wildlife Service is considering listing the Little Aguja pondweed as endangered . . . . We believe that with the understanding and cooperation of private landowners, we can prevent some unnecessary harm to this species, perhaps even prevent its demise."

"I had never heard of the Endangered Species Act or the pondweed," Mrs. Espy says. "So I just kept the letter. It didn't seem to require an answer."

Early in 1989, she received a call from Mr. Love, who told her that, indeed, the Little Aguja pondweed had been listed as an endangered species. The Fish and Wildlife Service apparently had made its decision on the basis of a specimen that an undergraduate student from Alpine's Sul Ross State University had obtained from Aguja Creek in Little Aguja Canyon by trespassing onto Mrs. Espy's Jeff Davis County ranch.

"I got in contact with my lawyer, who is in Fort Worth, and we worked with the Heritage Association for a year about the pondweed," Mrs. Espy says. "It cost me between eight thousand dollars and ten thousand dollars in legal fees."

They had to invoke the federal Freedom of Information Act to get the Department of the Interior to release information about its decision, and Mrs. Espy became involved in a lengthy correspondence with the department.

"Their letters were always quite courteous," she says, "but they also were quite vague. They said my responsibility for the pondweed would be very limited, but they also said in several letters that cattle would endanger it. They might eat it or their manure might affect it. Well, cattle have been using that pasture for a century at least, and if the pondweed is still there, they haven't bothered it, have they?"

Mrs. Espy invited Dr. Barton Warnock, retired Sul Ross botany professor and the acknowledged authority on Trans-Pecos flora, to come to the ranch and search along Aguja Creek for the pondweed. "We crawled up and down that creek," she says. "Dr. Warnock found a species of pondweed, but it wasn't the one that had been listed. He couldn't find it anywhere."

As the Endangered Species Act provides, Mrs. Espy and the Heritage Association requested a public hearing of the pondweed question. One was scheduled for July 17, 1990, in Fort Davis. But in June she received another letter from the Interior Department.

"The U.S. Fish and Wildlife Service recently received information that the pondweed specimen collected on your property by a Sul Ross State University student was misidentified as Little Aguja pondweed *(Potamogeton clystocarpus)*. This error was brought to our attention by this former student and has since been verified by our botanical experts."

"The pondweed wasn't there," Mrs. Espy says. "But there was no concern about the trouble I had to go through to protect my property. There was no apology for my having to spend all that money. They probably thought we would call off the hearing, but we went ahead with it. We were very prepared in every way. They sent people from Albuquerque, I believe it was, but they said they had no authority to answer any of our questions."

281

The turnout was almost as large as for the earlier national park hearing. "That little assembly building in Fort Davis was bulging at the seams," Mr. Love says.

Although Mrs. Espy won her fight, the Fish and Wildlife Service went ahead and declared the Little Aguja pondweed an endangered species, and said it was present in Aguja Creek on a ranch owned by the Buffalo Trails Council of the Boy Scouts, just upstream from Mrs. Espy's place.

Later, she learned that under the Endangered Species Act, the Fish and Wildlife Service has no authority to restrict the use of land to protect rare plants — something that the Fish and Wildlife Service never told her. But as a result of her fight, many ranchers who previously had welcomed scientists and students onto their land to study its geology, botany, zoology, and archaeology have shut their gates to such visitors and now prosecute trespassers.

Recently a number of ranchers rescinded permission they had given the army to come onto their land to improve roads used by the Border Patrol to fight smugglers of drugs and aliens. The reason: A rancher discovered a vehicle full of scientists on his land, sent there by the Corps of Engineers.

"The Army had to get an environmental assessment of what it was going to be doing," Mr. Love says. "So it brought those people in to do surveys. Well, the [ranch] people who gave them access granted it patriotically. But they didn't know they were opening themselves to having those people investigating their land."

Since the Little Aguja pondweed incident, the Fish and Wildlife Service hasn't bothered the Trans-Pecos much, Mr. Love says. He believes the Heritage Association is responsible for the respite. "The pondweed debate told the service that the folks out here are not going to allow themselves to be regulated without stirring up a little sandstorm," he says.

The Heritage Association's perceived enemy now is the Nature Conservancy, a private wildlife conservation group funded largely by corporations. The conservancy works for the conservation of rare species of plants and animals in all fifty states and in thirty-four other countries. It often buys land on which rare species occur, and recently purchased two small tracts in Jeff Davis County. The Heritage Association regards it as "nothing but a giant federal real estate agent," according to Mr. Frank.

"Over 90 percent of the land the conservancy has bought in Texas is now in government hands," he says. "The National Park Service and other federal agencies use it to acquire land when it would be controversial for them to try to get it themselves."

Last summer, the conservancy brought a group of its large donors to the Trans-Pecos to show them the Davis Mountains. Some members of the Heritage Association greeted them with signs on their ranch fences: "Private Property Yes, Nature Conservancy No."

David Braun, vice president and state director of the Nature Conservancy of Texas, led the tour. He says the Heritage Association's fear of his organization is unjustified and based on a lack of understanding of its mission.

"Our work in the United States is to locate places where those rare things still exist and in some way set up protected wildlife refuges," he says. "In Texas, about half the land we work on is owned by private landowners, and we cooperate with them and act as an adviser to them. We have about three hundred thousand acres in that status. The private landowner joins what we call the Texas Land Steward Society, a purely voluntary, cooperative organization. A number of Trans-Pecos landowners belong to it. And, yes, sometimes we buy properties. In Texas, we own

about forty-four thousand acres in two different reserves.
Almost every piece of land we buy will have rare plants,
animals or ecosystems on it. We use them as educational
and research sites. And, yes, the third leg of our work is to
help the park agencies like the National Park Service and
Texas Parks and Wildlife and the U.S. Fish and Wildlife
Service acquire reserves."

Those agencies often don't have the money to acquire
land when it comes on the market. They need someone to
buy it and hold it for them until they can get money
appropriated by Congress or the Texas Legislature. "So
we'll buy something and hold it sometimes as long as five
years," Mr. Braun says. "We owned Enchanted Rock State
Park for seven years before the state was able to get an
appropriation and buy it from us. We're a close partner of
the public lands organizations, whether federal or state or
local. I'm not ashamed of that. In fact, I'm proud of it."

But the 90 percent figure that the Heritage Association
cites is a distortion of the conservancy's record, he says. It
was calculated in the late 1980s, when the conservancy
was given a ranch in Brewster County, with the understanding that the conservancy would give it to the Big
Bend National Park, which it did.

"Since that time, we've bought twenty-five thousand
acres in Texas, which we're keeping ourselves," Mr. Braun
says. "In the spectrum of environmental groups, we're
considered off the chart on the conservative side. Our
membership is mainly business people who are very conservative politically and economically. It's just as likely
that we would sell to a private landowner as to a government agency. If we can get a private landowner to buy a
piece of property, and we know that person is committed
to conservation, that's our first choice, because they don't
have hoards of visitors coming in as the Park Service
does."

Nor is the Nature Conservancy interested in buying up the Trans-Pecos, neither for itself nor for the federal or state governments, he says. "I don't think we particularly need any more parks in West Texas. What we're trying to do is assemble some of the land at the very highest elevations of the Davis Mountains. There are very rare ecosystems up there. Plants found nowhere else in the world. When those ranches go on the market, we want to be in a position to buy some of that high land and just leave it alone. We want to make sure it never gets developed. For those few thousand acres at the top of that mountain that have those rare plants, we don't need a lot of people hiking around up there. We would prefer to manage that ourselves."

But some people in the Trans-Pecos fear the Nature Conservancy, he says, because they're threatened by the modern world that at last is intruding upon theirs, and the conservancy is one of the more visible intruders.

"What they're really afraid of is a change in their lifestyle. But what we're doing is similar to what they would like to do themselves. They would like to see things remain the same. We're much in agreement with that. We would like to see things in West Texas remain as close as possible to the way they are right now. I think the vocal ones — and I think they're a minority of the people — aren't willing to accept that there's going to be change in the Trans-Pecos. They haven't thought about what might be good change vs. bad change, and they aren't willing to talk about it. But changes are coming. You sit up on Mount Livermore now and you look out, and there are those damn drug balloons hanging all over Marfa — sophisticated radar watching for drug planes to go over. And you look in the other direction and there's a resort with hundreds of little trailers and cabins going in. You feel like you're in a wilderness until you really look, and there are all those weird things coming in."

In his office at the Jeff Davis County Courthouse, Judge Dillard is studying a large map of the county that hangs on the wall. "This is a very special place," he says. "What happens to it is at stake right now."

He points at large tracts of land on the map. "Here we've got a pipe salesman. Here we've got a lumber sales- man. Here we've got a Dos Equis beer salesman from Mexico. All big absentee owners. These are the kinds of guys who are owning this country now. Who knows what they're going to do with it? The old ranching families are in the fourth generation. They're beginning to break up. As they do, either a wealthy person like these men buys the land, or the conservancy — a group of wealthy per- sons — or they become five-acre 'ranchettes.' Well. What's best for the country?"

January 1994

Water, whether river, lake or creek or sea, puts me in a meditative mood. Even my condo swimming pool does. Although I'm an awful swimmer, I hurry home from work every day during the long, hot Dallas summers to loll in its water, chlorined and filtered as it is, and muse.

The Reflecting Pool

The brats who were shooting each other with water guns as big as bazookas finally have gone to their supper. So has their gold-chained dad, who expatiated loudly on which Wall Street stocks he considers good and which not so good, while his vacant-eyed wife or girlfriend rubbed coconut goop into her sun-parched hide and Neil Diamond caterwauled through the radio beside her.

I haven't seen them at the pool before. Maybe they're new in the condo. Or somebody's guests. Or maybe they sneaked in from the street for a dip, as people sometimes do, pretending to be residents. That would explain the noisy speechifying about stocks. Trespassers often overact, pretending to belong.

If they're residents, I hope they won't make a habit of coming to the pool at this hour, or remaining until the sun has sunk behind units 199 and 200, as they have today.

At twilight, the pool is mine. This has been so for eleven summers, and my ritual seldom varies, except when weather precludes a trip to the pool altogether.

I arrive home from work with the heat of July in my hair and clothes and weariness in my bones. I change into swimsuit and T-shirt, grab a towel, a book, and an ice-tea tumbler filled with ice, water, and a generous slug of bourbon. I march to the pool, arrange a deck chair and a small table in the place where I always sit, under a live oak at the southeast corner, then ease down the steps into the cool water and wallow like a hippopotamus.

Sometimes Isabel, my wife, joins me, and we stand in the water, discussing the events of the day, office gossip, what came in the mail, the books we're reading, and the latest brilliant thing that Ace has done that proves his intellectual superiority to all other cats. Then Isabel, a serious swimmer, ends the talk and begins her laps.

Having learned to swim in a West Texas stock tank of a diameter smaller than the width of this pool, I don't do laps. Did I say "swim"? It's far too generous a word for the splashing I do. I don't "swim" in the presence of others. Not even my wife.

When my skin begins to wrinkle, I climb into the deck chair and sip my bourbon and read. A Kinky Friedman mystery. A novel about Robert Falcon Scott and his men dying in Antarctica. An article about Texas Rangers in *The Southwestern Historical Quarterly*. Cormac McCarthy's latest masterpiece. A history of the Mexican Revolution. And then wallow again.

Sometimes Isabel doesn't come or leaves early, and the pool is left to me and the cats. The longhaired black-and-white one. The big tabby. The young black adolescent. They live in the units around the pool. The tabby may be a stray. Making their rounds, they spot me, halt, recognize me — "Oh. Only him." — and move on. Sometimes the black one comes over and says hello.

The birds are changing shifts by now. The day feeders roost in the trees, quarreling over which limb belongs to whom, and the night feeders are swooping out in search of bugs.

This is when the twilight thoughts come, long thoughts that slide into the mind only when the world is silent and the light failing, the kind of mental wandering that our ancestors called "reflection." It's an informal kind of meditation that people used to do as a matter of course during the quiet of their sewing or plowing, before technology trained us to crave moving color constantly before our eyes and constant noise in our ears, entertainment substituting for thought and memory.

The ghosts of my dead grandmother and my murdered stepson come to me sometimes, always smiling, laughing, enjoying some story or thing in the world. Images of my sons and my remaining stepson come, too, sometimes as they are now, sometimes younger. I marvel at their courage and humor, having to be young men in a world that was so thoroughly ruined before it was handed to them. "Here is your oyster, my sons. Try not to let it kill you."

And I remember friends I've enjoyed, and those I've lost to accident, heart attack, murder, suicide, AIDS, cancer, war. Quite a crowd. The world was no picnic ground for them, either. Maybe it never has been, for anybody.

My twilight thoughts often are intimations of mortality, but they aren't somber and I don't fear them. These memories enlarge my life as surely as the books I read. They make me aware of the sweetness of this fleeting, present moment. I am one with the birds, the trees, the cats, the very water in which I'm standing as the twilight dims, leaving the world to darkness and to me.

July 1994

In 1993, my mother sold the old adobe house in Fort Davis where I and my brothers and sisters grew up. It was the practical thing to do. My mother was growing old and living alone, far from her children, who had moved away long ago.

Our House

My family bought the house from George Grierson, the son of Benjamin Grierson, a famous Union general in the Civil War and the commander of the Buffalo Soldiers who served at the fort on the other side of Sleeping Lion Mountain.

The general had been dead for thirty-five years, but at least one of the soldiers who had served under him still lived in the town. So did a number of the men and women who had moved their families and herds into the lush Davis Mountains during the three decades following the fall of the Confederacy. In 1946, Fort Davis was still very close to its frontier beginnings.

The general's son was a gruff and highly eccentric old bachelor. He lived in only two rooms of the sprawling adobe, which an Englishman named Gleim had built during the 1890s. A dozen or so other rooms stood vacant, and Mr. Grierson had had all the electric wiring removed from the house because, he said, the wires made a noise that made him nervous. He had also removed all the vegetation — every tree, every shrub, every blade of grass, every weed — from the huge lot on which the house stood. We never learned the reason for this.

Oddities notwithstanding, Mr. Grierson had a kind heart. He hadn't intended to sell his home, but a friend told him that a young mother and a grandmother needed a house big enough to accommodate themselves and five children, so he agreed to let us have his. We bought it, and he moved to a smaller house on the other side of town.

The old adobe was the perfect place for us, just two blocks from the courthouse for my mother, who had been elected clerk of Jeff Davis County that summer, and about the same distance from the school where my grandmother taught and Linda, Dick, and I studied. (The younger kids, Mike and Sherry, would join us there later.) It was just across a fence from the Baptist Church, which we all attended, and in the middle of a neighborhood teeming with children.

Because it was so large and so many children lived in it, our house became a sort of community center for the other kids of the town. Even when we weren't there, they felt free to drop by, sit on our screened-in front porch and read the comic books we kept in a box by the swing. They came to our house to play baseball in the backyard, to spin tops, shoot marbles, play jacks, roller skate on the sidewalk, learn canasta, listen to football games on the radio, play poker for matchsticks, play dolls, play guns, fix bicycles, build forts and playhouses. Sometimes one or two of them would stay for supper. Sometimes they would spend the night, or the whole weekend.

Since I, the eldest, was nine when we moved in, and Sherry, the youngest, was only two, these activities continued for many years. And by the time the last of us was married and gone, the whole noisy whirl had been started all over again by the first arrivals of the new generation.

During the forty-seven years since we moved in, five generations of my family have lived or visited there. For all those years, it has been a house filled with love and laughter, and, from time to time, grief and pain. The memories of Christmases, family reunions, birthday parties, high school graduations, weddings, and the ordinary events of living that are contained within its walls are beyond number. And wherever the rest of us have lived, and however many years we've been gone, we've always thought of that house as home, as the headquarters of our family.

So when I drove a rental car out of the Midland airport a few weeks ago and pointed it toward the Davis Mountains, I already was feeling that emptiness in the pit of my stomach, that heaviness in the chest that makes one sigh. Our home had been sold. My mother had lived alone in the place for nine years and had decided, at age seventy-seven, that it was time to move into a smaller, more easily maintained house closer to her now middle-aged children, all of whom had drifted east of the Pecos.

A week earlier, she had held a yard sale so huge that she had hired professionals from Fort Stockton to run it. Hundreds of customers from scores of miles around hauled off truckloads of furniture, kitchen appliances, souvenirs of my mother's travels — including more than eight hundred coffee mugs — and just stuff that accumulates naturally in a large house if you live in it for half a century.

When I arrived, I immediately noticed the empty spaces where familiar objects had been, but I could see that Mother had kept too much. She admitted she would probably have to hold another yard sale at the other end of her move.

For the next few days, she and I sat on the front porch by the hour, remembering the years, listening to the call of a hoot owl over near the foot of Sleeping Lion and the town's dogs barking at the moon just as they always have. We walked about the yard, every foot of which had borne the brunt of all our boisterous childhoods. Mother picked an armload of ripe peaches from the tree on the west side of the house. I picked up three ordinary rocks near the fence to take back to Dallas as keepsakes, one for me, one for each of my sons, who had spent several blissful, unforgettable summers there. Together we visited my grandmother's grave in the cemetery on the hill.

A day or two before the movers were to arrive, the new owner — a rich man from East Texas — appeared. He walked about the house, bragging to Mother about the changes he was going to make. He was going to rip out this, tear out that, renovate this and replace that. He planned to undo the changes that had been made to modernize the old place over the years and restore it to its original condition, he said.

"Well," Mother said, "you'll have to dig a privy out back."

I wasn't there when the movers came. Mike had accepted the difficult duty of seeing the house empty, as it hadn't been since he was four.

We talked about it later on the phone. Mother had broken down a couple of times, he said, when old friends had come to say goodbye. But, all in all, she seemed happy to be moving on. We concluded that we should be happy along with her. We comforted each other with the thought that although our home now belonged to somebody else, its best memories would always be ours.

So why am I still sighing? Is it because my only remaining tie to the town I've always called home is my grandmother's grave? Is it because the next time I journey to my mountains, I'll go as a tourist and not as a home child returning? Is it because, in some deep corner of my heart, I believed I would live in Mr. Grierson's old adobe again someday, and would recapture some small part of that innocent, beautiful world I dwelt in as a child?

November 1993